"Absolutely," Cordy replied. It was refreshing to admit it, now that some of the other members of the group had confessed a willingness to believe, too. Things really were getting spookier by the day. So far, she didn't think there had been much actual danger, beyond Beth's attack—but if it came to that, it'd be good to know there were some others on her side. "I think they're restless spirits, with business left unfinished when they died. If they're prevented from doing what they need to do, that's when they're in trouble."

"Trouble?" Gordon echoed. His head was canted at an angle. It was his disbelieving head-cock, Cordelia decided. "So you think we're literally in danger here?"

"I don't know," she said honestly. *I hope not,* she thought, *but it's looking more and more like we could be.* "I really don't know."

"But I'd watch my step, just the same."

Angel™

City of
Not Forgotten
Redemption
Close to the Ground
Shakedown
Hollywood Noir
Avatar
Soul Trade
Bruja
The Summoned
Haunted

Available from Simon Pulse

The Essential Angel Posterbook

Available from Pocket Books

ANGEL™

haunted

Jeff Mariotte

An original novel based on the television series
created by Joss Whedon & David Greenwalt

New York London Toronto Sydney Singapore

First Simon Pulse edition February 2002

SIMON PULSE
An imprint of Simon & Schuster
Children's Publishing Division
1230 Avenue of the Americas
New York, NY 10020

The text of this book was set in New Caledonia.

Printed in USA
10 9 8 7 6 5 4 3 2 1

Library of Congress Control Number 2001097782

ISBN 0-7434-2748-3

To the *LATFB* gang, who can make the most grueling road trip seem like fun

Acknowledgments

Eternal gratitude goes out to those people who wrote the best haunted house stories I've ever read: Shirley Jackson, Richard Matheson, Anne Rivers Siddons, and Stephen King.

Thanks also to Joss Whedon, David Greenwalt, Tim Minear, and the cast and crew of *Angel;* Lisa Clancy, Micol Ostow, and Liz Shiflett of Pocket Books; Caroline Kallas and Debbie Olshan, and my family.

Chapter One

Monday

The house stood alone on the hill, as if no one else wanted to build or live within any reasonable proximity to it. Along most of Mulholland Drive—prime Los Angeles real estate—the houses, mansions though they might be, were all within a stone's throw of one another. But not this house. This house demanded solitude. Its grounds seemed to stretch forever, encompassing wooded hillsides of tangled manzanita and spreading live oaks, grassy swaths yellowed by sprays of tall mustard plants. A winding gravel drive led from rusted wrought-iron gates at Mulholland to the main house.

They had been on the driveway for several minutes before Cordelia Chase got her first glimpse of the house. She'd seen pictures of it, of course, and they'd all been warned that it was habitable but had not been consistently occupied for decades. As the van they rode in crested a rise to reveal the house atop the next hill, she craned her neck for a better view out the van's side window.

Not bad, was her first thought. From here, she could see that the house was even bigger than she'd believed from its photos, with large expanses of old stone walls, some ivy-covered, and steep roofs. To the right of the main doorway the wall angled toward a round turret with a conical roof. As the van drew closer, the chatter of her fellow passengers ceased, and there was no sound except the churning of the vehicle's wheels on gravel and the *thrum* of its motor. Not even birds sang in the late afternoon sunlight.

With nearness came clarity. The house was big, certainly, and had been luxurious at one time. But as the van approached, Cordelia could see more clearly the current condition of the house. Its stone walls were limned with a mossy green in spots, as if some lichen had taken a liking to them and called them home. Multipaned windows were covered with boards, their shutters broken or with gaps in their slatted fronts. Some of the stones from the crenellated battlement below the roofline, similarly, had vanished or chipped or disintegrated, leaving the battlements looking like an orthodontist's *before* picture. The place looked like a French château, brought over and reassembled piece by piece, but with part of the puzzle lost along the way, and then forgotten.

Or maybe, bad, Cordelia amended her earlier prognosis, as the van braked to a stop in a circular courtyard at the front of the building. *They certainly could use some Bob Vila around the place.* When her parents had had money, they never would have allowed their home to get so run-down. And after they'd stopped having money—after her father had run afoul of the IRS over that little matter of owing years of back taxes, she pretty much had stopped spending much time around the old homestead, anyway. She had left Sunnydale and her old life behind, and moved to L.A. in search of fame and fortune. She'd ended up working with a vampire detective, a British ex-Watcher, and the leader of a street gang dedicated to the eradication of vampires, but fame and fortune had been the initial goals.

And now, just maybe, she was on the cusp of both.

Thanks to the house. And *Haunted House.*

Rich Carson, the genial and handsome TV personality who would be the host of *Haunted House,* the TV show, emerged from the house's front door, a million-dollar smile pasted on his familiar, tanned face. He threw open the van's side door, and Cordelia and her eight fellow contestants piled out into the welcoming glow of TV lights. Rich spread his arms wide, encompassing contestants and structure alike, and said, "Welcome home!"

A shiver ran up Cordelia's spine as he said it. *Home*? For the next week, it would be, she knew. And after that, a brand-new world would open up to her.

As the group hit the gravel, conversation resumed and the air was full of sound again. Rich let it go on for a few moments, as everyone gathered their bags from the van's cargo area and got their bearings, then he held up his hands and called for quiet. Cameras rolled—a female camera operator with a Steadicam mounted on her shoulder knelt at Rich's side, shooting up toward him, while a male operator stood back at a distance, his camera mounted on a wheeled tripod.

"Okay, group. You all know who I am, and I'm getting to know who you are. But we all need to get to know the real star of our show." Here he gestured extravagantly at the structure behind him. "The house, right?"

There was a chorus of assent, which Cordelia joined. She was, she knew, as caught up in the moment as the rest of them. And even though the rules of the game would pit them against one another, she couldn't help feeling a kinship with the other contestants right now. *We're all in this together,* she thought. *At least until we stab each other in the backs.*

"So let's go on in and make ourselves at home," Rich continued. "We're taping now, as you can see, but we're not live yet—this'll be edited into an opening segment on tonight's show." Everyone lifted their backpacks, suitcases, or duffel bags, including Cordy, whose wheeled duffel weighed a ton, what with a week's worth of clothing changes, cosmetics, bottled water, and a few extras. She hung back, watching the others as they filed through the front door behind Rich, camera operators bringing up the rear. The group was as diverse as only a television production company could put together. Cordelia, Gordon, Beth, and Vince were Caucasian, Annemarie, Sharon, and Terry were African-American, Christy and Pat were Asian-American. The ages ran the gamut from late teens/early twenties, as in the case of Cordelia, Gordon, and Pat, to mid-forties, like Terry and Beth. The only things they all had in common were that they were all reasonably attractive and telegenic, and ambitious enough to put themselves through this experience for money, fame, or both. Unlike the crenellations above, they had all their teeth and would flash them for the right price.

Rich Carson led them through a grand entryway into a living room just to the right. The room was furnished with antiques, although they were the kind that looked like they'd been used since the day they were made rather than the kind that seemed to have been built and then put away for later sale at inflated prices in tony antique shops. Windows faced, Cordelia believed, out onto the drive, but they were covered with fresh sheets of plywood. Lights on stands provided more than adequate illumination, anyway, and there were cameras mounted at the roof and in various other points in addition to the ones operated by people.

"Take a seat," Rich suggested, and people grabbed spots on worn sofas, in straight-backed wooden chairs, or on the raised hearth of a stone fireplace. Cordy found herself on a sagging couch, between Gordon and Beth, looking expectantly toward the host.

Rich pointed to an oil painting above the hearth, a portrait of a white-haired man in formal wear. "That's Glenn Carstairs," he said. "He built this house, after buying the land in nineteen thirty-two. Until then, the land had been empty for centuries—cursed, or so the locals said. So he got it cheap. Anyone recognize the name? Glenn Carstairs?"

"Wasn't he a producer or something?" Cordelia piped up. "The name sounds familiar, and there's the Carstairs building in Hollywood."

Rich shook his head and wandered over toward Cordy. He was better looking in life than on the tube, and he was pretty hot there. He wore a simple off-white silk shirt and faded jeans. His blond hair was longish and a little unkempt, and he looked like he hadn't shaved in a few days. Cordelia figured he'd clean up before the evening's broadcast. *And he looks like he cleans up just fine.*

"He was a Hollywood fixture, all right, Cordelia. But not a producer. Carstairs worked behind the scenes, providing various services to the studios in Hollywood's Golden Age. Catering, trucks, costumes—anything studios needed to get their hands on, Carstairs was willing to provide. He'd made a few million in Los Angeles real estate, and then decided he wanted to get into the movies. But he wasn't particularly creative, so he opted for going a different route. By the end of his career, he had probably been involved with more pictures than Jack Warner."

"So what about the curse?" Pat Takenada asked. He was a muscular Asian man with close-cropped black hair. His body was wedge-shaped, with broad shoulders tapering to a narrow waist. His powerful arms stretched the sleeves of his polo shirt. "Did Carstairs know about it when he bought the place?"

Rich looked up at the portrait above the mantelpiece. "It's hard to imagine that he wouldn't have," he replied. "This is an expensive neighborhood. He would have wondered why no one had built here, and why the land was so inexpensive. Being in real estate, he would have heard stories."

"And what were the stories?" Pat pressed. "I mean, that's why we're here, right?"

It's not for the interior decorating tips, that's for sure, Cordelia thought. She thought she would sneeze from the room's layer of dust. *Or the fresh air.*

Rich turned to Pat, his visage suddenly serious, his voice hushed theatrically. "That's right," he answered. "That's exactly why we're here. So let me tell you the story."

"I like stories," Beth Ullman declared. She was a tall, thin woman with gray-streaked blond hair that fell almost to her waist, and pale skin, nearly as white as Angel's. She wore a long, flowing batik skirt, a purple silken chemise, and gold wire-rimmed glasses. *She just* screams *Summer of Love leftover,* Cordy thought. *Isn't a game like this a little materialistic for the hippie ethos?*

Rich squeezed onto the stone hearth, in between Christy Colquitt and Sharon Guthrie. All eyes in the room were on him, and he seemed to revel in that knowledge. He spoke quietly, forcing his audience to strain to hear his every word, even hushing their breathing for him.

Guy's a pro.

"According to the legend, this was the site of one of the Spanish land grants in the late sixteen hundreds," he began. "A family named Trujillo settled here, building a rancho. The house was right here on this ridge, and their land spread far and wide in every direction. Then, as now, there was not a lot of farmable land up here, so they needed a big spread to be able to raise much of anything. But they browsed cattle and sheep, they had some fields, they had chickens and pigs and ducks. The whole place, as was common at the time, was worked by Native American slaves. Don Trujillo was, word has it, very cruel to those slaves, while his wife was just as kind to them as he was cruel. They hated him, they loved her. There's a portrait upstairs, in one of the bedrooms—painted a couple of centuries later, so it's no doubt romanticized quite a bit—but if it's to be believed, she was beautiful as well as gracious and generous."

"So what was she doing with a loser like him?" Cordelia interrupted. "I know it's hard to find a decent guy in L.A. *now,* but that was a long time ago."

"There was barely an L.A. in L.A. at that time," Rich shot back with an easy grin. "The answer is, we don't know why she was with him, but it didn't seem to work out. She turned up mysteriously dead one morning. The Natives mourned her, but Don Trujillo barely seemed to notice that she was gone. Two weeks later, he had married again, and this new wife was every bit as nasty to the slaves as he was. He'd finally found his match.

"It didn't take long for this double-barreled cruelty to get old, and the slaves had a little surprise for the happy couple. They rose up, slaughtered the Trujillos and their various hangers-on, and burned the house to the ground. After that, stories began to spread that the land was haunted—people swore they saw the Trujillos wandering the grounds, looking for slaves so they could get their revenge."

"Sounds like they deserved what they got," Terry Watson pointed out. Another of the older contestants, he had skin as dark as a coffee bean, a receding hairline, and a thick, graying mustache. His voice boomed like a P.A. system with the bass turned all the way up.

"No doubt," Rich replied. "But from then on, things got weird around here. No one camped here for long. A couple of times, people tried to build on the land, but they were always driven away or suffered unexpected deaths. After a while, people just stopped trying." He rose, suddenly, from his hearth seat, and made an "up" gesture with his two hands, palms raised. "Let's walk around," he said. The others all stood, and he led them through a set of tall, double doors into a formal dining room. A vast wooden table stood in the center of the room, surrounded by two dozen chairs. Against the wall, dark sideboards and hutches held china, serving utensils, and linens. Crucifixes and old paintings decorated the plain plaster walls. The TV crew had already set up lights, microphones, and a couple of cameras that would cover the room. Here again the windows were boarded over. Cordelia wondered when Rich would get around to explaining that.

"This is where Carstairs entertained," Rich told them. "After he bought the land and built this house. He loved to give parties. And his parties, like just about everything else having to do with this place, were legendary, even by the standards of Hollywood in the thirties."

"They were wild?" Sharon asked. Something about the tone of her voice and the smile with which she said it made Cordelia think she wanted them to be. Sharon was a beautiful young woman, with rich, dark skin and a voluptuous body barely hidden by a baggy sweatshirt and jeans. Cordelia felt a twinge of concern. *I want to be the hot one on the show,* she thought. *I might need the adolescent vote.*

"As wild as it gets, according to the scandal sheets of the day," Rich answered. "Party spelled o-r-g-y, at times, or at least that's what the gossip columnists called them. Polite society complained about them, but everybody wanted to be invited. At least, until the bad one."

"Bad one?" Sharon echoed, still sounding intrigued.

"It was nineteen thirty-nine," Rich said. "Another in a long string of parties in this house, only this time there was a different energy to it, a kind of edge. Europe was slipping into war, and there was a feeling that America couldn't stay out of it forever. Times were tense. Maybe that tension carried through at the party, I don't know. But something happened. It's never really been explained what, exactly, even though the local authorities questioned everyone who was here. Well, everyone who survived."

"Who *survived*?" It was Cordy's turn to play echo chamber.

"That's right," Rich went on. "Sometime during the night, something went wrong. As I said, we don't know what. There were some guns on the property, I guess, and then a fire started. Eleven people died, and those who didn't were never very clear on exactly what happened. One of the dead was Jocelyn Carstairs, Glenn's wife. Her body was mostly burned, so they were never able to determine the cause of death. She was just twenty-seven."

This is not, Cordelia thought, *turning out to be exactly a fairy tale, is it? Or maybe it's the original kind, the kind where the kids get eaten by the witch, or the rats win, or whatever. Somebody's bones get ground to make somebody's bread, like* that *would bake up all smooth and fluffy.*

"Come on," Rich said. "We have a lot of ground to cover." He took them out of the dining room and into a kitchen that looked to Cordelia as big as most restaurant kitchens she'd seen. "Much like Don Trujillo, Carstairs remarried quickly, and he married a much younger woman than his first wife."

"How much younger could he find?" Gordon Shockley asked. Gordon was lean, tall, and handsome, with long dark hair and dark eyes that twinkled with mischief. Cordelia thought he'd be fun at a party, though possibly not the kind that ended in arson and homicide.

"The second Mrs. Carstairs was nineteen."

"You go, Carstairs," Vince Harralson said, but without genuine enthusiasm. Vince's age seemed to be close to that of the first Mrs. Carstairs. With his glasses, neat haircut, and expensive suit, he looked like a young tax accountant or a recent law school graduate. *He looks as uptight as Wesley used to,* Cordelia mused, thinking of the old days in Sunnydale when Wesley Wyndam-Pryce had been sent over by the Watchers Council to take Buffy under his wing. In those days, he'd been wound up tighter than a brand new Rolex. A couple of years on the front lines of demon-fighting had knocked some of the over-stuffing out of him, and as far as Cordelia was concerned, the change was definitely for the better.

"The theory was that he was trying to remake himself," Rich went on. They had passed through the kitchen and a giant pantry, and navigated a hallway with servants' quarters off the sides. "He stopped having parties."

"Duh," Cordelia interjected. "Probably couldn't get the A-list guests anymore after that."

"That was probably part of it. And the new Mrs. Carstairs was much more serious, even though she was younger—maybe *because* she was younger—than the first. Prim, even. Party Central became staid, quiet, and conservative. And a month later, his reputation irreparably sullied, Glenn Carstairs hanged himself." Rich stopped before a door, then threw it open and led them back out into the formal entryway. When the others had gathered on the marble floor, he pointed toward the sky. "From that."

Cordelia looked up. A giant crystal chandelier hung high overhead. Stairs swept up from the entryway, but the roof immediately overhead was three stories high. And the chandelier suspended from it must have been a dozen feet across.

"How'd he get up there?" Terry asked, incredulous.

"No one knows. Mrs. Carstairs found him in the morning as she headed downstairs for breakfast. He stayed there until the weight of his own body snapped his head off and he fell. Mrs. Carstairs had summoned the fire department, but it took them too long to get here. Somehow the household staff couldn't find a ladder tall enough to reach him up there, which is why they couldn't figure out how he got there in the first place. Some of them found a shorter ladder, but they could only reach his legs, which may have put additional strain on his neck."

Too bad Angel already found the Hyperion Hotel, Cordelia mused. *This place sounds right up his alley.*

"Come on," Rich said. "We have to get this done in time for everybody to get ready for tonight's big debut." Across the entryway they found a parlor, and then beyond that, a den for Mr. Carstairs and a sewing room for Mrs. Carstairs.

"That's the downstairs," Rich told them. "Upstairs are the bedrooms—you'll find name plates on the doors telling you which one you've been assigned to, though you can trade around if you want, and can find someone to swap with you."

"So what happened to the house after that?" Annemarie Torrance asked. Annemarie was a tiny woman, with chocolate-colored skin and hands barely bigger than Cordelia's palm. *She's probably petite enough to shop in the children's department,* Cordelia thought. *And really, they get to wear some of the coolest stuff.*

Rich gazed off into space, as if reading a TelePrompTer only he could see. "Young Mrs. Carstairs unloaded it to the first bidder and moved to Europe with some minor royal she'd hooked up with. Different people bought the place, moved in, but nobody stayed long. There were always strange sights and sounds reported—sometimes even smells. Phantom odors. People swore they saw Carstairs wandering the place, noose around his neck, looking for his wife, though we don't know which one. And others say they saw the first Mrs. Carstairs running hand in hand with a lover, who was not Mr. Carstairs. Which, given the nature of his parties, is not beyond belief."

"If you believe in ghosts," Christy said, shaking her head. Her black hair was shoulder-length and straight, and she wore sensible glasses, sensible clothes, and sensible shoes. Even her voice was sensible—she pronounced her words carefully, clipping them off as if unwilling to waste any more breath than necessary.

"If you don't now, Christy," Rich replied gently, "I can guarantee you that by the end of the week, you will."

Christy stood her ground, gaze locked on his. Finally, she shrugged. "Whatever."

"Let me wrap this up," Rich said. "The house changed hands several times. In the seventies, a murderous cult lived here, an offshoot, more or less, of the Manson family. They lured victims up here with tales of free drugs and free love, and then killed them. At least, they did until a meter reader for the power company came one day and found the whole bunch of them dead in what was apparently some kind of bizarre suicide rite. After that, no one was really interested in the place. It's been inhabited only briefly since then, and completely empty for more than a decade. And now it's our stage."

He turned the group around and herded them back toward the entryway. "Which gives me the perfect segue to go over the rules again, though I think you all know them."

"We do," Cordelia spoke up, thinking, *we'd better. We've had them drilled into us so much in the past few days I've been* dreaming *the rules.*

"Good, I'm glad. So I can be brief. Once the cameras start running tonight, cameras will be on twenty-four/seven. From six P.M. tonight until there's only one of you left in the House. We'll be live for one hour each weeknight. The rest of the time, there'll be live WebCams. You're guaranteed privacy in the bathrooms, but nowhere else. There'll be a van parked on the premises, but out of sight of the house, at all times, with a doctor inside. If you can't take it, if you're too scared, if you're sick, come outside. We'll see you on the WebCam, and the van will be in motion on the way to you as soon as you go through the door. If you don't want to leave the show, don't leave the house. You go out that door, you're off the show. Obviously, going out the windows—or even looking out the windows—is out of the question. Inside the house, for all intents and purposes—especially for the viewers at home—it's nighttime all the time.

"Each night on the live broadcast, whoever's left inside has to vote one of you out. You'll each have your own strategies, you'll try to form alliances. But there aren't a lot of you, and none of you want to stay longer than you have to, and a hundred grand is a lot of money. So my advice is, don't trust anyone. If there are two of you left for a period of three days and nights, then the home audience will vote for a winner via the Internet, so you'll be playing to them while you're here. But you'll never know which of the various WebCams is live at any given time."

"Big brother is watching us," Gordon said with a wry grin.

"We don't even mention that show," Rich joked. "We'll be much more popular."

A hundred thousand dollars, Cordy thought. *And better than that, national network exposure on a highly promoted show. This could be the chance I've been working for since I got to L.A.*

Rich took the group back into the living room. "One more thing," he said. "Once we're rolling, there's no communication with the outside world. That means no cell phones. If you've got one, I need to collect it now, please."

There was some generalized grumbling, but everyone fished theirs out and handed it to Rich, who placed them in a cloth bag that was lying on a sideboard. Cordy handed hers over happily. She'd anticipated this, and talked it over with Angel and Wesley. She was turning over her own cell phone, but she had Wesley's squirreled away in her suitcase. Angel wouldn't have agreed to this—and she wouldn't even have asked—if there weren't some way for her to get in touch in the event of a vision or an emergency.

"And just in case," Rich continued, "we have equipment hidden in the house that jams cell phone signals, so don't think any of you can pull a fast one. And you can't go outside to use them because then you're off the show."

Cordelia swallowed. This was unexpected. *Should I give it up now?* she wondered. *Just walk out on the money? And the fame?*

No, she decided. *We're live on the Web twenty-four hours a day. If anything happens, I can just write a note and hold it up to a WebCam, or something. There'll be a way. I just need to play along, and I'll figure something out before it becomes a problem.*

Anyway, this is a lock for me. A haunted house? Hello, Phantom Dennis? How many of these other contestants have a ghost for a roomie?

She almost felt bad for them, since they were going down to crushing defeats while she took the money and the stardom that went with it. She realized there was a chance she'd grow to like some of them, but that wasn't a handicap that couldn't be overcome if the price was right. She had become friendly with a girl name Kirsten St. Clair during the audition process, and had been looking forward to spending some more time getting to know her during the shooting. Only Kirsten, it turned out, had made the semifinals but not the final cut. *It would have been nice to have a buddy,* she knew. *But in the end, it'll be easier to vote the others off if they're not friends.*

"I'll let you guys go upstairs and get settled," Rich said. "If you want to change into something for the first broadcast, go for it. The WebCams aren't on yet, you have all the privacy you need. I'll be back at around five, and we'll run through the final details before we go live. Any questions?"

"What's for dinner?" Pat asked. The others laughed.

"Tonight is catered," Rich replied with a grin. "It'll show up in about an hour. After tonight, there's food in the kitchen, and you're on your own. Enjoy, gang."

Then he went out the front door, the camera operators following him, and the nine contestants were alone in the house for the first time.

Whatever the next few days would bring, Cordelia Chase was ready.

Chapter Two

Wesley Wyndam-Pryce carried a stack of freshly laundered blankets from Anne Steele's car trunk into the East Hills Teen Center, the youth shelter she ran. Three kids charged out of the door as he approached, and he had to swerve, narrowly missing them and even more narrowly avoiding dropping the clean blankets onto L.A.'s dirty pavement. He maintained his balance only through some fancy footwork, which was noted by Charles Gunn, holding the door open for him. Gunn wore an orange windbreaker, black jeans, and a smile on his dark, handsome face.

"You trying to give new meaning to the term 'hip-hop'?" Gunn asked him. "Ain't gonna go over with the ladies in the clubs, I can tell you."

"Thank you so much for the unsolicited critique," Wesley said, turning sideways to squeeze past Gunn and inside. "And for holding the door. Of course, you might have offered to carry something."

"I'm carryin', dog," Gunn said with a smile. He held up a brown paper bag, folded over at the top. "See? Chocolate chip cookies. You got your mission, I got mine."

Wesley trundled his blankets over to a table inside and set them down with a flourish. "Yes, I see. In the greater scheme of things, a much more vital commodity than mere warmth or shelter on a cool winter's night."

"Man, this is L.A.," Gunn argued. "How much warmth these kids need?"

Wesley just shook his head, knowing that Gunn had spent more than his share of nights on the street and understood how cold it could get. Los Angeles was not Chicago or even London, but outside was outside, and past a certain point, it was just uncomfortable.

Gunn carried the cookies off toward the center's kitchen, leaving Wesley to move the blankets from the common area into the bunk rooms. Wesley volunteered at Anne's center primarily because Anne had done Angel Investigations some favors, while Gunn appreciated her tireless effort to do some good for the kids on the streets. Besides, since Angel had come back from his long descent into darkness and Darla had finally been dispatched, things had been kind of quiet around Angel Investigations. And, though he didn't like to admit it, since Cordelia had been tied up with the auditions and preparations for her television show, not only had things been quiet but even a little boring.

"Thanks, Wesley," Anne said, emerging from a hallway and seeing him burdened with blankets.

"Oh, you're welcome, Anne. There's another load of linens, towels, and such. I'll fetch those in a moment."

"Don't bother," she said with a wave of her hand. "I'll send one of the guys for them. I know Angel's going to be getting up soon, and you men have big plans tonight, right?"

"Plans?"

Anne smiled. "A little popcorn, maybe a beer, and Cordelia on the tube?"

"Oh, right," Wesley said with a laugh. "That had nearly slipped my mind," he lied.

"You'd better not forget it," Gunn intoned from behind him. "She'd never let you live it down if you missed her big broadcast debut."

"I suppose that's true."

"Best believe it is, English."

The expression on Gunn's face was grim, in spite of the light mood of the conversation, and it worried Wesley. "Is, umm, something the matter?"

"Tell you about it later," Gunn replied. He ticked his eyes toward Anne. "Nothing to worry about."

"I have enough to worry about without looking

for more," she admitted. "Why don't you guys head out? I'll take care of the blankets. You've really been a big help today, both of you."

"I'm certain those cookies were a matter of life and death," Wesley said.

Gunn wagged a finger in Wesley's face. "Don't dis the cookies."

"Oh, no dissing intended, I assure you."

"She's right, we should get back to the hotel," Gunn continued. He started for the door. Wesley had to hurry to catch up with him. "Later, Annie."

"Bye, guys. And thanks!"

"You're quite welcome," Wesley replied.

"No problem," Gunn tossed behind him. He was already out the door.

A short time later, they were in the lobby of the Hyperion Hotel. Angel had taken one of the bolstered benches. Wesley found a seat behind the front desk. Gunn sat on the floor, arms resting on his knees, watching his friends trying hard not to look impatient as the minutes ticked toward nine o'clock.

"What was all that about?" Wesley asked. "At the teen center, I mean."

"I didn't want to say anything in front of Anne," Gunn confided. "But a couple of the kids told me an unpleasant rumor. Figured we should check it out before we worry her."

"What kind of rumor?" Angel asked.

"The kind with dead bodies in it," Gunn replied. "Well, one body anyway. So far."

"What do you mean, 'so far'?" Wesley queried.

"What I mean is, if the rumor's true, it sounds like it's not going to be an isolated incident. Maybe there'll be more turning up."

"Can we skip the twenty questions and get to the point?" Angel asked, stifling a yawn.

"I'm sorry you had to wake up," Gunn said confrontationally. "But don't take it out on us."

Angel glared at him for a moment, and he glared back. Then both broke into smiles. Sometimes they were so alike, it scared Gunn. *Of course,* he thought, *who wouldn't be scared to be like a vampire?* Vampires had killed his sister, and, present company excepted, he wished nothing more than for them all to die painful deaths. *Again.*

"As I was saying," Gunn went on, putting his most offended tone into it, "couple of the guys told me about a body discovered this morning, in a vacant lot not too far from the center. Had to be dumped there last night, because people use the lot all the time."

"Use it for what?" Wesley asked. His eyes blazed with curiosity behind his glasses. Occasionally, there were moments in which Gunn was amazed at Wesley's naiveté—as if English Guy's Watcher training had replaced, instead of enhanced, his knowledge of life in the real world.

"You know, sleeping, conducting business transactions, public rest room. Kind of an all-purpose area for the homeless. Anyway, they say it's a woman's body, but unless they can get a DNA match, there's no way they'll I.D. her. Face is gone, removed with acid, maybe. Teeth are gone. Fingerprints are gone. They said the cops were guessing forties, maybe fifties, in good shape, definitely female. Blond hair. Other than that, no identifying marks. No clothes."

"Cause of death?" Angel asked.

"Like takin' her face off with acid isn't cause enough?"

"Just asking."

"I don't know. Haven't read a police report. I just know what the kids told me."

"We should see if there have been any missing persons reports matching that description," Wesley suggested.

"The police will already have done that," Angel said.

"They're on it," Gunn told him. "I just figured you ought to know. You like to keep tabs on the weird ones."

"Nice to know you care," Angel said, utterly without sincerity.

Gunn was heartened to see Angel cracking wise. There had been a time—a long, bad time—when he would have sworn it would never happen again.

Now Angel seemed almost human again, which, since he only was almost human, was as it should be.

Wesley made a show of looking at his watch, as if he didn't already know precisely what time it was. He and Angel had both been acutely aware of the time—both pretending to a casual attitude toward Cordelia's television debut, but as nervous about it, Gunn thought, as a pair of mother hens. "If we hurry, we'll just have time to have some dinner before Cordelia's program comes on."

"I've already had a pint," Angel said.

"A step ahead of us, as usual," Wesley noted.

"That's why I'm the boss."

"No, actually, Wesley's the boss," Gunn pointed out.

"Right," Angel agreed. "Sorry, Wes."

"Quite all right," Wesley said. "Gunn? Do you have a dinner preference?"

"Anything, long as it ain't Type O," Gunn shot back with a grin.

Cordelia's room was almost livable, as long she would only have to live there for a short time. She had to share a bathroom, which she hated, but just with Annemarie, who had the room next door. *As if that wasn't reason enough to vote someone out, first thing,* she thought. But her bed was clean and comfortable, an antique four poster that she thought came from one of the various French Louis periods. *King Louis, or Louie Louie?* she mused, stifling a giggle. This whole thing was going to be fun, not least because everyone who'd ever doubted her would have to watch her on TV, or at least would know that everybody else was watching.

Besides the bed, the room held an armoire instead of a built-in closet, and she'd already hung up most of her clothes in it. Others had gone into a dresser. Both the armoire and dresser were built of a dark, rich-looking wood that was either genuine antique or well-distressed to look like it. The hardwood floor of her room was partially covered by a threadbare Oriental rug. A couple of landscape paintings—of unidentifiable hillsides with trees and winding country roads and farmhouses—decorated the walls and covered at least some of the truly awful red velvety wallpaper. *If this had ever been a brothel, they'd have told us, right?* Cordelia wondered.

Boards covered the two windows in here, which would have, if she'd gotten her bearings right, opened onto the front and the driveway. So she could hear, but not see, when the broadcast trucks pulled up outside and the crew banged in to start preparing for the live feed.

Because *Haunted House* was to be broadcast live, it would be shot earlier in the day than it really appeared to be. Six o'clock, California time, was nine on the East Coast. So they'd go on the air at six local time, and in the Pacific time zone, it would be shown "live on tape" at nine, a concept Cordy had never been too clear on. The best definition seemed to be "not live at all, but not as not-live as some other shows." She knew that it meant her family and friends would see her three hours late, in the "not live at all" category, but that was a small price to pay. Better than going on at midnight in New York, anyway. And the WebCams would be live everywhere.

A production assistant stormed down the hallway pounding on doors. "Five-minute warning, folks!" he shouted. Cordy heard him three doors down, but that didn't mean he skipped hers, hammering on it like Angel when he wanted in someplace. "Downstairs in five minutes! Let's get gorgeous!"

Cordy had already put on a yellow V-neck top and some killer black pants, in anticipation of this moment. They'd been warned against wearing checks or plaids, because those had a tendency to strobe on camera. *But really,* she thought, *anyone who would wear those on camera probably deserved to be eaten by a ghoul, anyway.* She stood before the foggy, gold-veined mirror on the armoire door and ran a brush through her hair a few times, then sat on the edge of the bed to slip on her ankle-strap heels.

And it was a good thing she was sitting down, because the vision slammed her like a runaway truck.

Cordy let out a scream, which she bit off immediately—even in the grip of intense pain, she didn't know if the room was miked and didn't want to take chances. But a moment later, even that much logical thinking was beyond her capability. The almost physical force of the vision flattened Cordelia on the bed, but she didn't know that because her mind was already full of images. She saw the back of a young blond woman—*Buffy*? she found herself wondering, but even as she did she knew that this was not the Slayer. This one was taller, well-proportioned, and muscular but heavier than Buffy had ever been, and her hair was longer. Then, the woman began to turn, and Cordelia knew it was Kirsten St. Clair, whom she had only known for a few days during the audition process for this show. Still, Kirsten turned, almost as if she were revolving on a lazy Susan, or a spit.

And as her face inched into view, Cordelia knew that there was something very wrong with her friend. Kirsten's eye sockets were empty, the big blue eyes missing. Her mouth drooped open; all the muscles of her face slack and lifeless. That was Kirsten's body, but it was hollow, empty of the person Cordelia knew Kirsten to be.

As they always did, this vision passed quickly. Cordy blinked a couple of times, recognizing her bedroom in the house. Out in the hall, the production assistant made his pass back toward the stairs, knocking on doors again. "Five-minute warning is down to four minutes! Let's move it out, people!"

Cordelia tried to make mental notes of what she had seen in the vision. The predominant image, the vacant husk of Kirsten St. Clair, was vivid, but there could always be clues, she knew, hidden in the folds and tucks of memory, so she had learned to deconstruct the visions while they were still fresh. Kirsten's body had been standing upright, supported via some artificial means beyond Cordelia's view. She had been in a room, an apartment, most likely. There had been a big window, no, a sliding-glass door, behind her, since she had been able to make out the line of a balcony rail through the glass.

An apartment, then, and near a beach—Cordelia could hear the distant crash of surf, and smell the tang of salt air.

She started to go for her cell phone and then remembered that there weren't any to be had. She had given hers up downstairs, and the backup phone she'd tucked into her bag was jammed, Rich had said, to keep the game fair. Maybe they haven't jammed it yet, she thought, since the game hadn't actually started yet. She scrounged through the bag until she came up with it, dialed the number of the Angel Investigations office, and pushed SEND. Nothing happened. She looked at the display. NO SIGNAL. She tossed the useless lump of plastic back into the bag.

From the corridor Cordy heard the unmistakable sounds of her fellow contestants heading down for the first show. Shaking her head to clear it, she fought back a wave of dizziness that threatened to knock her back onto the bed. She sucked in a deep breath, held it, and let it out slowly. A glance in the mirror—a little pale, but her color would return, she knew, in a few minutes.

Time for game face. Kirsten was in trouble, that was undeniable. But should Cordelia walk out on the game, at this stage? It would throw off the whole program if she walked out now, not only jettisoning her own career—she would never get work once word got out that she had bailed so early—but possibly harpooning the show itself.

As she headed downstairs on shaky legs, a plan worked itself out. Yes, there was the three-hour tape delay for California viewers. But if Angel, Wesley, and Gunn had any brains between them, they'd be checking out the Webcast while waiting for the television broadcast. So as soon as she had the opportunity, she would play to both the TV cameras and the WebCams, and she'd make herself be understood, by those who knew her, without coming across as too much of a schmoo by those who didn't.

I hope.

Calvin, the production assistant who'd been rapping on doors, waited at the bottom of the stairs. He looked at Cordelia with evident concern. "Everybody else is already here," he said. "Have you been sick?"

Cordy shook her head, not trusting herself to speak yet.

"Just nerves, huh? Don't worry, that'll go away after a little while. You'll forget the cameras are even there."

Not likely, Cordelia thought, though she just nodded at Calvin. *The cameras, right now, are the most important thing here.*

There was no makeup crew, no costuming department, no hairdresser, she knew. All part of creating the illusion of reality. The contestants had to be responsible for their own appearance—*the better to get across that haunted sensation,* Cordelia figured. So it was downstairs and right into the bright lights. Three cameras on rolling tripods faced the group from different angles, and a fourth, slung over the shoulder of the camerawoman who was once again down on one knee, faced Rich Carson. The contestants had taken up spots on couches and chairs, leaving only a narrow space between Pat and Terry on one of the sofas for her. She squeezed in, with smiles for her fellow travelers. Pat looked ill, probably worse than Cordy did, but Terry seemed to be relaxed and ready.

It seemed that Cordelia had only been sitting for a moment when the assistant director cued Rich, and the host broke into his famously winning smile.

"Good evening, and welcome to *Haunted House,*" he said to the camera and the presumably millions of people watching. "Tonight, you're being invited into a once-in-a-lifetime adventure, as we watch nine regular Americans, people like you and me, embark on an indefinite stay in a genuine haunted house. We'll be with them day and night, live on the air and on the World Wide Web. Everything they experience, you'll experience at home—except perhaps for the terror of actually being here."

He went on for a couple of minutes, explaining the rules to the home audience. Cordelia drifted off, trying to plan how she'd get her message delivered to the gang when her chance came. It looked like she was going to have to deal with it sooner rather than later—Rich was already introducing the contestants, giving each one the chance to say a few words about him or herself. Cordelia had already heard all these self-introductions in rehearsal sessions, trying to get everyone used to the cameras. She'd given hers a dozen times in practice, and now she was about to throw it out the window and try something entirely different.

Flying by the seat of my pants, she thought. *Good thing these pants are so darn cute.*

Then she heard Rich say her name, and the camerawoman with the handheld swung it around to her. Cordy smiled, looking into the handheld camera, then into the tripod-mounted one that focused on her, its red light glowing. "Thanks, Rich," she said brightly. "I'm Cordelia Chase, from right here in Los Angeles.

I love L.A., and would especially love an *apartment* by the *beach,* like my friend *Kirsten St. Clair*—who I just met while auditioning for *this show*—has. Kirsten, what a great girl she is. I could use a guardian *angel* like *Kirsten* has to look in on me from time to time, that's for sure. Someone to keep me out of *trouble.*"

She had a sense that she was making a fool of herself—the other contestants were looking at her, she thought, as if she had gone insane. But she could think of no better way to get the message out to Angel. Kirsten needed him more than Cordelia needed this moment on camera—there would be plenty more, over the next few days, in which to regain her pride.

"Thanks, Cordelia," Rich finally said. "It's, uh, good to know you made such a close friend on our show. I'm sure that within a few days you guys will all be friends—except when you have to vote each other out of the house."

"That's the challenge, Rich," Cordelia replied brightly.

"And sitting next to Cordelia is Terry," Rich continued. "Terry, why don't you tell us a little about yourself?"

Cordelia silently blew out the breath she'd been holding. That part was done. She could only hope that Angel was watching.

Chapter Three

Wesley served himself a second helping of spaghetti with a four-cheese sauce he'd learned to make years before. The secret to spaghetti, he knew, was to make the sauce and the spaghetti separately, but at the last minute, to drain the spaghetti, pour the sauce over it, stir them together over heat for just long enough to coat the spaghetti and trap in the heat of the sauce. *Cordelia loves my spaghetti,* he thought. The possibility struck him, suddenly, that she might not be around to share his spaghetti in the future, and he felt a wave of sadness wash over him.

Gunn broke off a piece of French bread, watched Angel sip from a tall glass of blood, and shivered. "Seconds, huh?" he said. "Man, I'm never gonna get used to seein' that."

"You will," Wesley assured him. "It's more or less second nature to me now. And Cordelia has even tried to spice it up—remember the cinnamon, Angel?"

Angel made a face. "Lumpy blood," he scowled. "Nasty."

"Speaking of Cordelia," Wesley said, "what time is it?" He looked at his watch, answering his own question. "Almost seven," he said. "She'll be on in a couple of hours."

"Wasn't there a Webcast, too?" Gunn reminded him. "That's supposed to be live, right?"

"That's right," Angel said. "That's what Cordelia told me."

"Well, do you think we should dial it up, or whatever it is one does with a Webcast?"

Angel looked at him blankly, and Wesley remembered Angel's notorious incompetence when it came to computers. "Perhaps later," he said quietly.

"Pass me that spaghetti," Gunn said. "We'll catch it the old-fashioned way, on the tube."

They were almost through Beth's intro—Beth had a tendency, Cordelia noted, to ramble, and she thought Rich was on the verge of cutting her off—when the lights went out.

Not just the house lights, but the TV lights, too. The room was plunged into sudden blackness. Despite the fact that it wasn't even dark outside yet, with the windows boarded over, the electric lights were the room's only illumination.

When the lights went out, a couple of the contestants screamed, so on edge were they about being on TV or just about being in the house. Cordy's breath caught, but she only tensed for a moment and then relaxed and sat on the sofa, waiting. *This is too pat,* she thought. *It's got to be rigged.* She heard Rich, using his most comforting tone, saying, "It's okay, it's all right, everybody just hang tight, okay?"

And a moment later, sure enough, the lights flickered and came back on.

"Emergency generator," Rich said. "We're ready for anything around here."

And then Annemarie screamed in horror.

I never thought the words "emergency generator" had the power to instill such fear in someone, Cordelia thought. But then she looked where Annemarie was pointing, and so did the rest of the people in the room, as suddenly there were a number of surprised gasps.

Painted on the wall above their heads—where someone would have had to practically stand on Cordelia's lap to paint it—in a still-wet red paint that looked uncomfortably like Angel's only food staple, were the words LEAVE HERE NOW in foot-high letters.

Annemarie was sobbing a little bit, and the camerawoman had crabwalked around to get a good shot of her. Cordy glanced at some of the others, seeing expressions that ranged from terror to wonder to near-hysteria.

These guys are good, Cordelia thought. *I wonder how they did that one.* She thought perhaps there had been a fake section of wall attached over the pre-painted letters, which was then yanked away remotely when the lights went out. However they'd done it, she appreciated the effect. It'd give her fellow contestants a sense of what the week would be like. *From the looks of her,* Cordy thought, *Annemarie might be ready to head out with the crew when they leave for the night. Which, considering the shared bathroom thing, would be just fine.*

"Hey, I can't see, man. Don't you have a widescreen or something?" Gunn asked.

"Believe me, we're lucky we're not trying to watch this on the computer," Wesley shot back.

"I've never been a big TV fan," Angel explained. He'd positioned himself so he had a good view of the TV set, perched on top of the hotel's front desk. Wesley had pulled up a chair next to him, and Gunn, who'd arrived back from dinner last, sat on one of the benches, trying to see past both of them.

"More of an illuminated manuscript kind of guy, I guess," Gunn suggested.

"Quiet," Angel said. "She's on." Cordelia had suddenly come onto the screen, and Angel found himself leaning forward, almost as if he might reach out and touch her. That was *his* Cordy on a national television show, the girl he'd known since she was a spoiled high school princess and had watched grow into a beautiful and confident woman. At this moment, though, she looked lovely but a little peaked. Then she was speaking, and the room settled into a hush.

". . . a guardian *angel* like *Kirsten* has to look in on me from time to time, that's for sure," Cordelia was saying. "Someone to keep me out of *trouble.*"

The camera cut back to the host, and Angel turned to Wesley.

"Has she taken leave of her senses?" Wesley asked, astonished.

"Naw," Gunn countered. "It's code."

"Code?"

Angel had already picked up on what Gunn called "code" and mentally noted the words she emphasized. *It must have taken a lot for her to do that, knowing it would make her look—well, nuts,* he realized.

When the next person was talking, Angel turned to Wesley. "Apartment. Beach. Kirsten St. Clair. Auditioning. This show. Angel. Kirsten. Trouble."

"So, this Kirsten chick, she's in trouble and she needs Angel," Gunn interpreted. "That's you."

"And she's in an apartment by the beach," Wesley said. "Brilliant."

"That's why Cordelia looks so pale," Angel said. "She had a vision."

"Right there on the screen?" Gunn asked.

"No, but probably shortly before. If it had happened while she was on camera she wouldn't have been able to get through her bit."

"Not the way they've been affecting her lately," Wesley agreed. "They're no longer just visions, they're . . . they're assaults."

"And she couldn't just call, because of what Carson explained about cell phones. So how we gonna track down this Kirsten?" Gunn asked.

Wesley was already on his feet and flipping through a phone book. "St. Clair, St. Clair," he muttered.

There had been a time when Angel would have simply called a friend on the LAPD, but that time was long past.

"There's no listing," Wesley declared.

"What about the Internet?" Gunn suggested. "Isn't that where Cordelia usually looks stuff up?"

"Yes, though I'm not precisely sure where," Wesley replied. "It's not like there's a www-dot-powers-that-be-dot-com, that I'm aware of." Even so, he went to the computer behind the hotel desk and turned it on. He sat in front of it, bathed in the glow from its monitor. From the TV, Angel could hear screams.

"Think there's something wrong with the set, man," Gunn said. "It's all dark."

Angel glanced at him. Gunn hadn't budged from

the big bench seat, a remnant of the hotel's earlier days as, well, a hotel. Those seats, Angel knew, were made to look comfortable, not to be comfortable. The hotel wanted to create the impression that guests and travelers were welcome to sit around in its lobby for hours on end, without having to deal with the reality of people sitting in its lobby for long stretches of time.

Gunn didn't seem to mind—he had an easy familiarity with his own body that allowed him to relax completely, almost anywhere, and then to snap back to coiled purpose when necessary at a moment's notice. It was something Angel almost envied him. To Angel, real relaxation was as much a memory as drawing breath or the pounding of a heart after a workout. There had been moments, over the past hundred years or so—but only moments.

He turned back to Wesley, who caught his gaze. "Thank God for bookmarks," Wesley uttered. "I must say, for whatever Cordy's faults, she's rather a well-organized Web surfer."

"That's great," Angel said. "But are you finding anything?"

"Just a moment," Wesley said. "Here it comes."

"Lights are back," Gunn told them. "Hey, that's cool, check it."

"What is it?" Wesley asked.

"Ghostly writing, in blood," Gunn responded. "Leave here now, it says."

Angel went around to the front of the counter so he could see the screen. Gunn was right, it was cool. *Looks real,* he thought.

"Got her," Wesley announced. "Kristin St. Clair. She's in Santa Monica."

"Let's roll," Angel said.

"What about Cordy's show?" Gunn protested.

"We'll catch it in reruns," Angel said.

"Reruns? On a game show?"

"What Angel means," Wesley offered, "is that as much as we'd like to see more of Cordelia's debut appearance on national television, there's a young woman in trouble severe enough that The Powers That Be sent Cordy a vision about her, and that reality must overrule our selfish desire to be entertained and amused."

In spite of his verbal protestations, Gunn was already on his feet and headed for the door. Wesley and Angel joined him. As they left, Gunn said, "Thanks for translating, Wes, but to tell you the truth, I don't know which of y'all is harder to understand."

Larry Mullins slammed the door of his BMW, then wished he could slam it again just to hear the sound it made. *Now that's a car,* he thought. He admired it for a moment, then noticed that Lilah Morgan, already halfway to the front door of the house, was staring at him, arms crossed over her chest. He knew that mentally she was tapping her foot impatiently, even though her feet were, in actuality, still.

"I'm coming," he told her. *A man can't even enjoy his car around these people,* he thought. *It's all about the career with them.*

Of course, he was no different, he understood. It was the career, for instance, that had bought him the BMW. Three years at Wolfram and Hart under his belt, and he had already traded up to German engineering. The next trade would be to Italian, he had already decided. Ferrari, Maserati . . . he hadn't picked the brand yet. It didn't matter. The important thing was the country of origin, and he knew that.

Lilah reached the door ahead of him and rang the bell. She turned, eyeing the briefcase he clutched. "You do have the papers?"

He wagged the case at her. "Right in here."

"Good. I'd hate to make this trip for nothing."

Larry looked around at the Beverly Hills mansion. The place resembled the White House. Floodlights splashed gleaming white columns that rose two or three stories overhead. They stood on a wide brick porch before a Colonial-style door. To either side of the door, bay windows jutted out toward the wide expanse of green lawn. *The color of money,* Larry thought. *Like this is a bad place to spend an evening.*

After a couple of minutes, and two rings, Parker McKay himself opened the door. Which was, after all, the way it was supposed to be. He had been instructed to dismiss the household staff for the night, and he appeared to have followed directions.

"I'm sorry," he said softly, a little out of breath. "I was all the way upstairs."

"In the west wing?" Larry asked.

"East, actually," Parker replied, missing the joke. Then he caught it, and forced a polite chuckle. "Oh, yes, right."

Larry had never liked the guy, but business was business, a client was a client. They couldn't all be gems.

"We just need to get this paperwork wrapped up, Mr. McKay," Lilah said. "Then we'll be out of your hair."

Which, Larry thought, *is pretty generous considering the man hardly has any.* Parker McKay wasn't ancient yet, but he was, by Larry's standards, getting old. He had read Parker's file and knew the man's vital statistics inside out. He was sixty-six years old. He'd made money in a variety of businesses, everything from aerospace to fossil fuels. He'd even had the presence of mind to get out of dot coms while the getting was good. His fortune was currently valued at $700 million, give or take. Not the wealthiest of Wolfram and Hart's clients, but certainly worth catering to.

Unconsciously, Parker rubbed a hand across his thinning white hair, and made a half-turn to invite them inside. He walked with a stoop, like a man older than he was. His face was tanned, and he had a tennis player's build—and he wore tennis whites, even indoors, to enhance the image, Larry noted—and his teeth testified to expensive dental work. Larry figured hair plugs were next, followed perhaps by a few tucks by a plastic surgeon. Parker McKay, he had a feeling, was a man desperately fighting the aging process.

"Come in, won't you?" he asked. "The staff is gone for the night, as you requested, so we have the place to ourselves. I don't need staff to mix a drink, though."

"Nothing for us," Lilah said quickly, cutting off Larry before he had a chance to ask for the Manhattan he craved so badly. "As I said, a few papers and we'll be out of your way."

Larry had the sense that McKay wanted the company, but he didn't press it. Lilah had seniority, she had Nathan Reed's ear, and Larry was, by comparison, a message boy. Sure, he had the car and the law degree and the condo in Westwood, but he knew the corporate culture at Wolfram and Hart was a complex one, and people had to earn their stripes. He was still earning his, so this project was primarily Lilah's show.

Parker led them through the house into a formal dining room. When he pressed a button on the wall, overhead chandeliers blazed to life. The walnut table would have seated twenty. "I think we can spread the papers out here, no?"

"This should be just fine, Mr. McKay," Larry said. "We'll be out of your way in no time."

Parking was at a premium a block from the beach in Santa Monica, so Angel just pulled his '67 Plymouth GTX into the alley behind the complex and they all piled out. The building was white stucco with aqua trim, three stories tall, with balconies on the side that faced toward the ocean. Across the street were shops and more expensive apartments, and beyond those was a strip of sand, and then the Pacific Ocean.

Wesley had determined that Kirsten St. Clair lived in apartment 311, so he led the way to an exterior staircase that climbed one end of the building and they went up. Lights shone in several of the windows, and the bluish glow of television sets illuminated others. A party seemed to be in progress on the second floor; the door was open, and people spilled out onto the concrete walkway with plastic cups and glass bottles in their hands. Several of them noted the three men rushing up to the third floor, but no one spoke to them. Wesley found himself hoping that Kirsten was inside, maybe watching the end of the program, and that they'd totally misinterpreted what Cordelia had said. *That's unlikely, though,* he thought. *Cordelia, bless her heart, is far too vain to make a fool on herself on national television without a very good reason.*

Angel stopped in front of 311 and pushed the doorbell, but it didn't work. He rapped on the door. There was no answer. He tried the knob, and it turned easily in his hand, so he pushed the door open and tried to step inside. He couldn't—an invisible wall blocked his passage.

"So she's alive?" Gunn asked, behind him. Angel stepped out of the way.

"Seems to be."

"Well, that's good news," Wesley said. He and Gunn entered the apartment.

"I'll wait here," Angel said.

"Right," Wesley agreed. It wasn't like Angel had a choice—he couldn't enter a human's home without being invited in by the resident, as long as she was alive. But in this case, she didn't seem to be here to extend that courtesy.

Wesley flipped on a light, and Gunn gave a low whistle. The apartment's décor could, Wesley thought, be graciously defined as "beach casual." The furnishings were eclectic at best, with the primary commonality seeming to be an ability to withstand wet swimsuits and sand. A sofa that appeared at a glance to be leather was really some leather-like plastic substance. Other seating options ranged from folding sun chairs to an inflatable rubber hand. Before the sofa was a coffee table made from a big chunk of driftwood, cut off and polished at the top, with a glass panel that rested on it. But the glass, just now, was on the floor, and the driftwood lay sideways next to it. A tumbler of some orange-colored beverage had apparently been on the table when it went over—a stain had spread out on the off-white economy carpeting from where the up-ended glass had landed. One of the folding chairs had half-collapsed nearby.

"Looks like someone left in a hurry," Gunn suggested.

"Yes," Wesley agreed. "A very large hurry."

"I'll check the bedroom," Gunn said, passing through a doorway into a short, dark hall.

"Watch yourself," Wesley said. The apartment looked as if it was empty, but there was nothing to say that whoever had disrupted it so wasn't still here.

"Always."

Wesley took a second, more detailed look around the living room. At the light switch near the door—the one he had just used to flip on the lights—he saw a streak of crimson.

Angel, standing just outside the door, watched him peer at it.

"It's blood," Angel confirmed. "I can smell it."

"I thought as much. So whoever took Kirsten St. Clair out of here either injured her, or she hurt him, or both."

"And one of them bothered to go to the trouble of turning out the lights on the way out."

"Well, electricity prices being what they are," Wesley said.

"No one's home," Gunn said. "But it doesn't look like she took a trip." Wesley turned and saw Gunn holding a woman's purse. He had her wallet out and open. "Kirsten St. Clair. She didn't even take her I.D. Is that . . . ?"

"Blood," Wesley told him. "Yes."

"So, put that together with the mess in the living room—"

"And you've got a kidnapping," Angel finished.

"We should call the cops," Gunn suggested.

"If this was anything the police could handle, The Powers That Be wouldn't have bothered Cordelia with it."

"What do we do, then?" Gunn asked. "I don't see anything that looks like a clue jumpin' out at me. Why can't Cordy's visions be a little more specific, so we know where Kirsten is now and not just where she was when she was snatched?"

"That's what our job is," Angel replied. "Figuring that out."

Chapter Four

The camera crew was gone, the production assistants and assistant directors, the director, the grips, Rich Carson . . . some of their equipment remained behind, but the house was completely empty except for the nine contestants.

Nothing in particular held them together in the living room, but nobody seemed to want to be the first one to go off by him or herself. So they sat around for more than an hour, chatting quietly, as if to raise their voices would summon the ghoulies and goblins.

". . . was watching when they packed up their gear," Gordon was saying. "If they rigged that writing on the wall, I don't know how." The words were still there—no one had been willing to even touch the lettering, but it seemed to be drying to the kind of rusty brown color one would expect if it really was blood.

"I was thinking maybe they had it covered, and snatched the covering off when the lights went out," Cordelia offered. "But I never saw anything that might have been covering it."

Gordon looked on the floor below the wall, and behind the couch in front of the lettering. "There's nothing down here. And to pull away some kind of covering, they'd have had to go right over your head."

"That's true," Cordelia admitted. She was less sure of her theory than she had been, but still believed it must have been a trick of some kind. Ghosts just weren't cooperative enough to perform such a stunt on cue, and the show's producers wouldn't have wanted their debut episode to be without some kind of spectral visitation.

"What if there are tiny holes in the wall, and they injected the paint, or blood, or whatever, from behind it?" Beth opined. She stood before the liquid lettering, peering at the wall over her wire-rimmed glasses. "Smells like blood to me."

"Secret passages behind the walls?" Christy asked.

"Why not," Beth said. "It's a haunted house, isn't it? I'd almost be surprised if it *didn't* have secret passages."

"Maybe more to the point," Pat put in, "the house was built by a guy who seems to have been a bit of a perv, or at least held some pretty wild parties. He might have put in secret passages so he could spy on his guests, right?"

"Nice theory. And my room is next to yours," Sharon told Pat. "I suppose you've already checked for peepholes."

"Hey, just because I thought of it doesn't mean I'd do it," Pat objected.

"Sure. I'll be changing in the bathroom, away from WebCams. With the lights off, just in case," Sharon shot back. She was smiling when she said it, though, and Cordelia understood that her remarks had been made in jest.

Still, she thought, *that's worth thinking about. This place could be honeycombed with passages.*

"So do you guys think the production crew is really going to be setting up 'haunting' events to scare us?" she asked the room in general.

"Oh, sure," Gordon said. "How can they not? They've got a TV show predicated on the idea that we're stuck in this haunted house. If the house doesn't manifest in spectacularly visual ways, they have to fake it."

"So how will we know what's real and what's phony?" Terry asked.

"Does it matter?" Annemarie responded. "If it's scary, it's scary."

"It matters to me," Terry said firmly. "Real ghosts scare me a lot more than Hollywood special effects."

"Just assume it's all real," Gordon said. "That way, we'll put on a better show for the home viewers."

"That's what I'm concerned about, all right," Terry said. "Never mind my own sanity, I just care what the couch potatoes think."

"Those 'couch potatoes' are the reason one of us will walk out of here with a big bag of money," Cordelia inserted, making air quotes around the words "couch potatoes." "And we're no doubt on WebCam right now, so we might want to be nice." She could barely believe she was saying that. She hoped no one in Sunnydale was watching the former Queen of Mean urging her fellow contestants to be nice. Her reputation would never recover.

But on the other hand, she hoped *everyone* in Sunnydale was glued to TV sets and computer monitors. So what she really hoped, she decided, was that they weren't actually on WebCam at this particular moment.

"Anyway, from what I've heard," Vince said, steering the conversation back to where it had been, "this house don't need any help providing the scares."

"You believe in haunted houses?" Annemarie asked him.

"I believe there's a lot more out there than our tiny minds can comprehend," Vince replied. His voice carried the slightest Southern inflection that Cordelia found a little charming. "I don't know as it's ghosts or what, or if it matters. But there's energies left behind, sometimes, in a place where bad things have happened. And this house has had more than its share of bad things. I'd be surprised if it wasn't haunted by something."

"I was hoping to get some sleep tonight," Annemarie said. "Maybe I should just give up on that now."

"Have any of you ever seen a ghost?" Christy ventured. "Or anything else like that?"

Cordelia kept mum. Phantom Dennis was her secret weapon. She knew how unlikely it was that any of them had anywhere near the experience she'd had with the supernatural, including sharing her apartment with an actual ghost. And, briefly, Dennis's ghostly mother, who had been a whole lot scarier.

She hadn't decided how she felt about this house yet—the lettering on the wall had been creepy, but it was not beyond the realm of possibility that it was a plant to add some chills to an otherwise not very scary first episode. The broadcast had summarized, with photos and even some reenactments, the history of the house that Rich had outlined for them earlier that day, and the handheld camera had taken a poorly lit tour of the property, in addition to showcasing each of the contestants and describing how the game would work.

Now, though, she was exhausted. She figured that the vision had a lot to do with it—they took more and more out of her, and they didn't let up, like they once had, until the crisis was over. Whatever was going on with Kirsten St. Clair, the situation was ongoing, she could tell, because her head still throbbed and her whole body felt like she had a grip on a live wire.

"I'm going to bed," she announced suddenly, stifling a yawn. "If any ghosts want me, they'll know where to look." She stood and headed for the stairs.

"G'night, Cordelia," Annemarie called after her.

"Sleep tight," Gordon added. "Don't hesitate to try a bloodcurdling scream if you see a spook."

"Trust me, not a problem," Cordelia tossed back over her shoulder.

Climbing the stairs, she heard their muffled voices below in the living room, but the long hallway at the top of the stairs was utterly silent, at first, and just the slightest bit creepy because of it. Candle-style lightbulbs burned in wall sconces between each door, but they didn't cast much illumination, so the hall was shadowed with just faint stripes of light falling across it. And as Cordy walked, her footsteps on the hardwood floor creaking with every step, she heard another set of footfalls, almost echoing hers.

She stopped suddenly. One more footfall sounded, and then the second set stopped as well. Cordy took one quick step. The echoing footfall followed suit. She couldn't tell where the sound came from; it seemed to be beside her, above her, beneath her. She turned and started for the stairs again, feeling suddenly like a little company might not be a bad idea. The footfalls copied her.

This is ridiculous, she thought. She spun again, and went straight to her room. The footsteps echoed her all the way, but after she opened her door and stepped into the privacy of her own room, they stopped. She closed the door, turned the big iron key in the lock, and checked the door. The lock held.

I'm perfectly safe in here, she told herself. *The show isn't going to let anyone be in real danger. Sure, a few scares, some goosebumps, a couple of sleepless nights. But no one's going to get hurt.*

She performed a quick mental check to see if she felt like she was being watched, from a secret passage or from some other plane of existence. Neither seemed to be the case—the only eye on her, she believed, was that of the WebCam in the corner. She smiled at it, tugged some pajamas from a dresser drawer, and went into the adjoining bathroom to change, locking the door on Annemarie's side when she went in.

"We do what the police would do if they were here," Angel instructed, standing outside Kirsten's apartment. He wished he could have gone inside, knowing that, as good as Wesley and Gunn were, his own senses were far sharper than theirs. "Door to door. See if anybody saw anything."

"There's a party going on downstairs," Wesley pointed out. "It's amazing that someone was able to kidnap her with all those people roaming about."

"Place like this, a lot of people don't pay much attention to their neighbors," Gunn observed. "Not exactly a security building. People want their own privacy, they demonstrate that by keeping their noses out of one another's business."

"Yes, but a kidnapping? Someone was bleeding," Wesley said. "You would think—"

"You'd think a lot of things when you're talking about people," Angel said. "The best you can say is that they usually come up with a way to surprise you."

"Split up by floors?" Gunn offered. "Three of us, three stories."

"Makes sense," Angel replied. *It'd be hard to physically haul a struggling woman from a third-floor apartment without somebody noticing something,* he thought. *But since The Powers That Be saw fit to send Cordy a vision about it, we're not necessarily dealing with humans, here. There could have been an invisibility spell cast, or something else that would fog people's perceptions or memories.*

"I'll start at the bottom," Wesley said. "You work up here, Gunn, and Angel in the middle?"

"Works for me," Gunn agreed.

They split up then, Wesley rattling down the stairs and Gunn moving to the apartment next door and pressing the doorbell button. Angel left him, moving to the second floor, the one on which a party was still underway. He decided to start there, since various partiers stood outside on the walkway looking at him. He approached the group. "Is the person who lives here around?"

One of the partiers, sitting on the walkway with his back against the apartment's stucco wall and a plastic cup in his hands, craned his neck to look in through the open door. "I don't see her, but she oughta be in there somewhere. Staci, that's her name. Staci with an 'i.'"

Without her specific invitation, Angel couldn't go in to look for her. "Could you find her?" he asked. "It's important."

Another party guest looked inside her own cup for a long time, as if ascertaining that it truly was empty. "I need a refill," she said. "I'll find Stace."

"Thanks."

Waiting outside, he decided to ask these guests if they'd seen anything, though he wasn't sure he trusted their perceptions. *Enough partying, and that invisibility spell wouldn't be needed.*

"Do any of you know Kirsten St. Clair? Lives upstairs?"

"She's the one who auditioned for that show, right," someone asked. "The lifeguard."

"She's a lifeguard?"

"Yeah, that's what Staci says."

"She's a hottie, I know that," another guest added.

A young woman came to the door and looked at Angel expectantly. She wore a tiger-patterned halter top, denim hip-huggers, and platform shoes that pushed her a little over five feet tall, and her brown hair was pulled back into a loose ponytail. "I'm Staci," she said. "You were looking for me? Are we making too much noise?"

"It's nothing like that. Can I talk to you privately for a moment?" Angel asked her. "It's about Kirsten."

She glanced behind her into the apartment. "There's kind of a party going on."

"I can see that. Maybe if we just step down the way a little."

Staci came out, giving him a questioning look.

"I'm sorry, I wouldn't bother you if it wasn't important."

"It's okay," she said. She walked with Angel down toward the staircase at the end of the building. "Is Kirsten in some kind of trouble?"

"I think she might be," Angel admitted. "When's the last time you've seen her?"

Staci thought for a moment. "This afternoon, I guess."

"And she seemed okay then?"

"Yeah, sure. She was fine. She was going to come down tonight, she said. We were going to watch *Haunted House,* that new reality show? She tried out for it, but she didn't make the cut."

"But she was going to watch it, anyway?"

"Yes, she was anxious to. She said she made some friends during the whole audition process, and she wanted to see what it turned out to be like. So we had the show on at nine, but she never showed up."

"Did you worry about her? Try to call her or see if she was there?"

Staci shook her head, ponytail whipping back and forth. "Why would I? I just figured she got a better offer. Have you seen her? A girl that looks like that gets a lot of better offers."

"No, I haven't," Angel said.

"You know that woman from *Baywatch,* the one who marries rock stars like a kid eats jelly beans? Kirsten looks like that, only it's all real. And she's nice, besides. Seems to have a real level head, you know? Unlike a lot of the beautiful beach bunnies you see around here."

"Someone said she's a lifeguard. Here in Santa Monica?"

Staci inclined her head to the west. "She walks to work."

"So you didn't see her leave with anybody? Maybe around six?" Angel asked.

"Didn't see a thing," Staci confirmed. "At six I

was taking a long shower, though, so I wouldn't have. Are you a cop or something?"

"Something," Angel said. He fished an Angel Investigations business card from a pocket of his long black coat and handed it to her. She seemed sincerely concerned for her friend, although anxious to get back to her party. He hoped the concern would win out, and she'd try to remember any more details. The hunt for Kirsten St. Clair was going to be a tough one if they couldn't get some kind of a handle to start with. "If you think of anything else, or hear from her, I'd appreciate it if you'd give me a call."

Staci examined the card. "You're Angel?"

"Yes."

She stuck out her hand, and he shook it. "I'm Staci. You want to come in for a while? Have a drink?"

"No, thanks," Angel said. "I appreciate the offer, though. You'll let me know?"

"I'll let you know," she said. "Maybe another time?"

"Maybe."

Angel met up with Wesley and Gunn twenty minutes later at the car. "Anything?" he asked.

Gunn broke into a wide grin. "That girl was hittin' on you, dog," he said.

"No, she wasn't."

"I heard her. I was upstairs."

Angel held back a smile. "Maybe she was, a little."

"But you know where that leads," Wesley said.

"Not necessarily," Angel argued. He knew Wesley understood his curse better than to believe that. As he recalled, Wesley himself had engaged in some amorous activity while posing as Angel, when he'd been bodyguarding Virginia Bryce.

"Yes, I know, I understand," Wesley admitted. "I was being overly general."

"So, if we could get back to Kirsten St. Clair," Angel tried. "Did you get anything?"

"Actually, yes," Wesley replied. "One of the neighbors downstairs saw a black stretch limo parked in the alley, about five forty-five, as he was coming in from a run on the beach. He showered and went back out a little after six, and it was gone. He thought it was odd because the usual types of car one sees around here, he said, are surfer vans, VW Beetles, and old station wagons."

"A stretch? Those are some upscale kidnappers," Gunn observed.

Angel climbed into the convertible, sliding behind the wheel. "Well, it gives us something to go on," he said. "We can try the limousine rental agencies in the morning. And someone should check out the beach, talk to Kirsten's coworkers. She's a lifeguard there."

"A lifeguard?" Gunn asked. "That sounds like me."

"Perhaps we'll flip for that," Wesley said. "Though I think Angel's out of the running."

Angel nodded and turned the key. The GTX roared to life.

On the way back to the Hyperion Hotel, they stopped at the vacant lot where a woman's body had been found that morning. They walked around the lot, outside the yellow crime scene tape that had been stretched around the discovery area. Light from nearby streetlamps spilled over some of the lot, but the cluttered, junk-strewn spot where the body had been dumped was dark and quiet. Angel ducked under the tape and walked the area, senses alert for anything out of the ordinary, any clues the forensic techs might have missed.

But there was nothing. Which, in itself, indicated to Angel that it had been merely a dumping spot and not the scene of the murder itself.

After a few minutes, he let himself out under the tape. "Nothing," he reported. "Let's go home."

"I'll take off from here," Gunn said. "Go check with the crew, see if anybody's heard anything about this lady or Kirsten St. Clair."

"I could use some sleep," Wesley admitted. "Being diurnal, and not nocturnal like the two of you."

"I'll drop you at the hotel, then," Angel said. He'd had an idea, but it would be easier to put into action solo, so he didn't mind leaving the others behind. "I've got another stop to make after," he said.

Chapter Five

Tuesday

Cordelia slept. And as she slept, she dreamed.

Not one of those dreams that she would later catch herself remembering at odd moments, wondering if it was real or imaginary. She knew, even as it happened, that she was dreaming.

Which didn't make it any less horrible.

She saw Kirsten St. Clair, on a beach in one of those red one-piece swimsuits that lifeguards wear. Not a great look for most people, but Cordy found herself feeling a twinge of aggravation at how well Kirsten pulled it off.

Suddenly, Kirsten saw or heard something that was beyond the range of Cordelia's vision or hearing. Something that scared her. Her wide eyes popped open wide, her jaw dropped, mouth gaping.

She screamed.

The scream went on forever.

Kirsten threw her head back, eyes closed now, veins showing at her temples, fists clenched at her sides, screaming toward the heavens. The noise built and built, until Cordy couldn't understand why she wasn't waking up from it.

Kirsten continued screaming, louder and louder, mouth opening wider and wider.

When it occurred to Cordy that her mouth was open too wide, that no one's mouth really stretched that far, Kirsten's opened still more, and the skin of her chin and forehead began to fold in on itself.

Then Kirsten's scream became soundless, because her mouth was clogged with something pink. But that pink mass expelled itself, shooting high into the air, and it was followed by more of the same, bits of pink and white and gray, and Cordelia knew that Kirsten was screaming herself empty, blasting organs and muscle and bone and brain out of herself. The gout of internal body parts formed a solid, grisly column extending out of Kirsten's impossibly wide maw like something meant to hold up the sky, and as it reached higher and higher, Kirsten's body started to collapse in on itself. Firm, toned flesh sagged like an empty sack. Finally, vacated, Kirsten's mouth closed and she fell over, eyes meeting Cordelia's and blinking once before she hit the ground with the sound of rustling paper.

Cordelia woke up drenched in cold, clammy sweat, seeing Kirsten's clear blue eyes burned into her mind. She shook all over, as if from a fever. *That poor girl,* she thought. *She's still in danger, and it's getting worse.*

Climbing out of bed, she turned on the overhead light. Sleep wouldn't come easily again this night, she knew. The dream had been almost as bad as a vision in its clarity and severity.

She glanced at a bedside clock. A little after three. The house was silent. She'd gone to bed in a white cotton nightgown, but it was soaked through with sweat now, so she went into what was now her private bathroom for a quick shower. She'd feel a little better after that, she knew, and maybe she'd still be able to salvage a few hours of rest.

With the hot water cranked up, the bathroom was soon filled with a thick cloud of steam. Cordelia drew back the shower curtain, ready for any of the various haunted house clichés that might await her: the body in the bathtub, the knife murderer hiding behind the curtain, the blood that sprayed from the showerhead. But this water wasn't red, and the tub was empty. She stood under the stinging spray, eyes closed, letting the pressure and warmth drum the memory of her awful dream away.

When she emerged, the mirrors were fogged and steam hung in the room like dense fog at the coast. But in the fog—no, more accurately, of the fog, carved from it as if from a slab of alabaster, a face stared at her as she stepped from the tub. She recognized this face—small eyes spaced wide, as if drawing away from a prominent, slightly bulbous nose, a heavy-lipped mouth set into a weak jaw, all topped with an unruly shock of white hair. It was the face of the man in the living room portrait. *What was his name? Carstairs. Glenn Carstairs.*

The man who had hanged himself—or been hanged—from the crystal chandelier.

By the time she reached for a towel, the mist had shifted, and the face—if it had been there at all—had vanished.

This night is just not going well for me.

They hadn't been able to find out much about Kirsten St. Clair from her neighbors, but Angel had thought of a way to get a little more information.

He had remembered that when Cordelia was applying and auditioning for the TV show, she'd complained about the amount of paperwork she'd had to fill out. Medical forms, insurance forms, references, questionnaires—the producers had wanted, she had suspected, to be able to get as clear a picture of their potential contestants as possible without having actually known them their whole lives.

That information, Angel thought, would be filed at the production company's offices. It would be considered private, and they'd never just hand it over to him without a search warrant, which he couldn't get. But if he could get inside while they were out, and find her file, he'd get friends' names and addresses, maybe learn some likely hangouts, and who knew what else?

The production company was located in Burbank, which was another thing Cordelia had complained about, the Valley being . . . well, the Valley. *At night, though,* Angel thought, *it's not so bad. Certainly not as bad as that winter in Irkutsk.*

He parked around the corner from the office building, in front of a Chinese restaurant. The production company, Laughing Pig Productions, was housed in a warehouse space. Cordy had said they kept a couple of soundstages there for other shows they produced, even though *Haunted House* was all location shooting. She had once auditioned for a pilot there, for a daytime soap called *Nights of Fire.* It had been, she said, about the lives and loves of a mixed-gender fire company. "Incredibly stupid," she said. "It'll probably be a monster hit."

She'd been wrong about that one, but it looked like *Haunted House* might pay Laughing Pig's rent for a while. Without a smash hit under their belts, though, their headquarters was nothing fancy.

Neither was their security system. Angel managed to snap the lock of a side door, off an alley, and walked right in. Strolling past the front, he'd seen a sleepy-looking security guard sitting at a card table just inside the front door, flipping through a hot rod magazine. Angel hoped the guard remained enthralled by that long enough for him to get what he needed and get out.

The side door had taken him into the soundstage area, though the stage wasn't set up for anything. He worked his way silently through the dark, deserted stages, into an open conference area surrounded by closed doors. Overhead lights were on in the open area. Angel stopped and listened, his keen senses attuned for any noises—breathing, heartbeats, the creak of a chair or a floorboard—that might tell him that somebody was inside.

Hearing nothing, he went in.

Next to the doors, placards with names and titles hung on the walls. He moved quickly, door to door, until he found Alexa Bratton, Casting Director. Putting an ear to her door, he listened intently. Nothing. He turned the knob of her door, breaking the weak lock. He slipped inside and closed the door behind him, but saw at a glance that this office wouldn't help. A few head shots, signed to her by successful actors, adorned the walls, and her desk was buried under manila file folders. But Angel didn't want those—those would be the under-consideration people. He wanted the passed-over people. There was only one filing cabinet in the room, and he knew he was looking for more than that. He left again, and tried the room next door.

Jackpot. This room was a warren of filing cabinets.

Angel opened one, skimming the names as he flipped through the files—Martin, Prosky, Shea, Tidwell. No St. Clair. But as he flipped back through the files, he realized how they were arranged, so he went to "H" for *Haunted House.* In this cabinet, there were two sets of files, one with names he recognized—Cordelia Chase among them, but also Terry, Pat, Christy, Sharon, and the rest. The other set was much bigger, and arranged alphabetically. The losers. He went straight to Kirsten's name, drew out her file, opened it. *Perfect.*

Terry Watson woke up because he felt the bed move, as if someone sleeping next to him had just sat up.

But there should be no one sleeping next to him. He for sure hadn't gotten that friendly with any of his fellow contestants, and in his own home no one had slept next to him since his wife had moved out, two years before, and filed for divorce from two states away. Still, the way the bed lurched when that action was performed wasn't something one forgot easily.

He opened his eyes.

Two someones, in fact, one on either side of him. A man and a woman, that much he could see in spite of the room's darkness. He couldn't make out much more than that—the only light seemed to come from the figures themselves, as if they emanated some inner glow, and looking straight at them made them appear vague and indistinct. He noticed that he could make out more details if he looked away a little; when he turned his head from one to the other, they came into sharpest focus.

But then he really woke up, and lunged from the bed in mortal terror. Gaining the relative safety of the room's farthest wall, he tried to calm his hammering heart and looked back at the bed. *I was just dreaming it,* he thought. *This house got the best of me, and I had a nightmare.*

They were still there, though—both still sitting up on the bed. Their nightclothes looked old-fashioned, maybe foreign. Their expressions were filled with horror. The woman slid herself across the room, and nestled herself under the man's arm, ghostly tears running down her face. It wasn't until the acrid tang of smoke hit Terry's nostrils that he realized what this tableau was. He was watching the last moments of the Trujillos, the property's original owners, as their house burned down around them.

Prepared for something like this, Terry hadn't even bothered to unpack. He tossed a couple of toiletries he'd left out into his leather suitcase and closed it. Sweat ran in rivers down his sides, pooled at the small of his back, and it wasn't from the flames—which didn't exist, he knew, but which he could now see reflected in the eyes of the Trujillos.

He tore his gaze away from them and started for the door. But before he could reach it, something grabbed his arm. He swiveled and found himself looking into the eyes of an Native American, holding a spear at Terry's neck. Terry shook his arm free and let out a scream.

The hot shower—and even the spectral face in the mirror—had helped Cordelia forget her dream a little. By the time she was dried off and dressed in a big, baggy T-shirt, she had almost decided that she might get some sleep after all.

She was just heading back to bed when she heard a bloodcurdling scream—much more masculine in tone than the one from her dream. Dashing into the hall, she was just in time to see Terry—older, heavyset Terry, whom she'd considered solid as a rock and serious competition for the prize money—charging down the hall with his suitcase banging against his leg. He couldn't exactly be said to have been white as a sheet, but there was a definite pallor beneath his brown skin.

"I am out of here," he snarled as Cordelia came out of her room. "I just can't take any more of this nonsense. This is j-just too m-much."

Beth and Sharon had also emerged, in various stages of disheveled sleepiness. "What happened?" Beth asked him.

He glanced over his shoulder toward the room

that had been his, as if all questions could be answered simply by passing through its doorway. Perhaps they could. He just shook his head. His voice quaked when he spoke. "Th-there isn't enough money in the w-world," he muttered. "And the rest of you should think about what I'm s-saying." He reached the staircase and descended without a look back, suitcase thumping all the way down.

From the bottom of the stairs, they heard the front door open and Terry thump outside, to the van that waited out there around the clock for just such an occasion.

"You going to look in his room?" Sharon asked. A couple more contestants had poked their heads out now, wondering at the commotion.

"Not me," Cordelia said, doubting that it would reveal much, if anything, now. But she added Terry's flight to her mental list of things that might be genuine supernatural manifestations—the guy had looked as scared as anyone she'd ever seen. Blood writing, spectral footfalls, the face in the mirror . . . it bothered her that the list was getting so long so quickly. "I have my own problems."

"I hear that," Sharon agreed.

Beth bit back a yawn. "Maybe I will in the morning," she said.

Cordy doubted that would happen. She had a hunch that Terry's door would just stay closed. She said her good nights and went back to bed.

* * *

Gunn sat across from Wesley in the hotel's interior courtyard, surrounded by plants and fresh air. The early morning sun filtered down around them, haloing Gunn with a yellow glow. Wesley cupped a mug of coffee in his hands—cupped it because, having tasted it, he didn't really want to drink it. *Cordelia's coffee can't be described as . . . well, good,* he thought. *But apparently it's much better than mine.*

"I talked to some of my boys last night," Gunn said. "About that body they found in the lot. Rondell had a good thought."

"What is that?" Wesley asked.

"We think this corpse looks like the work of a serial killer, right?"

"It does have the hallmarks," Wesley agreed. He'd been thinking along those lines himself, and had even done a little reading on the subject the night before. Quite different from his usual research, about demons and magical forces, but no less horrifying. *Humans can be every bit as nasty to one another as the powers of darkness are,* he thought. "It's quite rare that a single killing, which is usually done out of rage or for profit, leaves such a horribly disfigured corpse."

"That's right. Serial killers are the ones that murder ritualistically, and there's a pattern to the damage they do to their victims. We think the cops are going to be looking for that pattern."

"Correct." *Perhaps Gunn has been reading the same books.*

"But have you heard of a murder like this one since you've been in town?"

"No, I can't say that I have."

"Neither have I. So either this is a new lunatic's first victim, or we're looking at a killer who doesn't mind waiting awhile between victims."

Wesley wondered where Gunn was going with this, and began to wish his colleague would simply get to the point. "However, we don't know that this unfortunate woman's case is along the lines of the cases that we investigate. There's nothing to indicate that it's not strictly a—well, a 'natural' crime, I suppose, as opposed to a 'supernatural' one."

"Maybe not along your lines," Gunn argued. "But she was found in a neighborhood I protect. That makes her my business. And look at this." He reached into the pocket of his baggy pants and withdrew a piece of paper. It was a penciled rendition of bizarre markings, almost hieroglyphs, Wesley thought, but not in any ancient language he knew.

"Is that a demonic script?" he demanded.

"You tell me, man. All I know is, one of the street people who found the body said these marks were burned into the flesh of the woman's arm. I didn't hear about it until last night—cops haven't shared it with anyone, none of the guys at the center knew about it yesterday. It's one of those things the cops are holding back, be my guess, so they can weed out the crank confessions."

"Indeed."

"So this looks like it might make it Angel's kind of business, too, doesn't it?"

Wesley removed his glasses and scratched his temple with one of the earpieces. *Suddenly, we're back on more familiar ground,* he thought. "Well, it certainly might. I'll have to compare those markings to some of the texts—"

"Ain't got time," Gunn said. "We had a couple of things to do today, visiting limo rental agencies and the beach. Now all of a sudden we got more to do, and still just the two of us to do it."

"What exactly are you proposing, Gunn?"

"Go back to the cops. We think they'll realize this is a serial killer, same as we do. But they won't share that theory with us."

"Almost certainly not. Why would they?"

"Exactly," Gunn said firmly. "No reason. Angel had a friend on the force, but then she became an ex-friend, and then she got busted off the force altogether."

Wesley nodded. Gunn wasn't telling him anything he didn't already know.

"Police lady brought the heat down on herself 'cause she had a jones for investigatin' vamps, demons, and other freaks, right? She wouldn't let up, so the brass figured they had to squeeze her out. They don't want people turnin' up the wrong rocks."

"That's one interpretation," Wesley agreed.

"It's mine, anyway," Gunn said. "So they're going to be lookin' into this killing, but they won't be lookin' in the right places. But think about this—we know that Angel was livin' in L.A. back in the fifties, right?"

"That's right. Here in this hotel, in fact."

"Exactly. And we know that demons and vampires and all, that's nothing new, right? They've been around forever."

"Longer than we have," Wesley said. He thought he was beginning to comprehend what Gunn had in mind.

"So in all that time, there must have been other cops who stuck their noses in the wrong places. Policewoman can't be the first cop who's been busted out of the ranks for sniffing up the wrong tree."

"I suppose not."

"Here's my idea." *At last.* "I'll track down some of those other cops, ones who were booted off the force because they were looking into occult and supernatural events. If this killer has been working in town for a while, maybe these other ex-cops know something about earlier crimes. Maybe some of them still have contacts on the force, and would help us if we seemed like we took them seriously. Maybe they just want to settle a score with the P.D.

One way or another, I'll find out if this killer's M.O. has been seen before, and we can come at the investigation that way."

"*You're* going to visit a bunch of ex-police officers?"

Gunn smiled. "Think that's a problem?"

"Would you like copies of your rap sheet to present when you meet them?"

"You got copies?" Gunn laughed. "I'll be nice, friendly, straight up, all that. They'll never know what kind of element they're associatin' with."

"Somehow, I think they'll guess," Wesley said. "But you're right, it could prove to be valuable to have that kind of insight. It won't help us find Kirsten St. Clair, but if you're right about this murder having some demonic connection, then we certainly ought to look into it."

"I figure you can work on Kirsten and I'll work on Jane Doe."

"And you're really going to talk to these police officers?" Wesley still had a hard time envisioning Gunn getting along with that sort.

"I'll use the charm offensive," Gunn said. "Never fails."

"I'll anxiously await the results," Wesley told him.

Gunn rose and headed for the door, then stopped and looked at Wesley. "I tried your coffee, English."

"Yes?"

"If Cordy becomes some kind of superstar and

goes uptown on us, we're gonna have to work something out. Move next to a Starbucks. Something."

Wesley examined the brownish liquid sitting untouched in his own mug. "Yes, I suppose you're right," he said.

Is it wrong, he thought, *to hope that she* doesn't *succeed*? He wanted nothing but the best for her, but he truly missed having her around.

Kirsten St. Clair thought she would go insane.

The room they had her in could have fit inside her bedroom, and her bedroom was not huge by any means. Five times today, they had let her out of the room to use an adjoining bathroom, but other than that, she hadn't been allowed to leave. Virtually empty, the room contained the chair in which she sat, a flat video screen of some unbreakable glass, and speakers mounted into the wall, behind metal grates so she couldn't tear them out with her fingernails.

She had tried.

On the screen, she watched a man's life. Over the speakers, she listened to the same man's life. Nothing interesting, nothing unusual—just his day-to-day affairs, caught on tape. In the morning he got up, took a shower, ate breakfast, brushed his teeth, used the toilet, dressed, combed his hair . . . she had seen this part four times now, and knew every mannerism, every tic, every gesture. She could look away—nothing held her head in place and her eyes open—but in the utter emptiness of the room, even this mundane entertainment helped to pass the time.

Occasionally, the video monitor would go black. At those times, though, the voice over the speakers would continue. The man might be doing something as prosaic as reading out of a phone book, or reading classified ads from the newspaper. His voice was mild, reasonably pleasant, fortunately not grating or hard to understand. But Kirsten didn't know why she was being forced to listen to it nonstop, even when she slept, and she didn't know why she had to watch him on screen for most of the day, and she didn't know for how long this would continue.

They'd taken away everything she might be able to use to fight back, or to kill herself. Just like a prisoner in a cell. Her keys, her belt, her shoes. They'd left her in a T-shirt, canvas pants, and house slippers.

She found herself waiting for the click that signaled that the bathroom door was unlocked. Once, she had tried waiting in the bathroom, hoping that to stay in there too long would force someone to come in and haul her out. Just to see another human being, to maybe ask questions, engage in conversation.

Instead, the bathroom had filled, from a tiny vent, with something that she assumed must be tear gas. She'd been forced back into the empty room where the man's face filled the TV screen and his voice emanated from speakers, and the bathroom door had locked behind her. The next time she went in, the gas had been sucked out of the bathroom, but she hadn't made the mistake of lingering.

The closest she came to human contact was when her food came. Three times a day, when the bathroom door clicked, she went in to find a tray of fresh food waiting for her. She couldn't see another way into the bathroom, but there had to be one. So a live human being was within a few feet of her, at least three times a day. She wasn't, at least, forgotten in this torture chamber. And the food wasn't bad. It was plain; unflavored yogurt, creamy peanut butter on white bread, an apple, a banana, white rice. Water to drink. It would keep her alive.

When she finished, she left the empty tray in the bathroom, as she'd been instructed to do by a different voice that came over the speakers. The tray had always disappeared before she was let in again.

She had no way of knowing how long she'd been in this room, though she figured it couldn't have been more than twenty-four hours. Probably less—even though it seemed like much more, she understood that it would, given the stimuli she was exposed to. She didn't know how long she was expected to stay, she didn't know who had put her here, she didn't know what she was supposed to be learning or experiencing or remembering about this guy on the screen and the speakers.

The last thing she remembered, she had been sitting in her own living room, listening to music, drinking Gatorade, thinking about going out that evening to the party downstairs. The premiere of *Haunted House.* Then her memory got vague. She woke up in this chair, with the old guy's face on the screen in front of her. She had a dull headache, and her muscles felt sore from sitting too much, not getting enough exercise.

People, she assumed, would be looking for her. The police. Maybe the FBI. Her friends. She was clearly the victim of some sort of kidnapping. Which almost made her laugh—no one would pay the kind of ransom for her that would make a kidnapping worthwhile. Her mother was dead; her father hadn't even bothered to pay child support, which made the idea of ransom laughable.

Would her seekers know to look here? Was she still in L.A.? Was she still in the United States?

The things she didn't know were voluminous. The things she did know were few. There was only one thing she knew for certain.

If this lasted much longer, she would certainly go insane.

Chapter Six

The limousine rental agencies were a complete bust.

Wesley had received several discount offers. One of them even promised a beautiful female driver who would take him anywhere in the city for a three-hour minimum of only seventy-five dollars an hour. *A bargain,* he thought, and one he considered for almost two seconds before turning down. Most of the other services didn't make promises as to the gender of the chauffeur, and most of the minimums were higher.

But none of them reported having had a limousine anywhere near Kirsten St. Clair's Santa Monica apartment between five and six o'clock the evening before. Which simply meant that the limo was privately owned—no shortage of those around Los Angeles, he knew—or rented someplace out of the immediate area.

And it was astonishing just how many limousine rental agencies there were in Los Angeles. He decided to skip the Valley and South Bay and concentrate on Santa Monica, Brentwood, Beverly Hills, Hollywood, downtown, and the beach communities. Most of them he called on the phone, until he thought that his fingers would drop off and his ear swell to the size of a coconut. Then he went out visiting them, just for a change of pace.

He could hardly remember a more wasted day.

Finally, at four-thirty in the afternoon, he went to the beach. The sun was still high and hot and it made the water sparkle like handfuls of scattered diamonds, though it wouldn't really be beach season for another month or so.

Wesley had given a great deal of thought to his beach wardrobe. He didn't want to stand out like the proverbial sore thumb, so he decided to go for casual attire. When he arrived on the sand at Santa Monica—having parked several blocks away and walked—he realized that his version of casual differed from most other people's. *Or at least most southern Californians'*, he thought. *Still people, I suppose, but a unique breed just the same.* Wesley wore a pale blue short-sleeved shirt, tucked into a pair of cuffed brown trousers. His loafers were oxblood Italian leather and matched his belt.

The male uniform of the day seemed to be muscle

shirts and baggy shorts, or worse, Speedo swimsuits.

To further enhance his appearance as a beach bum, he'd stopped at a discount store and picked up a folding beach chair, the kind made of strands of rubber, like blue spaghetti, wrapped around an aluminum frame. He carried it under one arm, where it knocked against his hip with every step. Tags dangled from its frame and fluttered in the steady offshore breeze.

Sore thumb indeed, he thought. *Perhaps I just don't spend enough time at the beach.*

Of course, working with a vampire does put a crimp in that sort of activity.

But he was here now, so there was no point in delaying the inevitable. He had questions that needed answering, and these people were the ones who could do it.

He picked a spot a dozen feet from a lifeguard tower, unfolded his chair, and sat down in it. *"Casual" is the watchword,* he thought.

The chair groaned once and collapsed under his weight, spilling him onto the sand.

He rose, cheeks coloring, and dusted sand from his pants. Straightening out the chair, he opened it again, until he heard its frame lock into place, and parked it. He sat.

The chair held. He faced the ocean and watched the waves roll in. Surfers lined up on the water waiting for the perfect curl. Beautiful young women in skimpy bikinis strolled past as if on display just for him. *I really should do this more often,* he thought, emptying the sand from his loafers. *It's quite pleasant.*

But after a few minutes, Wesley realized he was no closer to having his questions answered than he had been before he'd come here. *If one wants a casual way to meet a lifeguard, one has to have a drowning incident,* he decided. The lifeguard wasn't going to come to him just because he happened to be sitting on the beach.

Well, he wasn't going into that water, he knew. So he was left with little choice. He got out of the chair, which nearly folded with him as he rose, and left it sitting in the sand. The lifeguard tower was behind him, and when he turned he saw that the lifeguard himself—a powerfully built young man with a blond crew cut, a tattoo of a dragon climbing his right shoulder, a deep tan, and the traditional zinc oxide whitening his nose—stared right at him. When the lifeguard smiled, his teeth fairly glowed in his sun-bronzed face.

"'Sup, brah?" the lifeguard asked him.

"Excuse me?" Wesley replied. Then realization dawned on him. "Oh, what's up, I see. Um, nothing. Just, you know, hanging, um . . . ten and . . . catching some beams, as it were."

"Primo, brah. So you're here to hit the surf? Spend some time in the green room? Maybe pick up a sand facial? You look like a shredder, kook. Where's your stick?"

Wesley just looked at the lifeguard, who began to climb down from his station. *Is he speaking English?* he wondered. From up the beach, another red-trunked lifeguard joined them, virtually indistinguishable from the first except that his blond hair was longer and more unkempt.

"Dude," this new lifeguard said upon reaching them. With a shake of his head he indicated Wesley. "What's with the hodad?"

Wesley was pretty sure they were making fun of him by now. The new arrival walked around him in a circle, as if he were a representative of some new species that had never before walked the Earth.

"I was—I'm looking for some information," he said, deciding the best approach was the straightforward one after all. "Do you happen to know a young lady named Kirsten St. Clair?"

"Oh," the first lifeguard said. "Another shark?"

"Shark? Was she attacked by a shark?" Wesley glanced nervously toward the water.

"Lawyer," the second lifeguard explained. "He wants to know if you're another lawyer."

"Me?" Wesley chuckled. "Oh, for God's sake, most certainly not. Why, have there been lawyers asking after her?"

"Couple days ago," lifeguard number one said. "Pair of 'em."

"How did you know they were lawyers?" When Wesley heard that lawyers were involved in anything underhanded, Wolfram and Hart were the ones who came to mind. "I mean, did they identify themselves? Did they leave you with a card, or any way to reach them?"

"Nobody comes to the beach in a wool suit unless they're a lawyer or a dweeb, or both," the second lifeguard said. "This was a dude and a dudette—kind of hot, if she'd lose the Barney and the briefcase, know what I mean?"

"Of course," Wesley replied, though he wasn't at all sure he did.

"Thought maybe it was about that TV show she bombed out of," the second lifeguard continued.

"*Haunted House?* You knew about that? The auditions, I mean?"

"Totally. Do you know where Kirsten is?" the first lifeguard asked him. "She didn't show up today. Totally bogus, you know, sticking me with a double shift when the heavies are breakin'."

"No, I don't. I was hoping you might."

"You see her, give her that message," the lifeguard insisted.

"Oh, I will, you can rest assured of that." If he could translate just what the message was supposed to be, he would deliver it.

"Excellent, kook." The lifeguard turned and climbed back into his tower. "Later days."

The second lifeguard had already wandered back up the beach toward his own station. Wesley glanced up at the first one. "And, um, cowabunga to you," he said.

Angel sat in front of the computer, watching the Webcast from *Haunted House.* On the desk was Kirsten's file, which he'd gone through page by page several times. It cleared up a few questions about her—mother deceased, father unknown, no brothers or sisters. The references listed were a clergyman and a high school friend in Illinois, where she had apparently lived before moving to L.A., and the downstairs neighbor, Staci, whom Angel had already spoken with. Big blank there, since it didn't seem likely that Kirsten had suddenly decided to move back to Illinois without even taking her purse.

The file included a head shot, and Angel saw that she really was a beautiful girl. Pure California beach bunny, even if she had come from the Midwest. *The photo might help if I accidentally run into her on the street somewhere, but all in all, breaking into the Laughing Pig offices was probably a wasted effort,* he thought.

He knew that what they needed were clues that might point to whatever had become of Kirsten, and he figured the best he could do just now was keep tabs on Cordy in case she came up with something new. The window on the computer's monitor was small, and the picture jerky, occasionally freezing or disappearing altogether as the legend "buffering" showed up on-screen.

All in all, not the highest quality video footage he'd ever seen.

But he could recognize Cordelia on occasion, when she happened to pass before one of the Web-Cams and whoever was making the decisions about which cam to air had chosen that one.

With a tall, frosty glass of pig's blood close at hand, watching was almost an entertaining experience. Almost, because the show didn't seem to be living up to its promise. He didn't see anything that looked particularly spooky. Mostly, what the WebCam showed was people's "private" moments, flirting with one another, or exploring the house, or arguing—Sharon and Christy got into an especially heated row over whose turn it was to do lunch dishes. Angel felt like a bit of a voyeur, which, he figured, was supposed to be a major part of the show's appeal.

He had the cup to his lips and was just taking a thirsty drink when Cordy suddenly filled the little media player's window.

"I wonder if my guardian *Angel* is watching over me," she said. At least, that's what he thought she said, but at the sudden and unexpected appearance of her face on-screen, huge compared to the distance with which everyone else had been seen, the blood had gone down the wrong pipe and Angel was choking and coughing over most of her monologue. *She must be right on top of the camera,* he thought. "Because if he is, he should also be looking in on my friend *Kirsten St. Clair* from *Santa Monica.* I have this *bad feeling* about her."

Angel fought to catch his breath and clear his throat. "Don't—don't worry, Cord," he told the screen. "We're on it." *Not making much headway yet, but we're trying,* he thought.

He could see from her appearance on his monitor that the vision was still taking its toll on her. She looked tired, and there were bags under her eyes that her makeup could only hide so well. *Maybe if someone didn't know her,* he thought, *they wouldn't be able to tell.*

He wished there were a way he could call the house, just to let her know that he'd received the message, loud and clear. Maybe if she knew that the guys were looking for Kirsten, it'd help with the vision hangover. *Probably not,* he figured. But it was worth hoping for, anyway. He didn't want her time on television to be spoiled by anything, and he didn't want people who knew her to think she came off as anything less than her best on the air.

Not that many people are watching, he thought. Wesley had found overnight ratings, and the debut episode hadn't exactly set the world on fire. In fact, the second half hour had scored considerably lower than the first, as people had switched channels in droves.

Then Cordelia was gone, and the scene switched to another part of the house, where other contestants played to the suddenly active camera. Angel turned away and wiped his mouth with the back of his hand. *She'll be glad to know she has an effect on me,* he thought.

"Were you talking to the WebCam?" Gordon asked her.

Cordelia turned away, embarrassed to be caught. "Oh, no—I was . . . I was just using it as a mirror to check and see if I had anything caught in my teeth," she lied. *Bad enough to humiliate myself in front of the computer-literate world,* she thought, *but I'd hate to have my temporary housemates think I'm a whack job, too. Especially the cute ones. Because, after all, the home audience is going to want to see some people hook up, and there'd be worse people here to hook up with.* "You know those poppy seed buns."

"Your teeth are fine," Gordon assured her.

"Yes, they are, aren't they?" She gave him a big smile, baring teeth and gums alike.

"Excellent teeth."

"I've always thought they were one of my best features," she said. "Along with . . . well, you know, everything else about me."

Gordon laughed. "I can see why you'd feel that way."

They were in a wing of the house that, to Cordelia's knowledge, none of the other contestants had explored so far. A side game to the main one of not being terrified out of the house was a game of exploration—there were small fabric rectangles, called flags, with bizarre symbols on them, hidden at various spots throughout the house. On that night's broadcast, whoever had found the most flags would be safe from being voted out of the house that night, if a vote became necessary. So most of the contestants were spending the day scouring the premises for flags. Cordelia and Gordon, having been chatting during lunch, decided to continue the quest together, splitting whatever they found fifty-fifty. Gordon had proven himself a gentleman by declaring that, in the event that they found an odd number of flags, Cordy could have the spare.

Forty minutes earlier, they'd come across a door more or less hidden underneath a servant's staircase, accessible only by passing through the kitchen's big walk-in pantry and out a door most people hadn't even noticed was there. The staircase led to a suite of rooms on the second floor they hadn't realized existed—what looked like a master bedroom suite, with a sitting room, a small office or library, a bedroom, a bath, and a dressing room.

Cordy walked through a doorway into the office/library, while Gordon looked under the cushions of chairs in the sitting room for stray flags.

"Brrr," she said. "They've really got the AC cranked." Taking a couple more steps into the room, she knew that wasn't the case at all. She'd felt a bit of a chill at first, but further in, the temperature was barely above freezing.

She stepped forward, two steps, then three. At three steps, the cold was behind her. "Gordon?" she said tentatively.

He didn't respond.

She glanced back at the door, but couldn't see him on the other side. The cold spot was between her and the door, and she wasn't sure she wanted to pass through it again. *Feels like it could freeze the blood in your veins,* she thought.

As she looked through it, she realized that, at its very core, the air carried a white tinge to it, as if the oxygen itself was lightly frosted by the cold. Staring at that icy core, she thought for a moment that it seemed to coalesce into an image, a man's face—maybe Carstairs again, though it was hard to tell—laughing or grimacing in pain. Watching that, she heard a distant sound, which could have been a roar of hoarse laughter or a bellow of agony. Then the sound was gone, and the image faded, if it had not been there at all. The air was just air, no white rime, no bizarre faces.

Gordon appeared in the doorway. "Did you say something, Cordy?"

She just looked at him for a moment, her mouth working, but nothing coming out. Then reason took over, and she remembered Dennis, her ghostly roommate, who had saved her life on more than one occasion. Even if she had seen something, it wasn't necessarily dangerous or malevolent.

But that doesn't mean it's not, she thought. She determined to be a little extra careful, just in case.

"I, umm . . . yes, I called you. Come here."

He gestured vaguely at the room. "In here?"

"Yeah, there's a cold spot here. Come see."

Gordon shrugged and stepped in.

"Farther," Cordelia urged.

He complied. When he reached the point where she remembered it had been most pronounced, he shivered and rubbed his arms. Goose bumps dotted his flesh. "You're not kidding," he said.

"It's not very big," she told him. "Just keep going and you'll be out of it in a second."

He walked toward her, smiling, as he cleared the cold spot. "That's better," he said with evident relief.

"Pretty strange, huh?"

He nodded. His sense of humor about the whole situation had appealed to Cordelia from the start, but here, faced with something genuinely creepy, it seemed to abandon him. The mischievous gleam that usually animated his eyes and his grin was gone, replaced by something that looked to Cordelia like fear. "You're not kidding," he said again. "That was just weird. Have you ever experienced anything like that?"

"Me?" she asked, all innocence. "No, of course not."

"We have to go through it again to get out," he declared. "No other exits I can see."

"It doesn't seem to be dangerous," she said. "Unless you're an orchid."

"An orchid?" He caught on a second later, and chuckled. "Oh, I get it. Hothouse flowers."

Okay, he's not as perfect as I thought at first, but he's not a complete stooge, Cordy thought. *And in terms of killing time while we're stuck in this house, he's probably the best I'm going to do.*

She turned her attention to the books filling the cases on the walls. No best-sellers here—these were old books, leather-bound, most of them, with brittle, yellowed pages. She thought she recognized some of the titles from the collections of Wesley and Giles, but others were unfamiliar to her. They sounded like more of the same type of thing, though: *De Vermis Mysteriis;* Danforth and Pym's *Through the Barrens;* the massive *Book of Eibon,* with the same brass fittings that Giles's copy had; Von Junzt's *Unaussprechlichen Kulten; Poligraphia,* by someone with the unlikely single name of Trithemius; and a slim volume called *Cryptomenisis Patefacta,* by Ian Wisdom Falconer. This last one had a ribbon in it, as a bookmark. Cordelia turned to that page, and the ribbon wasn't a ribbon at all, but a flag, emblazoned with a seal that resembled a snake eating itself. "Hey, Gordon," she said proudly. "Another flag!"

He glanced at it. "Ouroboros," he said.

"Ouro-what?"

"The Worm Ouroboros," he explained, brushing dark hair away from his eyes to take a closer look at it. "The mythological snake who eternally eats his own tail. No one quite agrees on what it represents. Maybe it's nature, continually restoring itself, recycling back to what it was before. Some think it symbolizes the human quest to integrate the physical and spiritual aspects of life. Or maybe it's the unchanging law that moves through all things, eternal and linking everything together with a common bond. It's found in some way in almost all cultures. You can find images of it from ancient China, Egypt, the Americas, Europe—it's one of those universal symbols that means different things to different people."

"I see," Cordelia said flatly. "Like a yellow light. Does it mean slow down, or speed up?" She shrugged. "Nobody knows." Gordon laughed and handed the flag back to her, and she tucked it into a pocket with the other two she'd found. "And you're studying what, again?"

"Getting my doctorate in astrophysics, at Irvine," Gordon said. "But with a wide-ranging curiosity, I guess you'd say."

"Don't forget what that did to the cat."

"Hey, what's one life when you've got eight more to go?"

Chapter Seven

Gunn was a little nervous about knocking on this particular door.

The bungalow was like a lot of others in this neighborhood, put up before the postwar housing boom that had spread Los Angeles across the landscape like a virus. These houses had a bit more individual style than those suburban tract homes that had become urban by dint of being swallowed by an ever-growing metropolitan area. The one Gunn stood before now had a deep porch with a glider chair on it, a bay window facing into the front yard, and dormers set into the roof upstairs. The bay window, Gunn thought, had to be a relatively recent addition—maybe the sign of a man with too much time on his hands looking to keep busy. The yard was neatly mowed, hedges trimmed, flower beds carefully tended.

Gunn knocked.

Cal Sullivan opened the door a minute later. He looked pretty much like Gunn remembered him, except for the apparel: steely gray hair and matching eyes; broad, powerful shoulders and arms; with a barrel chest that had, over the years, swollen into a gut barely restrained by a maroon polo shirt. The kind of blue jeans with a permanent crease, and well-worn moccasins finished off the ensemble, which couldn't have looked less like a police uniform. Those disconcerting gray eyes widened at the sight of Charles Gunn standing on his porch, and his mouth, a narrow, virtually lipless line, broke into something resembling a smile.

"If you're here to rob me, Charlie, you're too late. Between taxes, electricity bills, and alimony, you'll have to get in line."

"You got married, Sully?" Gunn asked him.

"Well, that part's a lie," Sully confessed. "But it sounds good, don't it?"

Gunn extended a hand. "I'll believe it if you want me to."

Sully took Gunn's hand in his own and squeezed it with a grip intended to crush. Gunn gave back as good as he could, but Sully had the advantage, and when Gunn got his hand back, it ached. "Come on in," Sully said. "You want a beer? Little early, but only by Pacific Time. East Coast, I figure it's at least five. Maybe in Newfoundland, anyway."

"No, thanks," Gunn said. "Glass of water, maybe, if you've got some."

"Water?" Sully said. "Deadly stuff. You know what they find in the water around here?"

"I'll take my chances."

Sully led Gunn into his kitchen, which was as immaculate as the yard had been. Countertops were wiped down, the floor was spotless, the appliances gleamed. "Nice place," Gunn offered.

"Thanks. I figure, I'm gonna spend the rest of my life here, might as well keep it the way I like it."

"You got a lot of years left to be thinking like that," Gunn said.

Sully examined him, as if looking for a visual representation of the reason for the surprise visit. When he didn't seem to see anything, he came right out and asked.

"Maybe not as many as you think." He handed Gunn a glass of tap water. "But that's not why you're here, Charlie. It's pretty rare for a con to visit his arresting officer at home, you know. So I figure you've got to have a pretty good reason for this unexpected pleasure. What is it?"

"Mind if I sit?" Gunn asked, inclining his head toward a fifties-style dinette set with genuine vinyl-covered chairs.

"Have at it," Sully invited him. "But don't think it's going to throw this old cop off his game. The interrogation continues."

Officer Cal Sullivan—Sully, as he was known to virtually everyone in the neighborhood, civilian and gangster alike—had patrolled Gunn's part of town for years. Gunn had made a mistake once—actually, he'd made several, resulting in a long string of arrests and an unpleasant amount of juvenile hall time served—but this one in particular had been dumb because it was virtually in his own front yard. A guy had made some remarks about Gunn's little sister Alonna, and Gunn decided that to avenge her honor, he had to go after the guy with a baseball bat. He'd done it in broad daylight, in a public place, and Sully had come around a corner and seen it. While he sympathized with Gunn's reasoning, the fact remained that Gunn had committed assault with a deadly weapon, and he already had a record of other petty crimes and misdemeanors.

Sully took him in, and Gunn went away again. He hadn't blamed Sully for doing his job, though, and both of them had felt a kind of grudging respect for the other.

Which still didn't mean they'd become fast friends. Gunn was almost as surprised as Sully was that he sat in the man's kitchen, drinking his water.

Tap water, even, he thought. *Cordy'd be mortified.*

He felt Sully's steady gaze on him. "Okay, here's the deal," he said finally. "I can't really explain why I need to know what I'm about to ask you—you wouldn't believe me if I did—but I need to ask it, anyway. Can you answer a question on those terms?"

"I'm not even sure I understand those terms," Sully replied. "But ask away, and let's see how it goes."

"You're a retired cop, right?" Sully nodded. "Retired early, too. Despite talkin' about the rest of your life, you could still be on the streets if you wanted to, right?"

Sully rubbed his chin with unexpectedly delicate fingers for such a big man. "I suppose I could be," he said.

"Yeah, well, I'm looking to find a retired cop who's off the force for a particular reason."

"What reason would that be?" Gunn noticed a skepticism come across Sully; his open face seemed to close off, eyes narrowing, lips pressing together. Gunn thought the man was gearing up to say no.

"It's gonna sound weird, maybe. But I need to find someone who was asked to retire because he or she was digging around in the supernatural."

"The supernatural?" Sully echoed.

"You know, vampires, demons, cults, stuff like that."

"I know what the word means," Sully said. "I'm a cop, not a moron."

"Can't always tell 'em apart," Gunn joked.

"You want my help, Charlie, you better be nicer than that."

Gunn knew that to apologize would only make things worse—showing any weakness would undermine the artificial antagonism on which their occasional relationship had been based for as long as he could remember. Once in a while, Gunn thought that he missed having the kind of education that Wesley obviously had, but he knew how to read people, and he wouldn't trade that and a lifetime of street smarts for anything.

"Why'd you retire so early?" he asked instead.

Sully crossed his arms and looked away. Gunn knew a defensive reaction when he saw one, and hoped he hadn't pressed too far too fast. The big man crossed to his clean white Frigidaire, tugged it open, and drew out a bottled beer. He offered it wordlessly to Gunn, who shook his head. Sully screwed the cap off and tilted the bottle to his lips, taking a long pull from it. Then he carried it back to the table, set it down, and sat heavily in the chair before it.

"Guess it won't hurt me to tell a con about it. You keeping out of trouble these days, Charlie?"

"The legal kind, yeah. Mostly. Trouble I find nowadays don't involve the laws of this world."

"You don't have to tell me any more. I get the feeling you're messing around in stuff that I don't want to have anything to do with."

"One way to look at it."

"The only way, as far as I'm concerned," Sully

said. He took another hit off the bottle. "You're with the LAPD long enough, you hear stuff. You can ignore it, or you can get obsessed with it. I tried to ignore it."

"So that's not what bought you early retirement."

"I bought it myself," Sully said. "Another problem with being on the force for too long, you start to think about how the crooks always seem to be living better than the cops. Then the crooks start making offers. I took one of those offers."

"You were dirty?" Gunn asked, the astonishment plain in his voice. That was the last thing he'd ever expected from Sully, who seemed like the straightest arrow he'd ever known.

"I made a mistake. I let a guy get away with something he shouldn't have, and in return he helped me out of a financial jam I was in. Happened once, and that's all. But I didn't want it to happen again, and I knew if I stayed where I was, it might. So I quit. Took early retirement and a reduced pension, but I removed myself from temptation before I gave in to it."

"Probably a good idea."

"It's the way I'm put together," Sully said. He spun the beer bottle on the tabletop. "I'm not good at resisting temptation, but I'm good at recognizing it. It's why I only keep one six-pack at home at any given time. It's why I supplement my pension by doing handyman work around the neighborhood instead of working security jobs or anything like that."

"So you're not the guy I need," Gunn admitted. "Got any idea who might be?"

Sully sat silent for a moment.

"It's important," Gunn said seriously. "It wasn't, I wouldn't be in your face about it."

"I heard there's a detective just recently that took a fall for that kind of thing."

"You're thinking about Lockley, she won't work," Gunn said. "Got to be someone with more history than that. And, anyway, she and I don't really see eye-to-eye on things."

"You don't see eye-to-eye with the law in general," Sully pointed out.

"Could be right. Anybody else come to mind?" Gunn pressed.

Another long moment of silence. Finally, Sully spread his hands wide. "Earl Monroe," he said.

"Earl Monroe."

"Earl Monroe took an early retirement back in the late eighties. He'd been on the job for almost twenty years, so it wasn't that early, but it was still unexpected. I knew him some. Good cop. Earnest about the job. He cared about what he did, took that whole 'to protect and serve' line to heart. But the rumors were, he got wrapped up in some cases that couldn't be closed in the traditional ways. Things no D.A. could prosecute in court, or would even try to. Monroe wouldn't let go; he was like a bulldog. The District Attorney's office warned him to lay off, and so did the brass. Finally, they reached an agreement. Earl would retire and keep his mouth shut, and they wouldn't take his badge and gun away from him and give him the boot. He cooperated in order to keep his pension, but he hated it. I didn't know him well enough to be close to him, but whenever I saw him after that, just around, you know, he looked like something was eating him from the inside out."

"Sounds like the kind of guy I'm looking for," Gunn said. "One who's willing to settle up some of those old scores."

"You sure you don't want to tell me what this is about?" Sully asked him.

"Let's just say I've got good reason," Gunn allowed. "A body turned up on turf I've taken under my protection. I want to see if maybe there have been others like it, over the years."

"Earl Monroe's your man, then, I think."

"Know how I can find him?"

Sully smiled. "You could track him down through police records, pension records, stuff like that, I guess. You could comb real estate records, see where he bought his house, find him that way—"

"I was hoping for something a little faster," Gunn said. "What with people dyin' and all."

"—or I could just call him up," Sully continued. "Ask him to meet you."

"That'd be better," Gunn agreed. "Let's go with that one."

Sully left his empty bottle on the table, stood, and went to the kitchen phone. "Why didn't you say so?"

He lifted the receiver and began to dial.

"Careful with that," Larry Mullins instructed. "Don't damage anything."

The two workmen shot death-glances at Larry. He didn't care. They were blue-collar workers on Wolfram and Hart's payroll—janitors, maintenance men, something like that, here to do a job and collect some overtime. They knew better than to complain. And Mullins wanted the things moved out of Parker McKay's house intact. They'd fetch a nice price someplace, probably in an out-of-town secondhand store that pretended to be raising funds for charity. Part of what he liked about the old firm was how well they had covered all the angles.

Lilah Morgan came into the bedroom then. She'd been having some kind of conversation downstairs with McKay, and now she marched in as if she needed to supervise Larry supervising the grunt workers. "Everything okay up here?" she asked.

"Fine," he said. "They're almost done with the removal."

"That's good," she told him. "The truck is downstairs with the new stuff, so when they're finished with this they can start bringing things in."

The workmen were removing women's clothing from dressers and the giant walk-in closet in Parker McKay's master bedroom suite. The truck Lilah mentioned would have come from a warehouse space leased, through a dummy corporation, by Wolfram and Hart. It would have inside it a brand-new set of women's clothes, in a different size, from a variety of stores. The clothes had been acquired over a period of weeks, never too much from one place, so as not to arouse suspicion. At the warehouse, it all would have been unwrapped, price tags would have been removed, folds ironed out, so they were like new but didn't look brand-new.

"They'll be done soon," he reiterated. "In and out."

"That's good. We don't want the client to be too disturbed by the process."

"I think he'll be okay with it in the end," Larry ventured. He thought about it for a moment. "I can't see ever doing it myself, though."

"How long have you been married?"

"Two years," he replied.

"So pretty much a newlywed, still."

"Yeah, I guess so."

"It's possible you'll change your mind someday."

"Maybe. I don't think so, though. Kat's pretty awesome."

"I'm sure Parker McKay thought that after two years as well."

"Yeah," Larry said. "He probably did."

"You never know what a couple of decades with the firm might bring," she said. "Make sure they're careful when they're unpacking." With that, she was gone and Larry was left upstairs with the men packing the rest of the clothes from the closet into big hanger boxes. *She just might be right,* he thought. *One never knows.*

Everybody in the room was jittery, mostly for reasons that had little to do with the live broadcast.

For Cordelia, and most of the other contestants, the house itself had been more creepy today than the day before—especially after the night, during which some unknown manifestation had chased Terry out of the house. Cordy and Gordon had found that cold spot upstairs, in the same room where she'd spotted a number of books on various occult topics—books that didn't seem, to her, to have been planted by the TV crew. They were genuinely old and dusty, and the dust on the shelves didn't seem to have been disturbed, except around the one book in which a flag had been planted. Other contestants reported strange noises or apparitions—the traditional clanking chains, high-pitched howls, and ghoulish laughter among the former, and a woman in a long white dress wandering otherwise empty hallways was observed separately by two different people.

Rich Carson was trying to lighten the mood a bit

before the cameras rolled. "So, everybody have a good day?" he asked. They'd gathered, as before, in the living room, where it would look like night even though it was not quite six o'clock in California. The usual camerawoman was there, hoisting her unit onto her shoulder to get ready for the shoot. Cordelia had learned that her name was Raquel. She was gorgeous, with exotic features and a lush figure, and looking at her reminded Cordelia that not all the beautiful people in Hollywood worked in front of the camera.

"If you include having the holy crap scared out of you as a good day," Annemarie related.

"No, no, save those stories for when we're on the air," Rich said, making crisscross motions with his hands as if to dissuade her. "Anything else?"

Cordelia had come in early enough to get one of the chairs, her flags tucked away in a pocket of her pants. Gordon had snagged one of the chairs, and the rest of the contestants filled in around them. "I had a very nice nap," Beth declared. "Quite relaxing, until I woke up because my bed was shaking."

"Like one of those motel beds you have to put a quarter in?" Christy asked her.

"Yes, only without the quarter. Or the motel."

Cordelia made a mental note of that, too—another ghostly occurrence that sounded like it could be real. She had come into this thinking that this whole show would be full of staged hauntings, but her opinion was quickly being altered.

One of the assistant directors signaled to Rich. "One minute."

"Okay, hold those thoughts," Rich said. He bowed his head, suddenly lost within himself, and Cordelia figured he was gathering himself for the upcoming intro.

At the A.D.'s sign, Rich launched into it. "Good evening, and welcome back to *Haunted House.* All of our contestants—except one—have, at this point, actually survived their first night in a haunted house. At least, we think they've survived it. Let's take a head count, just to be on the safe side."

Chapter Eight

Acting purely on a hunch, Angel abandoned the Webcast.

According to those who knew Kirsten, the only thing different or unusual in her life recently had been auditioning for *Haunted House.* So he plugged into the LAPD's internal Website, once again blessing Cordy for bookmarking her frequently hacked locales, and tried some of the other names he remembered seeing in the files at Laughing Pig Productions.

After several misses, he got a hit on Joan Martin.

Ms. Martin had vanished from her family's home in Westminster, just a few miles down the 405 in Orange County, four years before. There had been no trace of her since, according to her police report. No ransom demand had ever come, no letter or phone call from a distant city to indicate that she'd simply run away. She was there one day, gone the next, never heard from again.

Angel decided to try a different tactic, and began to look up similar crimes, using the key words he found in Joan Martin's report as a starting point. In this fashion, he managed to find two similar crimes, one nineteen years before, and one twelve. The missing women, Helen Lubitsch and Carrie Payzant, were both in their early twenties, as were Joan Martin and Kirsten St. Clair.

He needed another look at the Laughing Pig files.

He tried to access them from online. Hacking into their system proved easier than he expected, but apparently they only kept files online of people they'd used, not people who had auditioned and never made it. None of the names he looked up were there. But he knew Kirsten and Joan Martin were both in their files—*well,* he thought, *Kirsten had been, before I took her out.*

He glanced toward the window. Still broad daylight, and Gunn had his car. He took the sewers instead of the streets. It was shorter, anyway—from Hollywood to Burbank, going under the hills saved miles versus over or around them. When he got to the warehouse that Laughing Pig used as studio and office space, he worked his way up into their ventilation system, coming out in the same darkened studio space he'd been in before. This time, though, he was breaking in during business hours. He made his way back to the file storage room he'd found before, next to the casting office. No one seemed to be around, so he went inside, heading straight for the cabinet where he remembered having seen Joan Martin's name. He pulled her file.

The lovely head shot in the file matched the one in the police report. Same Joan Martin. She'd auditioned, five years before, for a role on a game show Laughing Pig produced called *What's The Deal?* She hadn't made the cut.

But then, a year after that, Angel knew, *she disappeared.*

Not knowing which shows to look under, it took him longer to find Carrie Payzant. Eventually, as the sun vanished from the sky and the single small window in this room grew dark, he found her. Like Joan Martin and Kirsten St. Clair, she had tried out for a game show, this one called *Liar's Dice.* And, like them, her head shot looked very familiar to the guy who had just been looking at it on a computer screen from the LAPD's intranet. Like the others, she was young and beautiful.

"You're not supposed to be in here."

Angel looked up from the file. Behind him, the door had opened and a young man in a baggy yellow shirt, with the collar of a white undershirt showing at the V of its neckline, and khaki pants, stood looking at him, several files under his arm. The man's hair was cut short, close to the scalp. Yellow-lensed wraparound glasses completed his look, which Angel classified as L.A. showbiz trendoid.

"Are you sure?" Angel asked.

"Dude, these records are my responsibility. I know who's supposed to be in here, and it's not you."

"I guess I just came in the wrong room," Angel said. "But if you're in charge of the records, maybe you can help me."

"I'll help you get arrested for trespassing," the guy threatened.

Angel knew he was a low-level flunky—but it occurred to him that a low-level flunky might be just the kind of guy he needed.

"Maybe I'm trespassing," Angel replied calmly. "But you've been doing things you aren't supposed to, either, so we're even."

The guy came the rest of the way into the room and closed the door behind him. *Guilty conscience,* Angel thought.

"What do you mean?"

"Carrie Payzant, Joan Martin, Kirsten St. Clair," Angel said. "You've been selling names and addresses, personal information, right? Who's the buyer?"

"You're nuts, dude," the guy said. "I am calling the cops."

"You sure you want to do that? It's okay, I'll wait here." Angel projected calm confidence. The young man, on the other hand, stood on wobbly knees.

Angel couldn't decide if he was more scared or more guilty. *Or a combination platter.*

"I haven't touched those files except for business reasons," the guy said.

"You haven't stood in here after hours, flipping through them, finding the prettiest girls? Passing their personal information on to someone else?"

"Dude, no way. That's, like, sick or something."

"Maybe," Angel said. "If you tell me who the buyer is, I won't turn you in, and you can get help for your sickness."

"No way, man," the guy continued. "You're just, I don't know, freaky deaky. Get out of here, dude, or I *will* call the cops."

That was the third time he'd threatened Angel with arrest, but he hadn't moved for a phone yet. So it was a good bet that he didn't really want to involve the law. Angel sniffed the air. Fear was palpable—even outweighing the guilt, he thought. Maybe the guy was telling the truth. Maybe it had been someone else in the organization. But he had a feeling about the trendoid, and it told him the guy was less afraid for his life than for his job.

Which means he's been doing something he could get fired for.

Angel knew he could figure the rest out, now that he knew the basics. But first he had to keep this guy quiet. He vamped out, letting his inner demon show through. The guy's face went white, and his eyes bulged behind his trendy yellow lenses.

"Okay," he said. "I'm going. I wouldn't tell anyone we had this conversation, though."

"Just . . . just . . . get out of here," the guy said again, his previous commanding tone changed to one of abject terror.

"Gone," Angel said. He squeezed past the young man and through the door, reverting to his human face as he did so.

When the visitor was gone, Curtis Tanner went to the telephone at his desk and punched out a number, his fingers trembling as he did. Twice he had to hang up and redial, to get it right. Finally, though, he made it to the end. He listened to the phone ring twice, and then click once as it was picked up.

"Wolfram and Hart," a voice said. "How may I direct your call?"

The show was just over forty-two minutes long, leaving plenty of time for commercials. The first fifteen minutes were eaten up by contestants relating their stories of the night before and of this day. After that, they were off camera as clips taped throughout the day aired. During this down time, Rich joked with them and they were allowed to leave for the bathrooms or to grab a bottle of water. When they came back, Rich settled them back into their places.

On cue, he looked at them with a somber expression on his handsome TV star face. "Sounds like you guys had an interesting day. And I know you're all looking forward to getting through the rest of tonight, and then tomorrow—but you're not all going to get to do that. Unless someone tells me right now that they're ready to chuck it all and get out of here, it's time for a vote."

He looked at them expectantly, one by one. "No takers?"

There weren't.

"Okay, then. Here's how it works. See that laptop over there?" He pointed at an open iBook that had been set up near one of the camera stations. *Nice product placement,* Cordy thought. *That must have cost a pretty penny.*

"That's hooked up to our broadcast feed. When you go over there and select one of the names, the home viewers will know immediately who you voted for. The screen will clear after your vote registers, so your fellow contestants won't know who you chose to dump. Everybody clear?"

His question was met by a chorus of affirmation.

"Just one more item of business, then. Who found the most flags? Anybody?"

"Six here," Cordelia said, tugging hers from her pocket and holding them up.

Gordon followed up with, "Five."

Pat revealed a fistful. "I found eight," he said.

After that, everyone else was quiet.

"No one can challenge Pat's eight, then?" Rich asked. "Good enough. Pat, congratulations. No one can vote against you."

The A.D. went to the open laptop and tapped at the keys for a moment, then cued Rich again.

"Pat's been removed from the voting list, so that leaves eight names. We might as well start here on the end. Cordelia? And remember, the audience at home will be able to see on-screen what name you pick."

Great, she thought. *No pressure—first to vote, first to look like a big fat meanie.*

There had been a time when she relished the role, but that was long ago and far away. And it was not on national television, which kind of made a big difference.

But it did no good to delay the inevitable, so she plastered a smile on her face and made her way to the computer. The camerawoman focused on her as she stood before the laptop, looking at the names on the screen. None of the contestants had really done anything to upset her yet, and none of them seemed to be a challenge to her ultimate victory. So she went with enlightened self-interest and chose Annemarie.

I want my own bathroom, she thought.

A few minutes later, the last contestant had voted, and the laptop found itself parked in front of Rich, who tapped on the keyboard. "Here are the results," he said. "Sharon, one vote. One for Cordelia. One for Vince. Beth, two. Annemarie, three votes."

Annemarie's face fell, mouth gaping, eyes going wide. "Me?" she asked sorrowfully. Cordelia felt a little sorry for her. *But just a little,* she thought. She wouldn't have been surprised to learn that Annemarie had voted for herself.

"I'm sorry, Annemarie," Rich said. "It looks like you're out of the house. There's a car waiting outside, so head on out. Your things will be brought down in a few minutes."

Hokey smokes, Cordelia thought. *Glad I didn't bring anything embarrassing with me, if the show staff is packing bags for the losers.*

Not that I'm going to lose, she silently amended. *Or own anything embarrassing.*

Another thought struck her then, watching Annemarie gather herself and say a quick good-bye.

Somebody voted against me! Grrr! What's up with that?

After that climactic moment, Rich wrapped the show up quickly. In minutes, the lights were shut down and the cameras turned off, and Rich had departed into the evening.

Gordon caught up to Cordelia on the stairs—unlike the previous night when they'd all hung together for a while, she hadn't wanted to sit around shooting the breeze with a bunch of people, one of whom had wanted her gone.

"Cordy, where're you going?" he asked.

"Up to my room," she said. "Somebody voted me out. Can you believe it?"

"I saw," he said. "I thought it was bizarre. Did you do something to tick somebody off?"

"Not that I know of. Unless they just wanted me gone because I collected the second highest number of flags. Or Annemarie voted against me because she wanted the bathroom to herself."

Gordon chuckled. "What a silly reason to vote," he said. "No one would do that, would they?"

"Well, if she did, it just makes me glad I voted for her."

"No way," Gordon said. "So did I!"

"That's two," Cordelia observed. "I wonder who the other one was."

"I guess we'll never know," he said. "Unless we watch ourselves on tape." He laughed again.

Since Cordy had every intention of doing just that, she kept quiet.

After an awkward moment, he changed the subject. "Sharon's making pasta for dinner. She said it'd be ready at quarter to eight. I hear she's a killer cook."

"Knock on my door if you don't see me?" Cordelia asked.

"Will do," Gordon replied. He turned around and rejoined the others in the living room.

* * *

Earl Monroe's home was in Simi Valley, otherwise known as the retirement community for ex-cops. Someone had once suggested that there were more ex-law enforcement types per capita there than in any other town in the United States, and Gunn believed it.

Which made it not the most comfortable place for him.

The streets were pure California suburban, one ranch home after another, all bathed in silvery light from a nearly full moon. American cars and SUVs filled driveways. Televisions and lights shone from windows, but there were people out, walking dogs, watering patches of green grass, or just enjoying the warm evening air. Gunn drove slowly, scanning the house numbers for the one that Sully had given him after he'd called Earl.

The house, when he found it, wasn't as neat as Sully's had been. Earl Monroe either had less free time or less patience for gardening and home maintenance. Either way, the house was in disrepair. Earl's garage door was canted at an unnatural angle, like a boxer with a broken jaw. The screens over his windows were so filthy, Gunn wondered if he could see outside, or if any light filtered in. The lawn, unlike those on either side of it, was a patchwork of yellow and brown—*dead grass and deader grass,* Gunn thought.

He parked Angel's car—the War Wagon would

have been as out of place in this neighborhood as Gunn himself was, but far more obvious—and walked up to the front door. A screen door in front of it wasn't quite closed, but hung from only two of its three hinges. A scrape mark on the sidewalk indicated that it had been this way for some time. Gunn tugged it—screaming across the sidewalk like a dentist's torture implement—until it was open all the way, and knocked on the front door.

The door swung open under his fist.

"Hello?" he called. "Mr. Monroe? It's Charles Gunn! Sully called you about me."

No one responded.

Gunn knew he'd been told to be here at eight. It was eight. He went to the side of the house, looked toward the back, and called again, in case Earl was in the yard. But there was no response there, either, so he went back to the door. It had swung open about a foot, and he could see a messy living room and a corner of a kitchen, through a doorway. White and yellow linoleum tiled the kitchen floor. White and yellow tile, Gunn noted, with a wet, red stain at the edge of it.

I know what that is, Gunn thought. *I don't want to know what that is, but I know what that is.*

He pushed the door the rest of the way open with his elbow, not wanting to touch anything with his fingers. The smell assailed his nostrils as soon as he was inside—rich, earthy, and sour—the tang of death.

Earl Monroe—at least, the man he assumed was Earl Monroe—was on the kitchen floor, except for that part of him that was on the kitchen wall and the refrigerator. It looked as if he'd been sitting at the kitchen table, which was oak and looked like something that would come with a furnished apartment a college student might rent, with his service revolver in his hand. He'd put the barrel of the gun into his mouth and pulled the trigger. The force of the blast had knocked him backward, chair and all, so both ended up sideways on the floor, with bits of blood and brain landing on the wall and fridge. His body had gone pale as the blood had run to his lower side and out the extremely large hole in the back of his head. Flies had come in through the open door and, fat and full, wandered about in the sticky pool and on Earl's wounds.

A yellow phone hung on the wall nearby, but Gunn hesitated about using it. Clearly, he was too late to do any good for Earl Monroe. The guy had been dead for hours. If he called in the suicide from here, he'd have to sit around waiting for the coroner and the cops. Then, since he had a record and Earl was an ex-cop, he'd have to answer a million questions, probably at the police station, and he might even be charged. No way he'd be convicted—Earl undoubtedly had powder residue all over his hand from having pulled the trigger, while a test of Gunn's hands would show he didn't even touch the .38. But did he want to put himself through the hassle? He didn't think so. Not with a killer still on the loose out there.

He was ready to turn and walk out when he saw the file folder that Earl had left on the table. It was almost half an inch thick, and the tab had been creased and folded so many times, it was almost torn off. Whatever label had been pasted on was long since worn off, and years of handwriting had obscured whatever it once might have said. But Gunn was able to recognize the papers showing at its edges, and they were police reports. He tugged a paper towel from a roll and used it to open the file and flip through some of the pages.

Apparently, Earl had prepared for Gunn's visit.

The reports documented, in the dry, clinical, overly precise language cops tended to use on paper to cover their tails, cases that no cop in his right mind would want to go near. Bodies found with tiny holes in their necks, drained of blood. Bodies incinerated, for no apparent reason, and without any detectable cause. A three-year period in which something very much like a large animal tore people into shreds, but only on nights when there had been full moons.

All of the cases were marked the same way: OPEN.

Unsolved.

Man, Gunn thought, *this is like a catalog of spook-*

iness. Wonder how many of these cases Angel has been involved with?

There were so many, he found himself being lulled by the sameness of them and the flatness of the language. But farther down in the stack, he came across a report that made him snap to attention. A woman's body had been found in a Dumpster in Culver City, with all possible traces of identification removed—fingers cut off, face burned off as if with a blowtorch, dental work knocked out. The date on this case was 1983. Gunn knew that was before DNA testing had been standard, so there would have been no way to determine who the victim was, and she was identified on the report only as Jane Doe.

On her forearm, strange symbols had been burned into her flesh, almost like a brand, according to the report.

Just like the woman in the vacant lot.

Gunn closed the file folder and picked it up.

A mile away from the house, he stopped at a gas station and called 911. Then he drove over the hill and into Hollywood, back to the hotel.

Chapter Nine

Angel was alone in the office, poring over the police report on Joan Martin's disappearance, when the phone rang. Distracted, he answered it. "Angel Investigations."

"Is this Angel?" a tremulous voice asked. It sounded familiar, but Angel couldn't place it immediately.

"Yes."

"Hey, man. This is—my name is Curtis. You don't know me, but you saw me before, at the Laughing Pig office."

Now Angel looked away from the computer monitor, recognizing the trendoid's frightened voice. "Right."

"Listen, man, you gotta help me."

"I do?"

"Yeah. I mean, I'm in trouble here."

"I believe it."

"I'm not messing around, man. You were right about this place. It stinks, and I'm . . . I'm in over my head, I'm not afraid to admit it."

I don't trust this guy, Angel thought. *His whole pitch sounds scripted.* "What do you need?" he asked.

"I need out. All the people I deal with on this stuff, it's like they're afraid of you, so I figured you were the guy who could help me."

"What's in it for me?" Angel asked.

Curtis hesitated. "I thought you just helped people. What . . . what do you mean?"

"I want names, details, you know. I want to be able to shut them down."

"I can't talk long," Curtis said. "They might be watching me now. Can you meet me, later tonight?"

"Okay," Angel agreed.

"How about . . . in Westwood, south of Wilshire. There's a big car lot, Royalty Motors."

"I know it."

"I'll meet you there, at midnight. Outside the lot." He hung up quickly, before Angel could even reply. Angel looked at the phone for a moment, then hung up his receiver.

Wesley sat in Anne Steele's cramped office at the East Hills Teen Center. She was on the other side of her metal, government-surplus desk, on the phone.

He occupied a secondhand stuffed chair, a remnant of some business that had failed and sold off leftover furniture cheap.

Every inch of her office seemed to be in use. A bookshelf overflowed with books—some popular fiction and nonfiction that Anne loaned out to teens who used the center, some sociological treatises on teen problems and urban blight, and a variety of binders holding articles on a wide range of topics. Her desktop was stacked with more of the same, along with Day-Glo file folders jammed with paperwork. A filing cabinet against the wall contained the rest of her files, and folded cardboard stands littered the top of it, filled with pamphlets on job opportunities and training, available social services, housing options, and other subjects of interest. To sit down in the guest chair, Wesley had needed to remove a stack of phone books and set them on the floor at his feet. *It's a wonder the walls don't explode outward from sheer pressure,* he thought. *If she tried to fit another thing in, they might.*

"I understand that," Anne was saying into her cordless phone. "But it's a little unsettling to us as well. I mean, I don't even know if my kids are safe on the streets at night." She listened for a moment, making funny faces at Wesley as she did to indicate her displeasure at the way she was being spoken to. "Okay. Do that. Thanks."

She hung up the phone.

"He says he can't tell me anything about the investigation that hasn't been in the newspapers," she reported. "Only he didn't say it in a very nice way."

"But we already knew everything that's been in the newspapers," Wesley responded, not bothering to hide his disappointment. "And more."

"Well, that's all the cops will give us," she went on. "They don't care if we're at risk down here. They don't want to, quote, jeopardize an ongoing investigation, unquote."

"So basically," Wesley said, "we're right back where we started."

"Looks that way. A dead body shows up a couple of blocks from my center, and the cops won't give me the time of day." She cocked her head, eyeing Wesley. "Don't you guys have contacts on the police force? Being, you know, like private eyes and all?"

"You'd be surprised at the lack of cooperation we get from the LAPD," Wesley told her. He'd been hoping she could find out more, especially about the symbols burned into the corpse's arm. The sketch Gunn had come up with was a good start, but the symbols didn't precisely match any known demonic language Wesley could pin down, and he was hoping for a photograph of the arm so he wouldn't have to rely on an untrained source's depiction of them. He'd thought that perhaps Anne, as a social worker who came into regular contact with the police, might have a better chance of getting something out of them.

Apparently, he'd been wrong.

Gunn parked Angel's car in its regular spot behind the hotel and went inside. The place seemed empty—though with sixty-eight rooms, one could never be entirely sure. But the lobby area was deserted, and so was the office. He had some time before his scheduled meeting with Wesley to catch up on the day's progress, so he went out the front door into the street.

By the time he'd gone three blocks, he was surrounded by young men.

"Hey, I think I know that dude," one of them said sarcastically. "Name starts with a G or something. Like Gull, or Gann, or Guff, something like that. 'Course, I never knowed him to spend so much time up in Hollywood instead of in his own 'hood."

"What's up, Rondell?" Gunn replied.

"Oh, he knows my name," Rondell continued in the same tone. "I don't have a name tag on, do I?" He slapped at his own chest, as if checking for one.

The others laughed.

"Listen, I know I ain't been around a lot lately," Gunn said, feeling defensive. "I been busy, okay?"

"Busy?" Joey echoed. "Busy forgettin' who your people are?"

"Hey, you guys are my family, you know that," Gunn protested.

"Seems like you don't remember who your family is most of the time," Rondell said. "You're turning into the kind of family that sends a card on Christmas and Easter and ignores folks the rest of the year."

"Yeah," Joey added. "You missed all the action this morning. Found us a nest over on Forty-third. Seven vamps, tough ones. Now you could pick 'em up with a Dustbuster."

I hate this, Gunn thought. He'd been over this ground with his crew before, but they never seemed to understand. *Or they're just not willing to make the effort.*

"You know there's more to keeping the neighborhood safe than dustin' vamps. I'm glad you took out the nest, and I'm sorry I wasn't there to help with it. I'm working on finding who killed that woman who ended up in the lot, you know? With the marks on her arm?"

"Right, that white lady," Rondell said. "She's a lot more important than any of those people the vamps been dining on for who knows how long."

"That's not what I mean!" Gunn exploded. "And you know it! Whoever wasted her, there's more going on there than just one dead woman. Those marks, they're some kind of demon language or something."

"Maybe you got to decide," Joey said, "if the demons you don't know are more dangerous than the ones you do."

"Don't be puttin' ultimatums on me," Gunn shot back. He felt suddenly weary—tired of being pulled in two directions, tired of working day and night to try to carve out a safe place in a dangerous world. "You dogs are my first family, but I got other obligations now, too. I can't just turn my back on those."

"No ultimatum, then," Rondell said. "We're out here, doing what we do. You want to join us, you can. Just don't think we're sittin' around waiting for you to lead us."

Gunn chewed that over for a moment. "That's fair," he said. "I can accept that." He slapped Rondell's proffered palm. "So tell me about this nest."

The tapes had been turned off. The strange man no longer flashed in front of her eyes every minute of the day, his voice no longer filled her ears. But still, she heard him in her head, saw him in her mind's eye. He had been her entire world for so long that she couldn't shake the memory, the image, the sound of him. She found herself wondering what he was doing now. Was he sleeping? She didn't know if it was day or night. Perhaps he was at work, sitting behind his big desk in his office, with a shiny notebook computer open on the desktop, three telephones lined up, writing on a legal pad with an expensive fountain pen. Maybe he swam in his private pool, one lap after another, working out his sixty-six-year-old body, staying lean and fit against the onset of age.

Parker, she thought. *Parker. The man has a name, and it's Parker. He's Parker, and I'm . . .*

Her mind was blank. She could remember Parker's name. She knew his address, his phone number, his birth date, even his Social Security number, she realized. But she couldn't even locate her own name in the jumble that her mind had become. She thought she knew, more or less, what she looked like. She couldn't remember anything about her home, though—when she tried, she saw instead mental glimpses of Parker's mansion. She couldn't picture her own family. When she tried to think about herself, she saw the ocean, waves rolling in, no two alike, crashing and washing up onto the beach and drawing out again, changing the face of the sand with each new attack. But that didn't tell her much—didn't tell her who she was or where she belonged.

She felt tears fill her eyes, run down her cheeks. *I've lost myself,* she thought. *I should know who I am, and I don't know why I don't. I don't know why I'm here or who put me here or how long I have to stay.*

If only Parker were here. Parker would help me.

She put her head in her hands and wept.

Chapter Ten

Wednesday

Angel drove down Wilshire, past the glittering high-rises of Westwood, and hung a right on Westwood Boulevard. A few blocks down, on the left, was the vast showroom and parking lot of Royalty Motors. In the glow of bright floodlights, dozens of luxury cars gleamed. As Angel pulled into a parallel parking place down the block from the dealership, he glanced over and recognized Rolls-Royces, Ferraris, Jaguars, Maseratis, Lamborghinis, Aston Martins, and a beautiful piece of automotive design that could only be a Bentley.

He climbed from the GTX without opening the door, slightly embarrassed by its relative shabbiness in the company of all these elegant machines. But the convertible served him well, and as long as the cloth top never got holes in it that let the sun through, he had no plans to trade up.

He was a few minutes early—he'd bailed on the broadcast of *Haunted House* after watching Cordelia's opening segment and finding that she didn't seem to be sending any new messages—and he saw no sign of the trendoid yet. He had a bad feeling about the whole meeting, a feeling that started when he was still on the phone with Curtis. He hadn't mentioned his name or left a phone number, so how had the guy known how to reach him? This was very likely a trap. But Angel trusted his own abilities to take care of himself, and even if it was a trap, he'd learn more than if he avoided the meet altogether. So he approached the dealership with his senses sharp, his muscles tensed and ready to jump, spring, or run, as the situation demanded. Just in case, he'd called Wesley and Gunn and told them where he'd be, though they had other projects going. Angel wanted this investigation to proceed on all fronts until Kirsten St. Clair was found and Cordelia's pain was alleviated, so he hadn't asked them to provide backup for this meet.

In the middle of the block, just past the driveway that led into a small parking lot for the elite customers of Royalty Motors, Angel stopped and turned away from the street, admiring the deep shine of the hand-washed and polished vehicles. *It'd be nice to have the kind of time to spend doing noth-*

ing but polishing a car, he thought. Lazy afternoons weren't really in his lexicon anymore.

As he stood there looking out over the sea of painted and polished metal, a movement from the middle of the lot caught his attention. He looked up and saw Curtis there, standing behind a low-slung sports car in a rich fire engine red. "Hey!" Curtis called in a loud whisper. "Angel!" He beckoned frantically, and Angel started toward him, weaving between the automobiles.

He was midway through the lot when he realized his mistake.

Car doors opened and shut behind him, and then in front of him. He turned his head and glanced over his shoulder. Two demons behind him, threading their way through the cars toward him. Up in front, where Curtis had been—but had now vanished from sight, he noted—two more faced him. Off to his sides, another pair emerged from their automotive hiding places. He was, more or less, surrounded.

At least I was right about the trap part, he thought. The knowledge gave him scant comfort.

Standing in the empty space between four cars—two Rolls Royces, a Jag, and a Ferrari—Angel made a slow turn, hands at his sides, ready to take on whichever demon came at him first. The cars were parked with plenty of space between them, to avoid dings from opening doors or overeager browsers, so he had some room to maneuver. He vamped, hoping his own demonic face might give them pause.

It didn't.

He didn't recognize the demons. They were all the same type, with brick-red skin that cracked and peeled like old paint or the flaking fabric from the spine of an ancient book, powerful builds with broad shoulders, and deep, muscular chests, long arms ending in dozen-fingered hands. Ridges of raw bone ran up the backs of their arms. One of them opened his mouth and hissed at Angel, extending a lengthy, nearly prehensile tongue and baring razor-like teeth.

Angel eyed that one just long enough to almost miss the sudden rush of feet from behind, but he spun as the demon over his left shoulder leapt onto the hood of a Rolls, crushing sheet metal under a heavy, clawed foot, and used it as a launching platform from which to hurl himself at Angel. The car's alarm began to whoop. Dropping into a crouch, Angel pushed himself out of it to meet the demon halfway, using his own momentum and the demon's to drive his shoulder deep into the beast's midsection. The demon grunted in pain, and Angel felt a rush of satisfaction. He straightened, slamming the demon backward into the rear of a Ferrari, which buckled under the impact. Another alarm blared.

A flurry of motion from every direction told Angel that the other demons were moving on him simultaneously. He leaped into the air, whirling and kicking out where he guessed one of the demons would be approaching. Miscalculating only slightly, his heel drove into the thick neck of one, missing the face that had been his intended target but doing the job just the same. When he landed he lashed out with both fists, each of them connecting with demon flesh. But another one closed on him and whipped the back of one hand through the air. The ridge of exposed bone on his arm caught Angel's cheek and tore the flesh. Lightning flashed in Angel's vision. He stumbled, falling backward into the side of one of the luxury cars.

"Do you like that, vampire?" the demon asked, its voice grating like a rock scraping glass. "Want some more?"

Angel didn't bother to reply. The demon pressed his advantage, charging Angel again, both fists pistoning into the vampire's face and body. Angel took the punishment, gathering himself in spite of the brutal assault. Finally, the demon, in close enough for Angel to see the square irises of his bloodred eyes, drove his fists toward Angel, and Angel reached out, catching them both and yanking the demon forward, chin connecting with Angel's oncoming knee. Angel felt the bones of the demon's jaw shatter. The thing staggered back, spitting blood and teeth.

Angel could smell hot, foul breath huffing at him

and feel the blows, but they were too close now, and too identical in appearance, to distinguish one from another. They weren't big talkers, taunting him occasionally but mostly quiet except for occasional grunts and moans when his blows found home. He swung with both fists, connecting now and again with tender spots, but there were so many of them, and the ridges of bone tore him again and again. Then, through a miasma of pain and blood, he felt a piercing jab at his ribs and looked down to see one of them withdraw a handful of wooden stakes from his torso.

Angel fell to his knees.

He had downed two of the six, but each of the remaining four filled a hand with a wooden stake from some hiding place and circled around him for the kill.

"Wood for you, soul-ed vampire," one of the demons said. "Prepare to die again."

Angel's back was up against a grand automobile, acres and acres of polished metal, it seemed, alarm shrieking into the cacophonous night air. Before the first demon could lunge at his heart with his stake, Angel slipped to the ground, seemingly defeated.

Writhing in pain, Angel thought the demon hesitated for a fraction of a second. It was all the time he needed.

He rolled under the huge car. The demons made sounds of surprise and jabbed at him with their stakes, but the car was broad enough that he was able to dodge their attacks by twisting out of the way. They spread out, surrounding the vehicle, shouting at him to come out.

Spreading out was just what Angel had wanted. He reached up and yanked off the exhaust-muffler unit from the car's underside. One of the demons had gone onto his belly, crawling under the car, stake clutched in his bony fist. Angel took careful aim and lanced the exhaust forward, driving it through the demon's forehead and eyes. The thing screamed in pain, bucked, and died in a burst of fire and smoke. Within a split second, nothing remained of him but a scorch mark on the pavement.

Angel crawled out from under the car where that demon had been, feeling the heat that the macadam still held from the demon's fiery disappearance. By the time the other demons came around the car at him, he was on his feet, exhaust pipe in his hands like a baseball bat. He took aim at one of them and did his best Barry Bonds, and the demon's head soared for the left-field fence, landing on a Maserati and kicking off an alarm in a whole new section of the lot. The demon's body burst into flames and disappeared as the other one had. Angel could only assume the head followed suit.

Another demon tried to use Angel's backswing as an opportunity, but instead of straightening out of the backswing, Angel just jabbed the near end of the exhaust pipe up under his own grip, past his bloody ribs, and caught the demon in the belly. The creature went down hard, his stake rolling out of his hand.

Now Angel faced the last demon, who backed away instead of coming toward him. A look that resembled panic washed across his face, replaced by a sudden expression of calm, almost serenity, Angel thought.

"You don't win, vampire," the demon said.

"Says who?" Angel asked. But the demon's sudden complacency was unnerving. *Reinforcements?* Angel wondered. Instead of continuing the battle, though, the demon turned the stake on himself, driving it deep into his own heart. Like the others, his body evaporated in a flash of white heat.

All around Angel now, the other surviving demons roused themselves into consciousness long enough to do the same, slaughtering themselves with their own weapons and vanishing in flame and smoke. Angel found himself suddenly alone in a luxury car lot in which at least a dozen cars had been damaged, dented, windows broken, streaks of flame bubbling paint and scorching metal, while their alarms wailed and whooped and whistled. He looked around quickly, ascertaining that Curtis was long gone, and then ran for his car just ahead of the oncoming sirens.

Jumping over the door and into the driver's seat,

he keyed the engine to life and pulled out into the lane. As he swung a right at the next corner, the lights of the first police car flashed down the street behind him.

In retrospect, he thought, *this old car isn't so bad after all. Those new ones just don't seem to be able to stand up to a little punishment.*

"I hope Angel's having better luck than we are," Wesley said. He and Gunn stood across the street from the lot in which the woman's body had been found two nights before. "Not only is this not helping locate Miss St. Clair, but I'm not sure it's doing any good for the dead woman, either."

"I'm working on that," Gunn said. "I'll follow up on that file I got from Earl Monroe tomorrow. But tonight, I figured it wouldn't hurt to find out who hangs out around here at nighttime. Maybe one of 'em will tell us something they wouldn't tell the police."

"That's possible," Wesley relented. "Though I can safely say that I'd feel somewhat better if there were a few police officers about."

"Streets are only as dangerous as you let 'em be," Gunn told him. "Stay alert, don't act like a fool, you'll most probably be fine."

"Playing the odds has never been my strongest suit."

Gunn put a silencing hand on Wesley's arm and

ticked his eyes toward the mouth of an alley that faced onto the lot. "Check it."

At the alley's mouth, an old man dressed in layers was spreading a threadbare blanket, his bed for the night. From a shopping cart he took a chunk of foam rubber that he'd use for a pillow and placed it just so. He seemed meticulous about how he made his bed, if not where.

"I bet he's there every night," Gunn ventured.

"Again, not big on betting."

"You must be a riot in Vegas," Gunn said.

"Perhaps one day we'll go and find out."

"Yeah, just as soon as we can take a vacation from fightin' evil. That seems likely, don't it?" Gunn didn't wait for an answer. "Come on."

He started across the street toward the alley. The man glanced up and saw Gunn coming toward him, with Wesley in his wake. His expression turned to one of fear, and he started toward his shopping cart as if to protect his valuables. His hair was long and unkempt, his chin grizzled, and his eyes shone with something like madness.

"Don't worry, pops," Gunn said. "We ain't here to mess you up."

"Quite right," Wesley assured him. "We're completely on the side of . . . well, the angels, you might say."

"Angels?" the old man repeated. His fear seemed to have left him. "I had an angel once, in Matamoros," he said. "Five foot two, eyes of blue. Lost her in a card game."

"You see?" Wesley said. "Gambling. It's bad news."

Gunn turned to Wesley and softly said, "Shut up, Wes." He faced the old man again. "We just want to ask you a couple of questions, gramps," he told the man. "Then we'll leave you alone, all right?"

"Ask whatever you want," the man replied. "Maybe I'll answer, maybe I won't. Maybe I'll turn into a jet plane and fly away."

Wesley sighed. *This is going to be a long night,* he thought.

"You sleep here every night?" Gunn asked the man.

"Most nights, yup," the man said. "Unless I have an invitation from the Queen of Hearts."

A very long night.

"What about two nights ago? Not last night, night before. You sleep here that night?"

The man scrunched up his face as if thinking it over demanded muscular gymnastics. "Yup," he said. "Right here on this spot. Warm night, too. Not as hot as those nights in Matamoros, but not as cold as some. A one-blanket night, that's all."

"You happen to see anyone in that lot?" Gunn asked him. "Anything freaky, anything seemed out of place?"

"Fireflies," the man said.

"You saw fireflies?"

"Naah, don't see those this side of the Mississippi," the man said. "I miss 'em, though."

"Yes," Wesley urged. "But did you see anything that . . . well, that you *did* see?"

"Sure," the man responded. "One of those big black cars. Long as a school bus, it was. Long as a freight train. Windows all blacked out so you can't see in. Could have been the Sheik of Araby and his entire harem inside there, all I know."

"You saw a limousine across the street?" Wesley wanted to clarify, if possible, what the man had really seen and what his fevered imagination had perceived.

"That's what they call it. A limo. Parked right there." He pointed to a spot in front of the vacant lot, near where the woman's body had been found. "Two nights ago. That's what you're asking about, ain't it?"

"That's right, sir," Wesley said. "Anything else?"

"Nothing else," the man replied. "Now leave me alone. It's past my bedtime."

Wesley pulled out his wallet and found a ten-dollar bill, the only cash he had with him. He handed it to the man, who sniffed it once and then tucked it into a pocket somewhere underneath the first few layers of clothes. Gunn and Wesley retreated back across the street.

"Great," Gunn said. "Another freakin' limo. Like that lead wasn't already a bust."

"Just what I was thinking," Wesley said. "We're right back where we were."

"Except for one thing," Gunn said suddenly. "The other limo was in the other case—Kirsten St. Clair. Think maybe they're connected?"

"I can't imagine that they could be," Wesley replied. "It's a long shot. But then, I'm no gambler, so what do I know?"

Chapter Eleven

Twenty-five minutes later, Angel stood on the third-floor landing of Kirsten St. Clair's apartment building. Lights shone in a few windows, but the building was mostly quiet. He made sure he wasn't watched, then went to her apartment and opened her door. He tried to step inside. He couldn't.

A faint smile crossed his face.

That's one thing, at least. I keep getting nowhere on finding her, but as long as she lives, there's hope.

Right now, a little hope was something to cling to, a lifeline to a drowning man.

He had never understood much about The Powers That Be. They didn't bother to explain themselves to him, or to anyone else—Angel and Doyle and now Cordelia seemed to be nothing more than tools to them, and who told their hammer or screwdriver what its purpose was when using it?

So he didn't know if they knew what was in his heart. But he didn't think they'd be pleased, if they even knew that sort of emotion. Angel was working hard to find Kirsten St. Clair. He wanted her to be safe. But mostly, he wanted it because he knew Cordelia was suffering, and would continue to until Kirsten's situation was resolved.

He was looking for Kirsten, but his mind was on Cordelia. She was what mattered. He realized that he might be losing her, anyway—if this TV show led to the kind of fame that she hoped for, he couldn't expect her to stick around with him and Wes and Gunn. She would have other demands on her time, other challenges and commitments. Angel hated the thought of losing her, but if he was going to, he wanted her to go comfortable and happy, not burdened with a vision hangover that wouldn't go away because he couldn't hold up his end of the job.

So he was glad that Kirsten was, at least, still alive. But he couldn't really claim, deep within himself, to be glad for Kirsten's sake.

It was all for Cordy.

Cordelia awoke to the smell of lilacs, strong and pungent. She hadn't fallen asleep to that smell, so she figured right away that something was wrong. She rolled over and turned on the light, blinking against its sudden glow.

Something seemed to stir at the edge of her vision.

When she turned her head, there was nothing there, but she continued to have the sense that it *was* there, just beyond where she could see. The effect was disconcerting. "Hello?" she asked. "Something I can do for you? Because if not, trying to get some sleep here, you know? It's hard enough to be cheerful and beautiful for the cameras without losing good mattress time, too."

There was no reply forthcoming. She kicked off the blankets and rose, frightened and wary. The floorboards were cool on her bare feet. She tried shaking her head fast, side to side, hoping to catch a glimpse of whatever was there. No luck. If there was anything there, it stayed just out of sight. *Not out of smell, though,* she thought. *Starting to get that old funeral home feeling in here.*

Suddenly aware of the cameras, she tugged on a robe over her nightgown, deciding that she probably wouldn't be sleeping again for a while. At least until the scent faded a little.

She had stayed up later than usual, talking to some of her fellow contestants. Overall, she liked them more than she'd expected to. She thought she should feel bad at the idea that there could only be one winner, that she had to vote others out, conspire against them, or hope that they were sufficiently terrified that they left voluntarily. *But that just wouldn't be me,* she realized. She decided that she was, if not exactly selfish, at least egocentric. *But honest about it,* she thought. *Which is better than pretending to care about everyone else while plotting their doom.*

It was the honest part, she knew, that really defined her. People had said she lacked tact, or concern for the feelings of others, when in fact she had just always been willing to say what she really felt. She was direct—*okay, blunt*—but not intentionally hurtful.

At least, not since high school.

She heard voices then, but these, she thought, were real, human voices, out in the hall. She opened the door, glad to have an excuse to get out of her room and away from the cloying floral fragrance. Gordon and Beth were there, both still dressed, talking in low tones. They turned, surprised, when Cordelia emerged.

"Secret meetings?" she asked.

"No worries here," Gordon said.

"I couldn't sleep," Beth said. "My bed kept shaking every time I closed my eyes. I decided to get back up again."

"Up and dressed," Cordelia observed.

"I've been dressing in the dark in my room," Beth explained. "Because of the cameras. I wanted company, but I didn't want to come out here in my PJs."

Beth was such a serious person, Cordelia thought, with her wire-rim glasses and batik skirts and midfortyish solemnity, that it struck her funny to hear the woman say "PJs." She chuckled and opened her robe, doing a little pirouette that revealed the nightgown underneath. "Guess I'm just shameless."

"So it would seem," Beth said.

"So, are you packing up?" Cordelia asked her.

"Sorry to disappoint you," Beth said. "I'm not scared so much as just disturbed by the shaking. If I could get some sleep, I'd be—" She stopped in the middle of her sentence and stood there, mouth open. After a few seconds, it became apparent that there was something wrong. Beth's eyes were beginning to bug, and the flesh of her face turned bright red.

"Cordy, she's choking!" Gordon shouted. He started for her, but then flew backward as if swatted by a powerful hand.

"Beth!" Cordelia called. She, too, tried to reach the woman. When she got near, an invisible hand smacked her away, shoving her into the wall. Beth's face was turning purple now, and her tongue bulged from her mouth.

Then, whatever held her in its grip released her, and Beth slumped to the hallway floor, gasping and wheezing. Cordelia hurried to her side. Gordon joined her there a moment later.

"Are you all right, Beth?" Cordelia asked.

Beth shook her head, her long hair flying. She looked up at Cordy and Gordon, tears in her eyes. "It—something had me," she managed. "Strangling me." She broke into a coughing fit. Cordelia could do nothing but rub the woman's back and wait for her to regain her composure.

Gordon stood, looking up and down the hall as if he'd be able to see whatever invisible force had attacked Beth.

"Do you need a doctor?" Cordelia asked. "Not that we have one, but I think there's a paramedic outside with the vans."

"I . . . I don't think so," Beth said weakly. "I just need to get out of here. That's what you wanted, anyway, isn't it?"

"Not this way," Cordelia replied. "I didn't want anyone to get hurt."

"Well, I did," Beth said. She sounded angry now, angry and hoarse. "I'm going. They can send my things."

She pushed herself to her feet. Her color had returned to normal. Gordon tried to take one of her arms, to help steady her, but she shook away his hand.

"I think that's a good idea," he said. "Maybe you should go, too, Cordy. This doesn't seem like such a big joke anymore."

"It was never a joke," Cordelia responded. *I know too much about the supernatural to dismiss it that way,* she thought. *And this incident proves that not only is it not a joke, but that the danger here is real.* "But I'm not going anywhere. You can leave, if you want. I'm sticking it out."

"Be careful, then," he said. They both watched Beth walk unsteadily to the stairs and then, gripping the banister, start down toward the door. "I'd hate to see anything happen to you."

"That makes two of us," Cordelia said. On shaky legs, she went back into her room. *I can do this,* she thought. *I've survived worse before. Lots worse. At least nothing's trying to impregnate me this time.* Inside her room, the lilac scent had faded somewhat, and she decided to try to get some more sleep before the morning came.

Curtis Tanner sat in his apartment, remote control in his hand, flipping through channels on his TV. He couldn't sleep, and he hadn't been able to eat anything since he'd had to go to Royalty Motors to set up the vampire. He wasn't used to physical violence, and he wasn't used to things like vampires and demons and creatures that could smash up a couple million dollars of luxury cars in five minutes, and the whole thing was just too much. He wanted out. And he didn't know how to do that, either.

So he sat on his couch and tried to focus on TV, but that didn't work. Nothing on at this hour but old, bad movies, self-improvement infomercials, and reruns of daytime talk shows. A movie sounded good, in theory—something to draw him in and make him forget about the evening's events. But there were only four on the air, and all four featured either Harry Hamlin or Corbin Bernsen, and that was just so wrong on so many levels, it made his head hurt.

He dreaded going to work in the morning. He'd unplugged his phone because he didn't want anyone to call him. One of these days his contact from Wolfram and Hart was going to want another favor, and what was he going to do then?

Maybe I should just leave town, he thought. *Canada is supposed to be nice this time of year. Or Tahiti.*

And I have just about enough cash to get me to Barstow.

Finally, he clicked the TV off in frustration. *This is getting me nowhere.* He went into his bedroom, found an old backpack in his closet, and started packing his clothes.

He didn't hear the front door open or the demon step inside silently, closing the door behind him.

He didn't hear the demon cross his apartment, taking each step carefully, in a measured, practiced stride. Didn't see the demon raise a hand, the fingers of which were each topped by a six-inch-long, razor-sharp bony claw.

Finally, at the very end, Curtis sensed the demon, and started to turn, and even began to shout something. But the demon swung his hand in a wide arc, and Curtis collapsed in a lifeless heap on top of his own backpack, his head spinning three times and bouncing off the wall before it landed in the middle of the floor.

Curtis wouldn't be doing any traveling after all. He had already arrived at his final destination.

* * *

Caritas had been closed for an hour, but the Host, like barkeeps and restaurateurs everywhere, didn't get to go home just because the door was locked. There was cleanup, there were dishes to be done and tables to be straightened, the night's bookkeeping needed to be performed, and the deposit readied to drop off at the bank's all-night deposit slot.

No rest for the wicked, he thought. *But then, better wicked than . . . whatever the opposite of wicked is. Boring?*

He punched the keys of the adding machine, adding up his figures for a third time, hoping against hope that this time his total would match one of the other totals he'd already reached. *I wonder if I'm going to have to replace that bartender,* he thought, grumpy at the prospect. *Ramon betrayed me, and endangered Wesley and Angel in the process, but at least he didn't dip into the till. Malkot demons are notoriously bad with money, and I guess this one's no exception.*

So when the pounding on his door started, he was in no mood for sociability. First, he waited a minute, to see if whoever it was would just go away. When they didn't, he snarled, "Cool your jets! We're closed! Do you know what closed means? It means come back tomorrow night, or better yet don't come back at all!"

"Open up," a voice replied, and the voice carried a familiar streetwise tang. "We know you're in there!"

"Of course you do!" the Host shouted, pushing back from the table and rising. "I just yelled at you. Doesn't take Hercule Poirot to figure that one out." He crossed to the bar and pressed the button that unlocked the door, which opened immediately. "Or Sherlock Holmes, either, for our English friends," he added, directing the comment at Wesley Wyndam-Pryce.

Wesley and Gunn paused at the threshold. "Well, are you coming in, or did you just hammer on my door to make me lose count?"

They entered. "Thank you," Wesley said. He sounded out of breath.

"Where's the smile and the friendly greeting?" Gunn asked. "You save those up for paying customers?"

"Sorry," the Host said glumly, leading them back to the table where his pile of receipts and his adding machine conspired against him. "I was just dealing with the realities of running a business. You know, trying to make a few dimes from the sweat of my brow." He touched the lapels of his fine French silk suit. "You don't think threads like these come cheap, do you? And that Malkot I hired is stealing, I just know he is."

He sat heavily in front of the machine. Gunn and Wesley pulled up chairs, and Gunn began to flip through the night's receipts. After a moment, he paused.

"Guy got the decimal in the wrong place," he said. "Unless you're sellin' White Russians for thirty-five bucks instead of three-fifty."

"Let me see that," the Host said. He took the receipt from Gunn's hand, peered at it, then tapped the adding machine's keys for a minute. "Oh, much better. Thank you, babycakes."

"I'm surprised, Gunn," Wesley added. "You have hidden depths I didn't know about."

"You knew about 'em, they wouldn't be very hidden. But it don't take Einstein to spot an overpriced drink."

"True," Wesley said.

"I'm appreciative," the Host said. "But I'm also sensing you gentlemen didn't pop by just to solve my mathematical mix-up. And I note the, in fact, extremely notable absence of everybody's favorite dark night avenger. What's the shakes?"

"Angel, um, called us," Wesley replied, suddenly grim. "He's gone to the hotel, to recuperate from a rather nasty brawl."

"Oh, dear," the Host said, sympathetic. "He'll be okay?"

"Long as he didn't get a splinter in his heart, he'll heal," Gunn offered. "And since a pile of dust don't got a pocket for a quarter to stick in a pay phone, we're thinkin' he's gonna pull through."

"But he wanted us to see if we could get a line on his attackers," Wesley went on.

"And since you're here to see me, I'm guessing these attackers were not of the Homo sapiens variety."

"Exactly," Gunn said. "He said they were ugly—"

"Always a subjective call," the Host said, suddenly sensitive of his hooked nose, jutting jaw, and overall emerald complexion. "And only skin-deep, after all."

"—ugly," Gunn continued as if the Host hadn't interrupted, "and big, barrel-chested. Bony ridges up the backs of their hands and arms."

"Right," Wesley put in. "Oh, and when it was apparent that they had failed in their objective, they killed themselves."

"Little fireworks show when they died," Gunn added. "Nothing left behind but some ash and burn marks on the ground."

"I see," the Host said.

"My guess is—" Wesley began.

"Branichor demons," the Host said.

"—precisely. Suicide demons. Obviously Branichor, as I was about to say."

"Strong silent types," the Host said. "Like me." He laughed loudly. "And very sore losers."

"Thanks for the analysis," Gunn said. "English here figured out who they were, what we need to know is where to find 'em. You ever get that kind in here?" He extended his hands to indicate Caritas. "Or is death by karaoke too slow for them?"

The Host ignored that last part, though it took some doing. "Occasionally," he said. "I know there's a population here, a small one. Mostly, they stay in Orange County. Land of theme parks, televangelists, and suicide demons. What they have in common is the pursuit of the almighty buck."

"They work for money?" Gunn asked.

"That's all they work for, darling," the Host replied. "If they don't finish the job, they don't get paid. Of course, if they don't finish the job, they're beyond caring about that."

"What we need to find out is who might have hired them," Wesley said.

The Host glanced about the club as if making sure it was empty. "Caritas is neutral ground," he reminded them. "And my readings have to be private. If I told you anything I'd seen in someone's soul—"

"They nearly killed Angel," Wesley said angrily, biting off the words.

"I'm only telling you so you'll appreciate the enormity of my good will," the Host assured him. "And the depths of my feelings for the dear vamp." He leaned close to them and spoke in conspiratorial tones. "Here's what I've heard. . . ."

Chapter Twelve

Larry Mullins had known since law school, of course, that a large part of being an attorney was writing. Legal writing was precise, almost ritualistic—sometimes literally ritualistic, when you worked for his firm—and incredibly detailed.

Along with the writing came the filling out of forms. Anytime a client had business with the government, for example, the forms came into play, dozens, maybe hundreds, of them. A lawyer had to know how to fill them out accurately and precisely and in such a way that they gave the barest minimum of information, never revealing any more than was asked but never enough less to raise questions nobody wanted to answer.

Often, a paralegal or a legal secretary could do a lot of this work. But that wouldn't do on this job. Larry wanted to do this himself. He had brought in his own electric typewriter, so there wouldn't even be a computer record, set it up on Parker McKay's dining room table, and typed out the answers that he and Parker agreed on, occasionally making mistakes and fixing them with Wite-Out to make the documents appear properly aged. In the computer age, he knew, it was possible to turn in a document with no errors. In the typewriter days, it had not been.

He made another mistake, a real one this time. He rolled the paper partway out and shook the tiny bottle, then withdrew the brush, coated with white goo. "You know who invented this stuff?" he asked Parker.

"Legal forms?" Parker asked back.

"Wite-Out, Liquid Paper, whatever," Larry explained. "This paint people used to use to fix mistakes."

"Apparently they still do," Parker pointed out.

"Yeah. Sales are probably down, but I guess they do."

"Not everyone's joined the digital age, Mr. Mullins."

"True."

"Anyway, who?"

"Who what?" Larry asked.

"Invented correction fluid."

"Oh," Larry said. He'd just been making conversation and had forgotten where he'd started. "Right. The mother of that guy in the Monkees."

"There were four of them, as I recall. Guys."

"Yeah, the tall guy. The one with the hat."

"The one with the hat," Parker echoed.

"Yeah, like a stocking cap? A wool hat."

Parker McKay looked at Larry for long enough to make the attorney uncomfortable. Larry found himself wishing Lilah would finish up her "feminizing" job upstairs and come back down to provide some buffer space. "Fascinating," Parker said finally. "Do you still need me here? Because, believe it or not, I have business interests that are suffering from the amount of time I am devoting to this enterprise."

"This enterprise is going to be very worthwhile in the long run," Larry assured him. "Maybe not so much financially, but emotionally. And I'm sure you'll agree that, important as money is, a happy and satisfying home life is really the most precious asset of all."

Parker sniffed once. "If I didn't think so, I guess we wouldn't be here."

"You won't regret it, Parker. I know I've said that before, but it's true."

"I'm sure you're right."

"Believe me, we've got many satisfied customers for this particular program," Larry said. "Even some of our own executives."

"Nathan Reed's wife?" Parker asked. "She's a lovely lady."

"I'm not sure about that," Larry said. *Like I*

would tell you even if I knew, he thought. The more time he spent with Parker McKay, the less he liked the man. But he appreciated Parker's contribution to Wolfram and Hart's annual bottom line, so he went out of his way to keep the man happy. "Anyway, we still have a lot of work to get through here," Larry continued. "What state do you want your wife to have been born in?"

"Holographic projectors, maybe," Gordon said. "But wouldn't we see them?"

"Depends on how well they hid them. Maybe some of the things we think are WebCams aren't."

Cordelia and Gordon had been scouting around the house, trying to determine how the production company had rigged the various hauntings—if, in fact, they had. Gordon still seemed convinced that it was all a fraud. Cordelia wasn't. There had already been too much—the mysterious writing in blood, the ghostly footfalls, the cold spot, whatever it was that had sent Terry packing in the night, and mostly the attack on Beth that she and Gordon had witnessed—for her to dismiss the possibility that something really was going on in this house.

She stood on tiptoes to look at one in the corner of a hallway, fingertips gripping the edge of the wainscoting that stopped halfway up the wall. The tiny lens set into the corner just looked like a lens, but there was no way to know if it was meant to take in light or beam it out. Assuming it really was a camera, though, Cordy hoped it wasn't a wide-angle lens, because it'd be projecting a very distorted view of her face from this distance. "I can't tell anything," she admitted.

"Well, and we haven't seen anything strange in this hall, that I know about," Gordon added. "So chances are that one's just a camera."

"I suppose so." She turned her back on it. "Then how do we figure out what's real and what's . . . surreal, I guess?"

Gordon wore a red T-shirt today that showed off his broad shoulders and powerful arms to their best effect, with a pair of faded jeans. He shrugged. Cordy liked the way it looked when he did that. "They have to have access to all the cameras, and whatever other equipment they've hidden around, right? It's all got to be wired in, remotely controlled somehow. So there must be secret passageways we haven't found. Maybe we should look for those."

"Or maybe the place really is haunted," she suggested, thinking that it might be time to share her theory.

Gordon threw her a dismissive look that made her think maybe she'd been premature after all. "You can't really believe that, can you?"

"Why not?" *The things you don't know about the world,* she thought, *would astonish you. If you'd seen half what I've seen, you wouldn't be so convinced.*

"For one thing, I know if I believed this house was really haunted, I wouldn't spend another night in it. The things we've all seen already would totally freak me out if I didn't think they were all rigged."

"I'm keeping an open mind," Cordelia said, "that's all."

Gordon started tapping on the wainscoting every few inches. Cordelia watched him for a moment, tapping and listening, listening and tapping.

"What are you doing?"

"Looking for hollow spots."

"I think the hollow spot is between your ears," she said, with a smile to disarm the effect.

He laughed. "You could be right, Cordy. But we're stuck inside this house for a while, and there's no DVD player, PlayStation, or Internet access. We have to keep busy somehow."

Good point, she thought. She picked a spot and started tapping. After she tapped a few times, she stopped and listened. She heard another tapping sound, and looked down the hall at Gordon. But he wasn't tapping, either.

Still, they both heard the noise—coming from inside the wall, like someone signaling to be let out.

"Okay," Gordon said. "That's just creepy."

Angel had a theory that when an investigation is at a dead end, one way to make progress is to go stir up trouble among those who might, through any twist of fate, have something to do with it. The idea being that when they—whoever they might be—saw that Angel was actively investigating, they'd come out of the woodwork. Usually that meant attacking him. In this particular case, though, they'd already done that—destroying several hundreds of thousands of dollars' worth of fine automobiles in the bargain. So what he needed now was to figure out who was behind the attack at Royalty Motors, which, if his theory held true, would point him to whoever had kidnapped Kirsten St. Clair.

There were two important points that supported this thesis. One, a definite tie existed between Kirsten and the attack—the trendoid, Curtis. Two, while he hadn't known for certain that Kirsten's kidnapping had a supernatural aspect—although the involvement of The Powers That Be certainly pointed to one—the demonic attack confirmed that there was.

With this theory in mind, he went out looking for trouble. Like himself, most demons tended toward the nocturnal lifestyle, so they were few and far between in the daylight. As the afternoon wore on, he tried a number of places—restaurants, saunas, gyms, and card games frequented by demons—with no success. But finally, he walked into Salvatore's.

Salvatore was a swordsmith in Toluca Lake whose primary business was making weapons for movies and TV shows. What those clients didn't know was that Salvatore had a secondary—and profitable—sideline going, creating swords and knives and axes and other edged implements for demons. His work was of uniformly high quality, and Angel Investigations was among his best clients.

The shop was on an alley off Alameda, close to some of the major movie studios but away from the street, since Salvatore had little patience for tourists or walk-in customers drawn by curiosity. Most of them wouldn't know how to use a real weapon, he believed, nor did they want to spend the money it took to make one. They wanted showpieces, if they bought at all, and that wasn't what he had apprenticed a dozen years in Toledo, Spain, to create.

Angel parked in the alley, just a few paces from Salvatore's door. The alley was shadowed from the afternoon sun, so Angel was able to make the walk quickly without risking spontaneous combustion. When he entered, Salvatore was bent over his work, honing the edge of a scimitar with a polishing stone and a damp rag. The swordsmith looked like a pirate, Angel thought. He was a short, round man, with a gleaming bald pate ringed by long, silver hair that grew from just above his ears. The hair was pulled back into a ponytail, and his gray beard was neatly trimmed to a point. Gold rings dangled from his earlobes. He wore a loose-fitting white shirt with ruffled sleeves, tucked into black pants held up by a wide black leather belt. Angel couldn't see his feet as he sat on his stool behind the counter, but he knew the man's pant-legs would be tucked into knee-high leather boots.

He glanced up at the sound of his door. "Angel," he said cheerfully. He held the scimitar up and looked at its edge, glinting in his bright work light. "Sharp enough to split a hair," he said. Laying the stone down on the oily rag, he rubbed a hand across his own polished dome. "I've got precious few to spare, though. Make me a gift of one of yours?"

"I'm keeping what I've got," Angel said. He trusted Salvatore, mostly. But the man had a lot of demons for customers, and it didn't seem like a good idea to willingly hand over a hair from his head to someone with such a disreputable clientele. Any number of spells required a victim's hair, and Angel had enough creatures after him already without adding to it.

"Good for you," Salvatore said with a chuckle. "You start giving it away, you'll wind up like me in no time." He looked at Angel, expectantly. "So, what brings you in today? Need a new sword? I've been working on a lovely Scottish basket-hilt, but the buyer canceled his order. Well, to be precise, he was disemboweled in an argument with a Tramaldon demon over the correct way to divide the marrow of a victim. So I could give you a deal."

Angel shook his head. "No weapons today, Salvatore. I'm just looking for information."

Salvatore blew out a sigh. "Get in line," he said.

"What do you mean?"

"Cops were just here, not half an hour ago, looking for the same thing."

Interesting, Angel thought. *They know about Salvatore?* "What were they investigating?"

"Apparently a young man was beheaded," Salvatore said. "They wanted to know if I had any ideas as to what kind of weapon it was."

"Did you?"

"No weapon I've ever sold, I told them. Here, they left me a copy of a crime scene photo, in case I had any ideas later." He slid a picture out from underneath the counter and put it down on the wooden surface, next to the scimitar.

The picture showed Curtis, the Hollywood trendoid who had worked at Laughing Pig Productions. *And set me up for an attack,* Angel thought.

"See the ragged edges where his neck is cut?" Salvatore demanded, stabbing a finger at the photo. "No blade of mine would make such an uneven cut, I told them. It just wouldn't happen."

"Do you have any idea what might have done it?"

"Of course," Salvatore said. "Which also, of course, I couldn't tell the police."

"What was it?"

"Angel, I can't tell you that."

Angel leaned on the counter, putting his face close to Salvatore's. "This kid set me up," he said.

"He tried to get me killed. Whoever killed him is probably behind the attempt on me, and is responsible for abducting a young woman whose life is in danger. Now I know you value your customers, but if you also value your life, tell me who did this."

Salvatore swallowed hard. "That was no blade, Angel. It was a Bextrian's claws. Look at the way the serrations tore the flesh instead of slicing cleanly."

"A Bextrian?" Angel asked, surprised. He hadn't heard of any even visiting North America in the last hundred years. They tended to stay in their native territory, on the Siberian steppe. "In L.A.?"

"If anyone finds out where you heard this, Angel, my life is over. Just so you understand that."

"Don't worry," Angel assured him.

"Worrying is what I do best. Well . . ."—he touched a finger to the edge of the scimitar's curved blade—". . . second best, anyway. Here's what I've heard. . . ."

Gunn found Phil Baxter sitting in a folding canvas chair on a dock in San Pedro, a fishing pole in his hands. An empty bucket stood beside him on the warped and uneven boards of the dock. Morning sun sparkled on the water, and the air was tinged with the scent of salt water, the way mornings by the ocean often smelled more strongly than the rest of the day. Gunn had never figured that out.

"Don't look like they're bitin'," he said.

The man didn't even look up. He was stocky, with

short gray hair and a ruddy face, dressed in a maroon and navy striped polo shirt, white duck pants, and deck shoes. The arms that held the pole were darkly tanned and muscular. For a guy in his sixties, he was in good shape. Only his face showed its age; his eyes were barely more than slits, heavy-lidded and crinkled at the corners. Deep creases extended from the sides of his nose to the corners of his mouth. His forehead was lined and folded in a frown. "Guess not," he said, as if he really hadn't been paying attention.

"But then, maybe you ain't here for the fishing."

"Could be right," Phil Baxter agreed.

"Guess I don't blame you," Gunn said. "Your partner's your partner, even after you both retire, right?"

The man sucked in a deep breath. "That's right."

"So when he swallows his own gun, that's gotta hurt."

Phil Baxter turned now, pinning Gunn with a steady gaze. What little showed of his eyes was clear blue, sky blue, and seemed to pierce Gunn like a sword. "I don't think I caught your name, son."

"I'm Gunn. Charles Gunn."

"Well, Charles Gunn, I'm fishing. You might have already noticed that, since you seem like the observant sort."

"I noticed."

"Something you might not have known about fishing. The fish like it quiet."

"You're not catchin' anything, anyway. Not like I scared 'em off."

Phil Baxter shifted in his seat, setting the end of his pole carefully in the empty bucket, and stood. He was an inch taller than Gunn, and that was going some, Gunn knew. He outweighed Gunn by a good forty pounds or more, but he was solid, not fat, and Gunn found himself hoping this didn't turn into a fight.

I could take him, he thought. *But it wouldn't be pretty.*

"There something I can do for you, Charles Gunn?"

"I hope so," Gunn said. "I want to talk about Jane Doe."

"I know a lot of Jane Does."

"This one's from nineteen eighty-three. And somebody marked her arm. You remember her."

Phil looked over Gunn's head as if checking to make sure he was alone. "I don't know what you're talking about."

"Earl Monroe left a file for me," Gunn said. "I was supposed to meet him yesterday. He didn't make the meeting. The file did."

Phil Baxter blew out a long breath and let his shoulders slump. He looked more like the aging ex-cop that he was now. "You're not a cop," he said simply.

Gunn laughed once. "Not even."

"Some things a man should take with him to the grave. Beyond the grave."

"I guess the pressure was a little too much for Earl."

Phil let his gaze travel up and down Gunn's body, sizing him up as if seeing him now for the first time. "What are you after?" he asked. "Why dredge up ancient history?"

"It's not so ancient," Gunn told him. "Body turned up a couple of nights ago. Face gone, prints gone, teeth gone. Markings on her arm. Whoever whacked Jane Doe in nineteen eighty-three is still out there, making new Janes."

Phil looked away, down at the fishing pole. Then he sat back down in his canvas chair. "Earl Monroe was my partner and my friend," he said. "I thought I'd catch a fish in his memory, barbecue it up for dinner tonight, maybe hoist a few in his memory. I thought it'd end there."

"People are getting killed," Gunn insisted. "It can't end."

"Who are you? Why do you care?"

"Just the way I am," Gunn replied. "Someone who cares. You might as well talk to me, 'cause I ain't goin' away."

"Pull up some dock then, because I'm tired of looking up at you." Phil sat quietly for a moment. "I don't even know where to start."

"You and your partner Earl, you guys came across

some weird stuff, according to the file I read," Gunn prompted, sitting on the edge of a nearby crate.

"That's right. We did. I guess every cop does, every one in Los Angeles, at least."

"Other places, too, believe me. Be glad you're not in Sunnydale."

"I've heard stories," Phil said. Gunn thought maybe the man was relaxing a little. "We ran across our share, I guess. But we kept quiet about it. You don't put in your official report that you think a wolf man ripped up a pair of teens necking up in the Hollywood Hills unless you want to find yourself walking a graveyard beat someplace that backup never seems to get to."

"So it's a career move, hushing up killings," Gunn said, unable to disguise his contempt.

"You haven't been out there, you don't know what it's like," Phil Baxter argued. "You see promising careers get shot down the tubes. You see cops, like Earl finally did, cashing out the easy way. You see the guys who don't make waves climbing up the ranks. I had alimony payments, a wife, a kid, then two alimony payments and child support."

So you're a bad husband and a bad father, and that excuses you, Gunn thought. This time, though, he managed to rein it in, and he let the man continue.

"But they can't touch my pension now, and Earl's gone, rest his soul. So I guess it can't hurt to tell you what I know about Janie. That's what we started to call her, Janie. Earl and I were obsessed with her, for the whole summer of nineteen eighty-three, and into the next year. We came at her every way we could but we kept running into roadblocks. It's not like we just let that one go, I'm telling you."

"I'm sure you knocked yourselves out."

"We did what we could," Phil insisted, an angry edge in his voice. "We even turned up a witness, eventually. Saw the body get dumped. Made a preliminary identification."

"So what happened?"

"The witness never got to make the I.D. official. She met with an accident."

"An accident?"

"Had her throat accidentally cut in her yard, with her own electric hedge-clippers."

"Hate it when that happens," Gunn said.

"Yeah." Phil picked up the fishing pole again and began to reel in his line.

"But you had a preliminary I.D.," Gunn said. "You couldn't find another way to make it stick?"

"We didn't have enough," Phil explained. "She never even got a chance to finger an individual. All we had was a guy in a suit, with a company car. We had a partial plate. Not much to go on."

"What was the company?" Gunn asked, thinking he already knew what the answer would be.

"A law firm, of all things," Phil said. "Wolfram and Hart. Real scumbags."

"So I've heard."

"Yeah?" Phil asked. "Glad they still have that reputation."

"They do."

Phil continued his story. "So, without the wit, there was no way to get a conviction. We kept poking, until word came down from upstairs that we should leave the lawyers alone. I never knew who got to whom, but we had to excise all mention of Wolfram and Hart from our report. I was in line for a promotion, so I didn't want to stir the pot, especially since it was clear the case was going nowhere."

"So you agreed, and you made the changes."

"And I got my promotion. So did Earl. I made it to Captain before I retired. I was able to pay the alimony as long as I needed to, and I put my son through college."

"And all it took was doctoring a report and giving up on Janie," Gunn prodded.

"Life's a series of trade-offs," Phil insisted. "This one wasn't perfect, but it worked out."

"For everybody except the new Jane Doe," Gunn argued. "And any between then and now we don't know about. And any still to come, unless we can get a handle on this."

Phil Baxter leaned forward, looking at Gunn over his shoulder. He didn't say anything for a long time, just looked at Gunn and finished reeling in his line, and then took the bait off his hook and tossed it into the water. Then he rose, and folded up his canvas chair, and picked up his bucket. "Guess I'm done fishing," he said.

Gunn shook his head. "I think you're just starting."

Chapter Thirteen

The young lady who had once been Kirsten St. Clair sat on her chair and watched without expression or visible emotion as the flurry of activity went on around her. Any activity in this small room was new and different, but she found it no more or less interesting than anything else. When people spoke directly to her, she looked at them. Nothing occurred to her to say in return, though. She couldn't answer the simplest questions. Someone said, "You okay?" and she could only shrug.

There were others in the room now, who couldn't reasonably be classified as "people." There were three of them that she had seen. They were tall and gaunt, one could even say sepulchral, and their skin was as white as tissue paper and appeared to be of a similar texture. Through the skin, she could see veins, a networks of red veins like worms wriggling under the earth, and beneath the veins she thought she could see their muscles expand and contract with every motion. They wore loose white robes, belted at the waist, made of a fabric that looked like linen, and their chests were bare and exposed and their long, thin legs were visible, and everywhere was the white skin stretched over veins and muscles and what may have been, just the ghost of a shadow visible, their skeletons underneath everything else. Their hair, worn shoulder-length and straight and unencumbered, was just as white as their skin and their robes. Even their eyes were a pale gray that was almost white. The only thing that wasn't white was their teeth; their teeth, she noted, were yellow, not mustard yellow but almost baby corn yellow, and she could see them show through the papery white flesh even when their mouths were closed.

At another time, the person who had been Kirsten St. Clair would have found this very unpleasant. Now, though, she just looked at them, without curiosity, like she looked at the people milling about who were actually people. It didn't occur to her to wonder what these strange white creatures were or why they were here.

Some of the activity seemed to involve the young lady, but she didn't question it. When they moved her, she agreed pliantly, staying where she was positioned until they moved her again. Her long blond hair had been pinned up, leaving her neck exposed.

She had not consented to this, nor did she argue.

Although she had never in her life been a part of this sort of situation, she no longer had any knowledge of that fact. So she sat quietly by, a moderately interested observer, as lines were painted on the floor around her—it occurred to her that she was in the exact center of the diagram, but that fact failed to stir her in any way—and candles were lit and incense was burned, tendrils of smoke snaking toward the ceiling and coalescing there, gradually forming a cloud that grew thicker and thicker as the day or the night wore on. In addition to the incense, flame burned in a metal brazier of some kind, and sticking out from the brazier she saw a metal rod with a wooden handle on it. She didn't really think anything of that, either, at the time.

After an indeterminate period, the people who had been in the room with them left, and she was alone with the three white creatures. To Kirsten St. Clair, this would have seemed strange, even terrifying, but to the young lady who sat here now, it was hardly noteworthy. For all she knew, every other day of her life had been like this one, and only somewhere deep in the farthest recesses of her mind did she feel that something was wrong, that maybe she really ought to be scared of what they would do to her in here. That thought flickered across her consciousness and then was gone, making no more impact than a single fly on a herd of elephants.

The white men—she thought of them as men, for some reason, though they seemed without gender at all, as far as she could tell—took up positions in the room, one directly in front of her, one directly behind her, one off to the side, near the brazier. The one in front of her closed his gray-white eyes and began a chant, tuneless and senseless, as far as she was concerned, making sounds but not recognizable words. After a moment, the one behind her started up, chanting what seemed to be the exact same sounds in the same order, but since he started later the effect was like an echo of the first one, not a harmony. Then the third one joined in, so the sounds were repeated again and again moments after the first one called them out.

She began to feel sleepy, as if the cloud of incense and the sputtering of the brazier and the chanting of the white men were conspiring to make her shut her eyes, to drift off to sleep. She saw no reason why she shouldn't. Her eyelids grew heavy, and she didn't fight it, just blinked a few times. Her breathing slowed. She felt her muscles go loose. The chanting continued, and she barely noticed the white man nearest the brazier remove the thing with the wooden handle, genuflecting with it and then passing it on to the white man in front of her. The end of it that had been in the brazier glowed white-hot. This man performed the same ritualistic gesture and passed it back to the white man behind her.

She couldn't see what he did with it, and it didn't strike her as important to turn around to find out. If she had, she would have seen the third white man perform the same genuflection and then bring the white-hot end of the iron toward the back of her neck, and as the chanting reached a specific phrase—a phrase that echoed what was written in a form of pictographs on the brand itself—he pressed the heated end of the iron rod, the pictograph end, into the flesh of the back of the young lady's neck.

This, finally, elicited a reaction. She screamed in agony as her skin sizzled and popped and the acrid stink of burning flesh and hair overpowered the incense, and then she fainted dead away.

Christy Colquitt's bathroom was across the hall from her bedroom, not adjoining, as she knew some of the other rooms had. She'd retired to her room for a brief nap, and then, upon awakening, had brushed her teeth and washed her face in preparation for rejoining the rest of the world.

But when she opened the bathroom door, a panther glared at her, teeth flashing, yellow eyes glaring with malice.

She slammed the door and tried to scream. She opened her mouth, clenched her fists, and made an attempt at a really good, curl-your-hairs B-movie-actress scream. But nothing came out. Her throat felt closed up with panic, her voice gone.

She heard the beast's claws clicking against the hardwood floor on the other side.

It was waiting there for her to try again.

Fighting back the welling panic that threatened to overtake her, she glanced quickly around the bathroom. There didn't seem to be anything to use as a weapon. She wasn't even sure what one would use as a weapon against such a beast—a rifle, she guessed, if one knew how to shoot one, which she didn't.

It's not real, she told herself. *It looks real, but it's a trick of some kind, a projection. There's no real panther in the house with you. How could there be?*

She almost managed to convince herself.

If she couldn't scream, she couldn't alert the others. It was the middle of the day, and there was no telling where anybody else was, but it was possible that it would be an hour or more before anybody bothered to come upstairs for any reason.

She couldn't be trapped in here for that long. She didn't like enclosed spaces to begin with—she blamed a childhood run-in with a piece of playground equipment that had looked bigger than it had, and in which she'd ended up stuck for several hours—and she knew that staying in this bathroom for very long would drive her mad.

So her choice was, stay in and lose it, or face the no-doubt imaginary jungle cat.

She swallowed and opened the door with trembling hands.

The panther looked at her, its coat black velvet in the faint light of the flame-style bulbs of the hallway, and uttered a low growl.

She wanted to say soothing words, but found that her voice still wouldn't work. All she could do was squeak incoherently.

The thing was, she realized, the panther made no move to attack her. It looked threatening, but it wasn't coming toward her.

She stepped through the doorway, eyes on the cat's eyes.

Its muscles tensed. She took another step into the hall and it coiled, ready to spring.

It really doesn't want me to leave the bathroom, she thought, stepping back across the threshold as quickly as she could. When she did that, the panther relaxed. But its eyes never left her.

Standoff, she thought. She didn't even bother to close the door. If it really wanted her, it could have taken her. It just didn't want her to leave. With the door open, her low-grade claustrophobia wasn't so bad. She thought she could take it until someone came by, and maybe the panther would give up on her then.

But as it turned out, she didn't have to wait that long. A few minutes passed, and then she saw movement in the hall. A beautiful, pale woman, all in white—hair, eyes, skin, clothing—drifted past, and spoke a word to the panther. Christy couldn't make out the word, but the panther apparently approved. As the woman continued down the hall—her feet never touching the floor, Christy noted—the panther stood and followed her. When they reached the end of the hall, where the stairs were, they both disappeared.

The address the Host had given them was an upstairs apartment in Beverly Hills, down on Robertson, south of Wilshire, where they had the name Beverly Hills but not the wealth and prestige to go with it. On the corner was a gas station that also sold tacos and beer and rented videos. Behind that, a two-story brick building housed a Chinese restaurant and a massage parlor. A wooden staircase off the alley led upstairs to the place where the Host had told them they'd find Kraal.

Not knowing precisely what to expect, Wesley was glad that Gunn had brought along some of his crew, even though there had been grumbling on the way down about taking time away from the neighborhood to go help out Angel. Wesley had the definite sensation that some of them resented the time that Gunn spent with Angel and the others instead of with his old friends. But the man's courage and street smarts had proven invaluable to the team. *And to me,* Wesley thought. *If it wasn't for Gunn, I wouldn't be risking my life here today.* When Wesley had been shot by an evil reanimated police officer, it had been Gunn who'd rushed him to safety and, eventually, medical assistance. In addition, there was no telling if Cordelia would be rejoining the team after her television stardom took hold. If she didn't, then Gunn's participation would be needed more than ever.

Wesley believed it was entirely possible that some of Gunn's crew would look fondly upon demons who tried to kill Angel, since Angel was, after all, a vampire, and vampires seemed to be the group's primary target. But there were bad vampires and there were . . . *well,* he amended, *there was* one *good vampire, and that one good vampire is responsible for an awful lot of decent acts.*

The staircase was rickety, and seven men climbing it unavoidably made some noise. He and Gunn stopped at the top, before a nondescript door. The other guys were bunched on the steps below. "Just barge in?" Gunn suggested.

"Do you think we ought to knock?"

"Figure he heard us about when we hit the first stair," Gunn said. "He don't know we're coming, he ain't gonna hear a knock on the door, either."

"Good point," Wesley agreed. He and Gunn were stepping back to launch simultaneous kicks at the door when the knob turned and it opened.

A shabbily dressed demon stood in the doorway, clad in a stained white T-shirt and gray drawstring sweatpants. At first, Wesley thought he also wore slippers shaped like a bear's claws, but then he realized that those furry, brown, taloned feet were actually the demon's. His hands were equally furry, as were the arms that vanished into the T-shirt sleeves, and the powerful neck that supported a squarish head with a corona of horns at the top, rising away from the forehead. The face, surprisingly, was smooth and hairless, almost reptilian, in contrast with the definitely mammalian body. Its skin was a magenta tone, with deep red eyes. A pink tongue darted over thin violet lips, and then it spoke in a voice that was unexpectedly smooth, almost silky. "My name is Kraal," the demon said. "Is there something I can do for you gentlemen?"

Wesley and Gunn glanced at each other. They'd been geared up for opposition, probably a fight, but not a polite greeting.

Recovering his composure, Wesley started in. "We believe you recently arranged for some Branichor demons—"

"Suicide demons," Gunn added.

"I know what they are," Kraal said.

"—to attack a friend of ours."

"It's quite possible," Kraal admitted.

"So you did," Wesley pursued.

"I said that it's possible, nothing more. I've been known to hire Branichors for a variety of tasks. It's what I do."

"What's what you do?" Gunn demanded.

“I’m a broker,” Kraal said. “I thought you’d have known that. You knew where to find me, after all.”

“We know much more than you think,” Wesley bluffed. “But just now, we’d like to talk about the Branichors, if you don’t mind.”

“Yes, of course,” Kraal said. “Would you like to come inside?”

“Nothing wrong with right here,” Gunn said.

“The neighbors . . .,” Kraal began.

“Neighborhood like this ain’t gonna be too surprised by anything,” Gunn observed. He glanced at his crew, leaning on the railing, watching him talk to the demon with expressions ranging from disdain to downright fury. “They ain’t called the cops on my boys, they ain’t too observant, anyway.”

“It’s a fine neighborhood,” Kraal protested. “Within a few steps of my front door I can have all my physical and material needs met. People are polite and respectful. A person can’t ask for much more than that.”

“But then, you’re not a person,” Wesley reminded him. “May we continue?”

“Certainly,” Kraal agreed. “Branichor demons are a most unsavory lot. You know they are quite happy to kill themselves rather than face failure?”

“So we’ve heard,” Wesley said. “Go on.”

“Yes, well, they’re good for fighting and not much else, I’m afraid. So when I’m contracted to provide Branichors, I usually assume that someone is to be attacked. But since it is not my business to ask who the intended target might be, I don't know that for an absolute fact."

"So you just provide the muscle and you don't care who gets hurt?" Gunn asked, anger in his tone.

Kraal looked at him as if sizing him up for a suit or a snack, and blinked a couple of times. "Yes, precisely. That's what a broker does. I provide demons for clients who need demons for their own purposes. If I constantly asked them what the demons were to be used for, I doubt I'd have many customers, would I?"

"Having had very little experience with demon brokerage houses, we'll have to take your word for that," Wesley said. "But about these Branichors. The job was last night. Certainly you don't hire so many Branichors that you can't keep them all straight?"

Kraal shook his head. "No, not at all. Branichor jobs are relatively rare, in fact. I know the crew you mean. I was guessing that none of them survived, since they never showed up for their final payment. That's the good thing about hiring Branichors—they don't expect to get paid if they don't get the job done. They do like a larger initial payment, though."

"These didn't get the job done," Gunn said. "Which is why we're not looking for the Branichors. We're looking for whoever hired them."

"Well, that would have been me."

Wesley was quickly losing patience with this demon. He touched his forehead, exasperated. "Yes, we know that. But on behalf of whom?"

"Well, I'm afraid I can't tell you that," Kraal said. "My clientele insists on absolute anonymity, of course."

"Hey, Gunn," Chain said from behind them. "We can make him talk. Let us at him."

The demon looked startled. "Is he threatening me with violence?" he asked.

Gunn laughed. "That's one way to look at it. In fact, that's the only way to look at it." He stepped to the side and cocked his thumb at the demon. "He's all yours, guys."

Kraal started to back into his doorway, but Wesley shoved a foot in front of the door, blocking it. Inside, he could see that the apartment was carpeted in a thick orange shag—floors, walls, and ceilings. He supposed the furry demon found it comforting, but he shuddered nonetheless.

The guys from Gunn's crew charged up the stairs, knives and stakes at the ready. Kraal took another step back, but then held his ground, palms out. "Please," he said, "there's absolutely no need for violence."

"Only good demon is a dead demon," one of the crew said. "So let's just finish this one right now."

"Kraal," Wesley suggested, holding up a hand to Chain and the others, "I'm sorry to say that we're not going to be able to restrain these gentlemen unless you give us what we need. They're a good lot, but a bit bloodthirsty when it comes to your kind." *And to tell the truth,* he thought, *I wouldn't mind seeing them rough this one up a bit. Might not be bad to get a few shots of my own in.*

"It's not that I don't want to tell you," Kraal said. "Well, all right, to some extent it is, I admit. But in fact, I don't know *what* to tell you. My clients frequently insist on anonymity, and they get it, partially by not revealing their identities even to me. I don't ask questions, I get paid in cash, I deliver the demons as contracted. End of transaction. The demons don't work for my clients, they work for me, and I pay them—when they survive—in cash. This is not a difficult concept, is it?"

"So what you're trying to tell us is that you don't know who you provided the Branichors to?"

Kraal touched the end of his nose as if playing Charades. "Now you've got it," he said happily. "I haven't a clue."

"You must know something about them," Wesley urged. "You met them in person, I presume, to collect the cash."

"They came to the door, just as you did," Kraal told them. "They told me what they needed. I decided Branichors would fill the bill. They came back at the appointed hour, paid me in cash, and took the Branichors away in a limousine. That's it, in a nutshell."

"A limousine?" Wesley asked. "What were the clients dressed like?"

"Lawyers," Kraal said quickly. "I just assumed they were lawyers, from the way they talked, the clothes they wore."

"Lawyers," Gunn echoed. "Figures."

"Is your friend, the one they attacked, in trouble with some lawyers?" Kraal asked.

"Constantly," Wesley replied. "Let's go, gents. I think we've got what we came for."

"We don't get to stick him?" Joey asked pleadingly.

"We might need him again," Gunn said. "We do come back, Kraal, we'll expect cooperation, all right?"

"To the best of my abilities," Kraal agreed. "Just keep your barbarians at bay."

Sharon found Cordelia and Gordon in the library, where they'd gone to get away from the ghostly tapping. Cordelia browsed the bookshelves looking for anything published more recently than the late 1960s, without success. Gordon sprawled in one of the easy chairs, staring up at the pressed-tin ceiling. Sharon stopped just inside the door. "Okay if I join you?" she asked.

"It's not our house, either," Cordelia said. "Feel free."

"Thanks." Sharon crossed to another of the easy

chairs and sat. She wore a yellow ribbed shirt that clung to her curves, and black pants. Her hair was done in beaded braids, and the overall effect was stunning. "Seems like you guys have gotten pretty close."

"I guess you could say that," Cordelia said, feeling suddenly ill at ease to have someone else point it out.

"The way I see it," Sharon went on, "no one is going to make it to the end of this game without teaming up with someone else. You've got to have a strategy. If you guys are allied in your voting, I want to get in on it with you."

"We haven't been," Gordon replied, sitting up straighter. "I mean, we told each other how we voted after the fact, but we didn't discuss it beforehand."

Sharon looked at him as if she wasn't sure whether to believe him. Finally, she said, "Well, the first vote, I can see that. But from here on out, you've got to play the game carefully. The fewer people left, the more complex the strategy's going to be. Anyone not playing smart just isn't going to make it."

"Just as a point of information," Cordelia said, "assuming Gordon and I were allied, why would we want to let anyone else in? If we could keep it to just two of us until the end, the home audience would have to pick one of us. We split the hundred thousand dollars and each go home fifty thousand dollars richer."

"If all you want is fifty grand," Sharon said. "Which I doubt is the case. Plus, two isn't a very solid voting block. Other folks line up against you, they can vote both of you out. Three, though, is a good number. We could put up a united front, pull each other through till we're all that's left, and then it's every woman for herself. And man," she added with a nod toward Gordon.

"There's some merit to that idea, Cordy," Gordon said. "Won't do either of us any good to be voted out before our time."

"I suppose," Cordelia agreed, somewhat hesitantly. "But remember what Rich said? Not to trust anyone."

"He's getting paid no matter what," Sharon said. "The rest of us want to make this whole thing worthwhile, we have to look out for ourselves."

"So what you're suggesting is we target someone to vote out each night."

"That's right," Sharon explained. "Whoever looks like the strongest player gets the boot. The others, the house itself will take care of, I figure."

"So we're really . . . just helping the house along with the elimination process," Cordy said slowly. She was starting to like the idea.

"Exactly," Sharon agreed.

"Do you have someone in mind?" Cordelia asked her.

Sharon paused. "Well . . . the first night, I would have said Terry."

"I know," Cordelia said with a chuckle. "Who'd have thought he'd be the first one scared out? He looked like a tough guy to me."

"I would have put my money on Beth," Gordon said. "She seemed like a lady with a lot of backbone. So I guess my judgment can't be trusted either."

"I say Vince," Sharon suggested. "Call me old-fashioned, but I think when it gets really tough, the women are going to bail first. I think Christy's going to bolt, but we need to take Vince out."

"Not this woman," Cordelia declared. *I think there's more going on here than he does,* she thought. In spite of her generally positive association with Phantom Dennis, the idea that there were real ghosts in the house made her nervous. But also, she recognized, curious. And so far, curiosity and ambition more than won out over the little shiver of fear she felt.

"Me either," Sharon said. "But in general, I think women tend to be more sensible, and less money-hungry, than men. Add those two factors, and you'll have guys sticking it out even if they're terrified."

"You're making me ashamed of my gender," Gordon said, laughing to show he wasn't *too* ashamed. "But, yeah, that sounds like us."

"Don't count Pat out, then, either," Cordelia reminded them. "He won the flag contest, after all."

"And there's another contest tomorrow," Sharon pointed out. "Maybe it should be Pat. He's vulnerable tonight."

This is such a bad idea, Cordelia thought. *For one thing, we could be on the WebCams right now, talking about this, which will definitely lose us votes. And for another, the other three people left in the house could be in another room working out a way to get rid of us.*

She went to the library's leather-topped writing desk and pulled a slip of paper from a leather square notepad holder. A quill pen turned out to have a ballpoint pen in place of the nib it had once had. She felt a bit awkward writing with the feather bobbing in her face, but she went through with it, anyway.

When she was finished, she replaced the pen and took the note over to show Gordon and Sharon, palming it so the camera couldn't see what it said. She put it in front of them, waited for their nods of understanding, and then scrunched it up and tucked it into a pocket.

The note read: "The walls have eyes and ears. We say no, but we vote for Pat."

Chapter Fourteen

"Lawyers and limos," Angel said. "It keeps coming back around to that."

"Sorry, Angel?"

Wesley had used his cell phone to call Angel on the drive back, and was having a hard time hearing.

"Nothing, Wes. Good job."

"Excuse me?"

"I'll talk to you when you get back here!" Angel shouted.

"No, I think my ear is fine," Wesley replied. "It's just this phone, I think. Bad signal."

"Good-bye, Wesley!" Angel yelled. Presumably Wesley would understand that part.

"I can't hear you, Angel," Wesley said. "Gunn has an appointment, so he'll drop me at the hotel in a bit and we can talk more then." He hung up. Which was what Angel was about to do, anyway, so he followed suit.

Lawyers and limousines. In Angel's world, that only meant one thing. *But it still could be coincidence,* he supposed. He paced the hotel lobby, thinking. There needed to be something that would tie it all together, and he was missing that link. A limo had been seen outside Kirsten St. Clair's apartment building the night she vanished. A limo had been seen near the lot where the unidentifiable body had been dumped, with demonic markings burned into its flesh. Lawyers had been at the beach, asking about Kirsten St. Clair, before her disappearance. Lawyers with a limo had hired the suicide demons who attacked him at the luxury car lot.

A lot of common threads, but nothing concrete. He needed a smoking gun.

He picked up the phone again and dialed the East Hills Teen Center.

Anne answered.

"It's Angel," he said. "Can you ask your friend on the cops for another favor?"

"I can try," Anne said. "It's important?"

"If it wasn't, I wouldn't ask you."

"Okay," Anne agreed. "What do you need?

Angel told her.

The crew showed up later than before, having become accustomed to the setup process in the house's living room. By five-fifty, though, they were all ready to shoot and, just killing time, were telling jokes and shooting the breeze, until Rich Carson came in from outside and the A.D. gathered the cast.

At six sharp, they were rolling. Rich did his now-standard intro.

"Good evening, and welcome to *Haunted House,*" he began. Cordelia tuned him out at that point. Her mind was racing, wondering if the deal she'd struck with Sharon and Gordon had been witnessed, if it would come around to bite them on their collective butt before they were done. Sharon played Miss Innocent, sitting on the other side of the room from Cordy and Gordon. Cordy noted that Sharon had traded in the tight yellow top for a silky purple one with a plunging neckline. *Going for the sex appeal vote, huh?* she thought. *Two can play that game.*

She remained distracted, intent on handicapping the game instead of what was going on around, which was basically just a summing up of the day's activities, anyway. When they played clips from the WebCams, Cordelia held her breath, fingernails biting into her palms, until it was over and she hadn't seen the library confab. *But that doesn't mean it didn't go out online,* she thought.

And, anyway, it was mortifying enough that they showed the close-up of her looking into the fish-eye lens in the hallway. The lens distorted her features, but even distorted she realized that she was looking kind of worn out. The unresolved Kirsten situation was really taking a toll on her. She hoped that Angel was making some progress on that. The thought occurred to her, on a regular basis, that maybe she should drop out and go see if there was something she could do to help. But Angel had told her before she went not to worry about such things, promising that he and the guys would take care of anything that came up. She felt like if she quit now she'd be letting him down, implying that she lacked confidence in his abilities, as well as giving up on the prize.

"We're a somewhat smaller group than when we started," Rich Carson said toward the end of the show. "Beth, Terry, and Annemarie are gone. That leaves us with Christy, Pat, Gordon, Sharon, Vince, and Cordelia. And tonight, one more of you will be voted out. But before we get to that, we have a little competition. The winner of this one can't be voted out tonight."

"What do we have to do?" Vince asked.

"It's simple," Rich told them. He took a drink from a glass bottle of mineral water, emptying it. "I'm sure you've all played spin the bottle before, right?"

"You want us to kiss each other?" Cordelia asked, surprised. *I know where I'd want to start,* she thought.

Rich chuckled. "No, we won't be playing it that way," he said. He put the bottle on the floor. A handheld camera followed his moves. "It's actually pretty simple. There are five of you. You'll sit in a circle, and you'll each get a turn to spin the bottle. Whoever the bottle points to most often gets spared tonight. If it points to each of you once, then I get a turn to spin it to break the tie. If the house itself wants someone to stick around, then this is the house's chance to show us, by controlling the spin."

The group left their chairs and sat in a circle on the floor, spin the bottle-style. The green glass bottle lay on its side between them. "Sharon," Rich said, "why don't you spin first?"

"Okay," Sharon agreed. She leaned into the circle and put her fingertips on the bottle. "Just like high school," she said with a giggle. She gave the bottle a spin.

It whirled eight or nine times, finally coming to a rest with the mouth pointing squarely at Gordon.

"Gordon, looks like you're up. Spin the bottle," Rich instructed.

Gordon did so. The bottle went around and around, slowing as it reached Cordelia, but continuing on past her and landing, once again, on Gordon, sitting next to her.

"Did you make a deal with the bottle?" Rich asked. "You've spun, so Cordelia, you go next."

The bottle felt unexpectedly cold to Cordelia's fingers. She gave it her best high school wrist snap and watched it twirl like a flung baton. She counted fourteen circuits before it slowed to a stop right between Sharon and Christy.

But it didn't really stop—it must have hit a snag on the hardwood floor, Cordelia thought, because it started to move again, skipping past Christy, past Cordelia, and coming to a stop, once again, pointing clearly at Gordon.

"It looks like you have a friend in the house, Gordon," Rich said.

"Or an enemy," Gordon said with a nervous laugh.

"Either way, no one can beat you now, so you're safe for tonight," Rich said. "You'll be removed from the voting list. Pat, Christy, there's no need for you to spin."

"But I *want* to," Christy said, laughing. She grabbed the bottle and gave it a whirl. The bottle began to spin, but erratically, wobbling as if it had gone off-balance somehow. Then it increased speed instead of slowing.

This doesn't look good at all, Cordelia thought. She raised her hands to ward off any breaking glass if the thing shattered.

But it didn't. Instead, the bottle took flight, lifting off the floor and rocketing away, narrowly missing Vince's head when the young man ducked just in time. The bottle sailed past him and slammed into the wall, not breaking but impaling itself in the plaster.

Rich Carson, face blanched, looked at the camera operators. "Did someone get that?"

"We got it, Rich," one of them assured him.

"Okay, folks," Rich said, trying to recover his composure. "Looks like it's time to vote. You can't vote for Gordon. But before we do, does anyone want to walk out now, in light of what just happened?"

Cordelia looked around the circle, her heart pounding. Everyone was frightened, especially Vince, who surely was thinking about what his face would look like now if the bottle had connected with him the way it had with the wall. But Vince wasn't the one who spoke up.

"Yes," Christy said. "I'm out. Between that and the panther, it's getting a little too spooky for me."

"Are you sure, Christy?" Rich asked her.

"I'm positive," she said. "You know I wasn't trying to do that—right, Vince?" she asked, putting a hand on the still clearly disturbed Vince.

"Believe me," he said. "If I thought you were able to intentionally do that, I'd worry about you."

"Well, I'm sorry." She turned to Rich. "It's just too much," she said. "I'm going."

"There's a car waiting outside," Rich said. "We'll pack you up and send your stuff later. But you won't be leaving just yet, because we're still going to have our scheduled vote, and whoever gets voted out will be joining you in that car."

"Okay," Christy agreed. She stood, patting Vince's shoulder as she did, and headed for the door without looking back.

"Good-bye, Christy," Rich said. "And good-bye, someone else. It's time for you to vote. Gordon, you can't be voted against, but you still get a vote, so why don't you go first?"

Gordon rose and, with a subtle shrug at Cordelia, went to the laptop computer. Cordelia went third this time, and when she got to the computer, she hesitated but then dutifully voted for Pat. Sharon didn't so much as glance at either one of them, but strode, full of confidence and grace, to the computer to cast her own vote.

When they had all gone, Rich got the computer and clicked some keys. He looked around the room, one by one. A camera did the same, pausing on each of them in turn. *You can almost hear the drum-roll,* Cordy thought.

"I have the results," Rich said suddenly, "and it's time to say good-bye to another contestant. The final tally is, Vince, two votes."

Vince looked stricken, but Rich didn't even slow down.

"Cordelia, two votes. And Pat, three votes. I'm sorry, Pat, but it's time for you to leave the House. There's a car waiting outside the front door to take you home."

"Okay, Rich," Pat said flatly. "I'm gone." He rose

and walked out of the room without looking at the others. After a moment, they heard the front door slam.

Cordelia was stunned—at the fact that the alliance had worked, and the toughest competition was gone, but also that two people had voted against her! *Who could it be?* she wondered. After the first wave of shock passed, she realized that one way to interpret it was that she was a contender, so somebody else wanted her out of the way, as she and the others in her alliance wanted Pat gone.

But, still . . . she looked at the others, trying to see who looked guilty. No one did.

Vince surprised the others by standing up, on legs that didn't look too secure. "You know what?" he said. "I've had enough. That bottle could have killed me, and then to get two votes against me . . . I don't need this. I'll go with Pat and Christy."

Rich was obviously caught off-guard, but he carried on. "Okay, Vince," he said. "You played a good game, but it's your decision. That's three down, in one evening. Anyone else?"

Gordon shook his head. "We can take it."

"Speak for yourself," Sharon said with a half-hearted chuckle. "Some of us are ready to change our pants."

Rich looked at his watch—for show, since he'd already noted the assistant director's hand signal to wrap the broadcast. "Our time's up," he intoned.

"Be here tomorrow night for the big finale—right here in our own *Haunted House*!"

As the crew packed up, Rich came to each cast member in turn and shared a few quiet words. When he got to Cordelia, he put a hand on her arm. "You sure you're okay, Cordy?" he asked her. "From what I've seen on the WebCams, you've had a pretty rough few days."

She put on a brave smile. "Oh, I'm fine, Rich. Some headaches, but nothing I can't handle. It takes more than a few ghosts to scare me."

"Somehow, I believe you," Rich said, giving her arm a friendly squeeze before letting go. "But you be careful, okay? There's more going on in this house than we thought, at first. We're not going to let it affect the show, but I can tell you, we won't be filming any other programs here."

He took off then. Cordelia appreciated his concern, but part of her thought that he was only trying to put one final scare into them by sharing that little bit of information at this late date. She believed that the house was more haunted than the production company had expected, but Rich couldn't possibly think that it was dangerous or he'd want the plug pulled right now. Nobody wanted to be associated with a reality TV show where people really died, did they? *What's really got me concerned,* she thought, *is getting two votes cast against me.*

The first time a vote had gone against her, Cordelia

had felt a rush of anger that sent her up to her room. This time, she took it almost as a badge of pride, and she was in no hurry to go upstairs. She stayed on the couch, and several of the other contestants hung around, too, watching the crew coil their cables and shut off their lights and make ready to go. Cordelia wondered, seeing them work, what the show looked like on the air. Here, behind the scenes, there was no music, no flashy computer graphics, not even little labels popping up underneath her chin to identify her when she was in close-up. *Which had better be happening a lot,* she thought. *And all my friends and enemies—especially the enemies—had better be watching. Along with casting agents. Lots of casting agents.*

She wondered briefly how she was being perceived by the public. She'd wanted to be the fun one, or maybe the sexy one. But she was afraid the vision fatigue was making her look like the hypochondriac one, which was not the image she wanted to project. *Still,* she thought, *if naked guy could win the first* Survivor, *who knows what characteristics will carry the day?*

Sharon and Gordon were involved in a serious conversation.

"What do you think they are?" Sharon asked.

"What are?"

"Ghosts, spirits. Whatever is haunting this place."

"Change of heart?" Cordelia asked. "I thought you didn't believe in ghosts."

"I'm starting to believe," Sharon stated. "The choking incident. What Christy saw—"

"The panther?" Cordelia interrupted. Christy had described her encounter with the big cat and the woman in white on camera, in the matter-of-fact, plainspoken way that matched her sensible clothes and glasses and shoes and haircut.

That's way freaky, Cordelia thought when she heard the story. She sat on the living room couch, arms wrapped around her folded legs, suppressing a shiver when she replayed it in her head. The whole panther thing was odd, but she remembered having heard that, in times gone by, bringing exotic animals to parties was sometimes considered a way to enliven them. It wasn't at all impossible that someone would have included a panther at a Hollywood party, even before the Siegfried and Roy days.

None of the others had heard anything, but any of them could have happened into that hallway during the time that Christy had been trapped. What would they have seen, if anything? she wondered. The panther might have been a purely visual hallucination, presenting no physical danger at all.

But for the first time, she found herself kind of wishing for Angel's presence here.

"Yes, the panther."

"Weren't you a devoted skeptic in the beginning?" Gordon asked her.

"I'm sensible, not skeptical," Sharon objected.

"Before, I hadn't seen anything that would cause me to believe. Now I have."

"I understand completely," Cordelia said.

"You believe in ghosts, too?" Gordon asked, sounding surprised.

"Absolutely," Cordy replied. It was refreshing to admit it, now that some of the other members of the group had confessed a willingness to believe too. Things really were getting spookier by the day. So far, she didn't think there had been much actual danger, beyond Beth's attack—but if it came to that, it'd be good to know there were some believers on her side. "I think they're restless spirits, with business left unfinished when they died. If they're allowed to complete that business, then they can get their peace. But if they're prevented from doing what they need to do, that's when they're trouble."

"Trouble?" Gordon echoed. His head was canted at an angle, and Cordelia realized he had held it at the same angle when cross-examining Sharon before. It was his disbelieving head-cock, she decided. "So you think we're literally in danger here?"

"I don't know," Cordelia said honestly. *I hope not*, she thought, *but it's looking more and more like we could be.* But she didn't want to share that possibility until it became absolutely necessary—if it did. She was naturally optimistic, and wanted to maintain that attitude if she could. "But I'd watch my step, just the same."

Chapter Fifteen

Gunn met Phil Baxter a block from Parker Center, the LAPD's downtown headquarters. They went to a nearby coffee shop, ordered, and took a table near the window, as far from the other patrons as they could get. Phil took his coffee black and hot.

"I put a bug in a few ears," he told Gunn. "I still have a lot of friends in that building. Some of them weren't too thrilled to hear that I was poking around in that Jane Doe case again, I can tell you that."

"But will they help you?"

"Hard to say. I think some of them will, if they can. Some of them won't want anything to do with me or that case. But there are others—cops who know their careers are stalled out, or cops who remember why they went into law enforcement in the first place, who will come through with what we need. In the meantime, I did get one piece of interesting information."

Gunn took the little white plastic lid off his own cup. He hated sipping through that little hole. He downed a swallow that felt like it was igniting his throat with napalm. "That's hot," he gasped. "What'd you get?"

Phil chugged most of his coffee, unfazed. "A connection I never made until you showed it to me," he said. "We had occasional bodies turning up with all their identifying characteristics removed, and those strange symbols. And of course, this is Los Angeles, so there are always disappearances. There are tens of thousands of people missing in the country at any given time, about five thousand young women who've vanished. L.A. isn't immune from that. Young people run away, they change their names, they move here to become stars and it doesn't happen so they go back to Iowa or Kansas or Ukraine or wherever they came from. But I never made the leap that there might be something connecting the bodies and the disappearances. The bodies were always older women, and older women tend not to run away. Plus, no one was reporting women of their age missing, just the young kids."

"How many of these things you think we're talking about?"

"Over the past thirty years, at least fifty. Sometimes as many as five or six a year, sometimes just one or two."

"And you're sure there's a connection between the bodies and the missing girls?" Gunn asked. He stirred his coffee with a plastic stirrer, to cool it faster.

"I had a friend in Parker run a computer check," Phil confirmed. "Each time one of these Jane Does turned up, there is a corresponding disappearance of a young woman. Not only that, but hair color matches up. If the Jane Doe is a redhead, a redhead disappeared. If the Jane is a brunette, a brunette was reported missing. Every time, the events were no more than a week apart."

"Sounds like a trend."

"Sounds like a problem. I can't believe we didn't catch on earlier. But like I said, with so many runaways and no particular reason to look for that tie-in, we missed it. I left my contact those names your friend mentioned, and she'll let us know if they turn up matching any of these incidents." He looked at Gunn over the rim of his paper cup. "You ever thought about being a cop?"

Gunn laughed. "No, I can honestly say that's never really crossed my mind."

"Think maybe you'd be a good one."

Gunn shook his head. "There was a time I'd have slugged you for saying that," he said. "I guess it's okay now, but somehow, I don't think the LAPD would want me anywhere near a badge."

"It's got some problems, but it's mostly a good

department," Phil assured him. "You might be surprised."

Gunn finished off his cup. "Yeah, I might be," he confessed. "Listen, I got to go, but you'll let me know what you hear, right?"

"You'll be the first to know," Phil promised.

Gunn left him sitting at the table, and shook his head slowly as he headed out the door. He laughed again.

Me, a good cop.

Security in the office building Wolfram and Hart occupied was intense, but Angel had been in the building often enough to have come up with his own ways in and out.

Well, in mostly, he reflected. Out was usually a matter of being escorted to the door or going out the nearest window just ahead of the guards, who bore batons spring-loaded with wooden stakes, and tasers that could take him down, though not kill him.

His usual route of entry was through sewer tunnels and into the parking garage, then up the elevators, or else into an air-conditioning duct and out through the floor in a hallway. The building was equipped with vampire detectors, and there was really no avoiding them—just evading as long as possible. He had waited until after the night's *Haunted House* broadcast, figuring that the building would be fairly empty this late. He went up through the duct and emerged into a hallway, dashing for a nearby elevator and ringing the call button. It opened almost immediately and he stepped in, aware that the clock was already ticking. Security would know by now that there was a vampire on the premises, and they'd be fanning out, trying to locate him.

He punched a button and rode up, prisoner for now of the elevator box. The only other way in involved going up the outside of the building and in through a window, and while that wasn't out of the question, it was more of a statement than he wanted to make tonight.

Lawyers and limos, he thought again. *Put them together and they point to Wolfram and Hart, frequent bane of my existence.* It was Wolfram and Hart who had brought Darla back from the dead and, through her, had almost sent Angel into a darkness from which there was no return. He hadn't quite forgiven them for that—would never forgive them, in fact.

He couldn't shake the hunch that they were involved in the case he was concerned with now. Or cases, depending on if they were really connected or not. He leaned toward the connected theory, though. There were few links between Kirsten St. Clair and the unidentified corpse in the vacant lot, but there were some—the presence of black stretch limousines being the strongest. So he thought it might be worth going to the source, to see if he could find out anything this way.

And for now, the source was one Lilah Morgan—as beautiful and coldhearted as anyone who had ever passed the California State Bar Exam. He didn't know for sure if she was in the building, but he knew that she tended to work late hours and didn't seem to have much of a social life, so he suspected that she probably would be.

He was right. When he approached the door to her office, he saw light leaking beneath it. He pushed the door open without knocking. Every second counted now. "Hello, Lilah," he said, putting a warmth into it he didn't really feel.

"Oh, it's you," she said, glancing up only briefly from the paperwork on her desk. Her response was just as cool as his approach had been heated.

"You don't sound surprised to see me."

Now she did look up, as if resigned that he wasn't going away. "I'm not," she said. "I'm working against a stiff deadline here. That's always when annoyances crop up."

"Now I'm just an annoyance?" he asked. "I'm wounded."

"Only metaphorically, I'm sure," she said. She was dressed in a gray cashmere suit as flinty and stylish as she was. "Did you have a reason for coming in here, Angel, or are you just trying to bother me?"

"I have several reasons, Lilah," Angel replied. "After all, you're my favorite Wolfram and Hart contact."

"At least now that poor Lindsey's hit the highway, right?" She held up her right hand. "Want to cut it off now? Or wait until I anger you in some way?"

"I'm looking for a young lady who's missing, Lilah. Her name is Kirsten St. Clair, and she's in trouble. Maybe you can help me to help her. Then I'm also trying to find out the identity of a woman who was abandoned, dead, in a vacant lot. And to top it off, a bunch of suicide demons attacked me last night when I started getting close to some answers. Does any of this sound familiar to you?"

She had returned to her paperwork. When Angel paused, she looked up.

"I'm sorry life is so difficult for you, Angel. I'm afraid I don't know anything about your various issues, though. Maybe your vision girl can find you someone who cares."

"Have you ever employed a Bextrian demon?"

Lilah thought for a brief moment, then shook her head. "I've never even heard of them."

"Is Wolfram and Hart behind all this?" he pressed.

"Why would we attack you?" Lilah responded, setting down her pen and looking straight at him. She was either playing it very frosty, or she really was an iceberg. He suspected it was a front, though.

"You were a project, that's all. We thought we had a way to get to you, through Darla. In fact, we did get to you, but it didn't turn out the way we wanted. That's all. End of story. You've been downgraded, Angel, from priority to nuisance. Now, guards are going to come through that door in about forty seconds. If you don't want to be an ex-nuisance, I'd recommend that you get out of here in a hurry."

Maybe I should *cut off her hand,* Angel thought. *Just to get some kind of reaction out of her.*

But he knew Lilah was right—he could even hear the guards headed toward her office. *She's not going to tell me anything until I have more of the pieces,* he thought. The best he could realistically hope for was to rule the law firm out, if it turned out they weren't involved with one or another of the various threads he was dealing with. But even that would be a help. He moved to the shadows behind her door and waited for the guards to come in.

Three of them entered, stake-batons in their fists. Lilah cocked her head toward Angel, behind the door, but he was already in motion. He swept his arm down, grabbing the first guard's baton. Spinning it in midair, he brought it up again and the club end caught the guard in the chin, knocking him back into his two colleagues. One of the guards tried to jab his stake past the guy but missed, and the stake drove straight into the guard's ribs. The man screamed in pain and doubled over, the baton jutting from his back. As he bent forward, Angel swung his baton over the guy's head and into the second guard, nailing him at the bridge of his nose. He felt bone break and cartilage tear, and by the time that guard got his hands to his face, his nose was gushing bright red arterial blood.

Angel stepped over the two downed guards. The third one was already backing away. He tossed his baton aside and yanked a taser from his belt, but it didn't look like he actually intended to get close enough to use it. Angel walked straight past him—the guy had literally backed up against a wall—and pushed the DOWN button for the elevator.

From her office, Lilah called after him. "When we decide to go after you again, Angel, you'll know it!"

Angel ignored her, turning to face the guard who cowered against the wall. Angel let his vampiric face overcome his human features, and he bared his fangs at the frightened security officer. "Boo!" Angel said with a demonic grin. The guard, in his terror, raised his hands to cover his eyes and jammed the taser into his own face. He gave a little shriek and collapsed onto the floor as Angel stepped onto the elevator.

Cordelia sat alone in the house's library, absently flipping through old books without really seeing the pages. Her head throbbed almost constantly now. No one in the house was sleeping much, she knew, but she was pretty sure that no one else had to deal with vision hangover, which made her a special case. Then there was the state of perpetual tension from being in the house, which she was more and more convinced was genuinely haunted by some kind of malevolent force. She was never free of the feeling that some . . . entity, she guessed, hovered at the edges of her awareness, just out of sight, just out of hearing. If she snapped her head fast enough, she was sure, she could catch sight of it. But moving her head the slightest bit made it ache worse; turning it rapidly was just begging for blinding pain. *I should be in front of the WebCams acting vivacious,* she thought. *But if I so much as smile my head will crack open and my brains will fall out on the floor.* If there were Cordelia fans out there—*Cordelia fans, what a great combination of words*—they'd be pretty disappointed to see her sitting here like a lump of agony. She wondered if there were threads on Internet message boards titled "Cordelia: Lunatic or Head Case?"

The library door creaked open, and Cordy steeled herself long enough to glance up. Gordon walked in, smile plastered on, wearing a nice purple silk shirt and black dress pants. *He does have a great smile,* she thought. *Kind of goes with the great rest of the package.*

"Hey, Cord," he said. "I wondered where you were. You okay?"

"Headache," she admitted. "Bad."

"Headache bad," he agreed. "Can I bring you some aspirin or something? A cup of tea? Caffeine's good for headaches, you know. Expands the blood vessels in your head. Or contracts them. Something like that."

"I took some," she lied. *Aspirin won't do any good for this one,* she knew. Rescuing Kirsten St. Clair from whatever trouble she was in would help it, but nothing else would do much. She hoped Angel had understood her numerous messages. *He had to,* she thought. *He's no dummy. And he's got Wes and Gunn there—between the three of them, they're practically a genius.* "But, thanks."

"Hey, what are friends for?" He knelt next to her chair. "Head massage? Back rub?"

"A head rub might be nice," she said. Ignoring the pain, she shifted in the big chair so that her head rested on the arm, exposing the top and sides of her head to Gordon. "If you don't mind."

"Not at all," he said. "Besides, the WebCam will see me being nice, and maybe I'll pick up some votes." With the fingertips of both hands, he began to rub her scalp, like ten pressure points moving independently of one another. She felt some relief almost instantly.

"And they'll have heard you being so manipulative," she reminded him, "that you'll lose even more."

"Price one pays," he said, "to get into the head of a pretty girl. Or *onto* the head, anyway."

"If that's all you wanted, I would have let you rub my head days ago."

"I didn't say it was all I wanted," he said. "But it's a start."

She let it drop there, and closed her eyes, just enjoying the sensation of his fingers caressing her scalp. After a little while, he spoke again, softly. "If you win, what are you going to do with the money?"

"I guess live on it," she said. "I mean, I have a job, but it doesn't pay all that well. And I'm kind of used to nice things, you know, designer clothes and good food, and I could definitely use a new car, like one of those cute little Mazda convertibles or something." She stopped before the old, greedy Cordelia could rear up and suggest that a hundred thousand dollars really didn't go that far in the old, rich Cordelia's world. "What about you?"

He was silent for a moment, as if shy about answering. His fingers stopped their massage, then resumed. "Well, grad school's not cheap," he said finally. "And then my mom's house is pretty run-down, you know? I'd like to help her fix it up, or move someplace else. Then there's this charity I do some volunteer work for, providing books and reading instruction for the underprivileged. Do you know what the adult illiteracy rate is among the working poor?"

Cordy pulled her head away, pushing herself up

onto one elbow to look at him. "Are you for real?" she asked.

"What do you mean?"

"Well, you're handsome, you're polite, you're smart, you're generous, you're . . . nice. Do you know how rare that is in L.A.? And did I mention good looking?"

"I think so," he said. He looked embarrassed at the attention, his cheeks coloring.

"And modest," she went on, knowing that she was maybe going a little overboard but unable to stop herself. She figured it was the tension, getting to her, making her lose whatever inhibitions she might have had. *That, and the possibility that we could both die at any time,* she thought. "And gorgeous. Stop me if I'm repeating myself."

"I'm just a regular guy," Gordon protested.

"Not in this town. You're about as far from regular as it's possible to get."

"Well, thanks, I guess," he said. "I think you're making too much out of it, but thanks just the same. I think . . . I think you're pretty special, too, Cordelia. And did I mention a total babe?"

"Now that you mention it, no, you didn't. But feel free."

"A total babe," he repeated.

"Let's continue along those lines for a while," she said. "But, keep in mind, the cameras are on us. Let me move so it can shoot my good side."

* * *

Angel parked in the alley behind Kirsten's apartment building for his nightly pilgrimage. He couldn't say exactly why he was so obsessed with finding this young woman. Obviously the impact her disappearance was no doubt having on Cordelia was part of it. For a long time—too long, he knew, now—he had hurt Cordelia, and Wesley and Gunn, by turning his back on them. He'd fired them at the time he'd probably needed them most. He'd gone into a pit of despair, spurred by Darla's reappearance in his life, and he'd shut out those who had been most able to throw him a lifeline. It was almost as if he hadn't wanted to be saved.

But saved he had been, and the guilt he still felt over the way he'd treated his best friends—his family, really—was enormous. In spite of his own worst efforts, it really had been his concern for them that had dragged him back into the light. He'd tried to make it up to them since coming back. He'd agreed to work for Wesley instead of the other way around, and that seemed to be working out well. Wesley had changed since he'd come to Los Angeles from Sunnydale. The new Wesley made hard choices, and he made them soundly.

But it seemed like he'd just gotten his family back when Cordelia had gone off to be on this TV show, and her week's enforced absence just pointed out to Angel how much he'd missed her. Her wit was caustic and knew no boundaries. She would say anything that popped into her head to absolutely anyone. She had grown past the stage where she did it specifically to be mean, and now there was, he believed, actually an innocence to the way she didn't bother with the kind of self-editing that other people did. And he missed that. He missed the sound of her ready laughter, the arch of her voice when she was annoyed, the shriek when she was startled. He even—though he hated to admit it to himself—missed the way she and Wesley bickered like adolescent siblings or some elderly couples he'd known.

Soon, he thought. *The game can't last forever, and then she'll come back.*

And I'll find Kirsten St. Clair, and I'll figure out who the body in the alley is, and everything will be okay.

He knew it was a lot to ask of himself. But he'd never shirked from tough jobs before, and he wouldn't now. He climbed the stairs as quietly as he could, and went to Kirsten's door. As always, he felt a sudden wave of anxiety when he reached for the knob. One of these days he might open the door and walk right in, and that would mean he was too late, whatever had taken her away had killed her.

But not tonight. He opened the door, tried to go in, and was prevented from doing so by the invisible barrier that prevented vampires from entering unbidden. He had never felt such relief over that stupid rule in his life.

He'd been frustrated by it more than once in his Angelus days, when chasing a tasty morsel who slipped away from him by dashing across her own threshold. But now he was glad that it existed, one of the inviolate rules of vampirism, because it confirmed for him that Kirsten yet lived. As long as she did, he could find her. As long as she did, he hadn't let Cordelia down.

Chapter Sixteen

Thursday

In the little room where the woman who had been known as Kirsten St. Clair was kept, three pale figures standing at three specific points chanted their tuneless, seemingly endless chant. These figures never seemed to tire, never stopped, never even seemed to need to catch their breath.

Ignoring them as best he could, Larry Mullins wiped the young woman's head with a damp cloth. He brushed the hair off her neck. The skin there was still blistered, but it looked like it would heal nicely in a few weeks, and the brand would last forever. It allowed the former Mrs. McKay's personality traits and memories to be transferred, via the symbols burned into her own flesh, and its permanence would help to secure her new identity. She had a high fever, he knew, but that was to be expected. She'd sleep a while longer, and then tomorrow it would all be over and she'd be a new woman. *Literally,* he thought.

"Sleep, Audrey," he said, calling her by her new name. "Sleep tonight. I know you can't hear me, and they"—he nodded toward the chanting demons—"they don't care, they don't listen to the likes of us. Tomorrow, not only will things be better for you, but for me as well. The bonus I'll be getting after I bring this off will pay my law school loans and give me a nice down payment on my future. Kat'll be able to quit her job at Macy's. Maybe it's time to start thinking about kids, what do you think?"

He knew that Lilah would get most of the credit for the success of this transaction. That was okay with Larry; he didn't mind sharing when it was warranted. The fee Parker McKay was paying at the successful conclusion of the deal would be big enough to make an impact on the firm's bottom line, and that would reflect well on both Lilah and Larry.

Looking at Kirsten—*sorry, Audrey*—in the loose white cotton gown she'd been dressed in for tomorrow's big event, he admired her form, her muscle tone, her firm build. "You're a beautiful girl," he told her. "Lilah asked me once if I'd ever replace Kat this way, and I told her no. But you know . . . when you step in for the former Mrs. McKay, you'll have many of her memories, Parker's favorite aspects of her personality without some of the annoying ones, and you'll be young and sexy and totally devoted to the old guy. Not such a bad deal. Maybe I'll have to give it a little more thought in a few years."

He mopped the girl's head again, and then wadded up the towel and tossed it into a corner. Nodding a farewell to the three chanting, oblivious demons, he exited through the open doorway and down the long tunnel that led to the outside world. His step was light. He whistled a happy little tune. He'd been recruited straight out of law school by a hard-charging law firm that billed at top rates, and he was making his mark on that firm. This was a great day for the Mullins family; tomorrow would be better yet.

Gordon's tender ministrations had actually helped Cordelia's throbbing headache, and Cordelia thought she might actually be able to get some sleep tonight after all. She said good night and went to bed shortly after midnight.

When she woke up, the digital clock by her bed glowed 2:17. At first she didn't know why she'd awakened, but then she heard them again: loud footsteps in the hall. They stopped outside her door, and her knob rattled. *Did I lock it?* she had time to wonder, and the question answered itself when the door creaked open and the footsteps continued, into her room, directly toward the bed. She'd been flirting with Gordon, she remembered, but didn't think she'd done anything to merit such a straightforward approach tonight. She was about to sit up and switch on the light when the bedsprings shifted and moaned under the weight of someone sitting on the foot of the mattress.

"Usually a girl likes some dinner first, and maybe even an actual date," she complained.

"Hey, I bought you dinner once," Doyle said. "You told me it was the best greasy fried chicken you'd ever consumed on a stakeout."

Doyle?

Now she did lurch to a seated position, grabbing at the bedside lamp until she found the push button and bathed the room in light. Sure enough, Francis Doyle perched on the end of the bed, black-haired, blue-eyed, leather-jacket-clad Doyle, grinning that mischievous smile at her, eyes twinkling with some knowledge that only he had.

"Doyle? It's . . ."

"Hey, I know, sweetcheeks, it's an unexpected pleasure for me, too. And I can't stay long, I'm afraid. I just came to warn you, really."

"Warn me?" she repeated. "About what?"

"This place, Cord. It's bad. There's stuff goin' on, forces—well, here *I* am, right? That alone tells you that things ain't natural in this house. People are messin' with things they don't understand. If you can still get out, I guess what I'm sayin' is it'd be a good idea."

"What forces, Doyle, what things? And you . . ."

A noise in the hall woke Cordelia, and she glanced at the bedside clock. 2:15. *But Doyle,* she thought, and then decided that he must have been a dream. *Did he ever call me sweetcheeks?* she wondered. *Did he really buy me fried chicken on a stakeout?* She was ashamed to realize that she was forgetting things about him. She could still call up his face and his voice, his enchanting Irish brogue, could still see sometimes, in the sky or the sea, the pure deep blue of his eyes. *But so much has happened since he sacrificed himself, and really I only knew him for a short time,* she thought. The half-demon had been a huge part of her life for a time, hers and Angel's—leading Angel into what had really become his calling, leaving Cordelia, through the magic of a kiss, with the power and the gift of visions. But now, Doyle was already part of her past, the days that slipped inexorably into flawed memory and had more to do with who she had been than who she was in the process of becoming.

The noise in the hall repeated itself again, becoming recognizably footfalls. *At least this time, I know the door's locked,* she thought. Instinctively, she looked at the clock again, just as it flashed over to 2:17. The footsteps paused outside her door, the knob rattled, the door swung open with a rasp and a low sigh, and the footsteps crossed the floor. Then she felt the unmistakable weight of someone settling at the end of the bed, and she reached out and switched on the lamp, thinking, *he's back!*

But it wasn't Doyle sitting on her bed. She could only assume that it was Carstairs, because the torso was thick and heavy, with powerful arms and shoulders, but where there should have been a neck and a head there was only torn, ragged flesh. The body at the end of the bed turned, in such a way that Cordelia thought that if there had been a head on those shoulders it would have been looking at her. But there was no head, and she remembered the story Rich had told about him hanging from the chandelier until the body had torn free of its own weight, and she remembered the disembodied head she'd seen in the cold spot, and in her bathroom mirror. Then the body that could only be Carstairs leaned forward, like a lover might, and reached out with one hand and caressed Cordy's leg, and she could feel the icy chill of his hand through the blankets and sheet, and then it just was too much and she closed her eyes and opened her mouth and screamed.

When she opened her eyes again, her own scream still ringing in her ears, the apparition was gone. She was sitting up in bed and her light was on and her door was wide open, so she knew she hadn't been dreaming this time. It had been here. Something had been here.

She got out of bed, shivering in spite of herself. She lived with a ghost, she'd faced demons and had even been pregnant with the spawn of one, for a time. *This shouldn't scare me,* she thought, *but it does.*

A lot.

Nervously, she glanced about the room, not knowing what to expect, what vision might present itself next. She wasn't sure if she wanted to close the door, thereby trapping herself in the room with whatever might be inside it, or go out into the hall with whatever might lurk beyond the relative safety of her own space.

Out there, at least, were other people. *Not that any of them bothered to come and see what I was screaming about,* she thought. And the idea occurred to her that maybe there weren't people there anymore, maybe they'd all fallen victim to the house and she was the only one left who still lived. So the question became, *if they're dead, do I want to see their bodies?*

But that's nonsense, she thought. *They're sound asleep in their rooms, just like I'd be if it wasn't like the Spookville Freeway at rush hour in here.*

Still, since sleep was a lost cause in her present state, she thought she'd go check it out. Starting with Gordon's room—after all, if the house had indeed wanted him to stay for some reason, as their spin the bottle game seemed to indicate, could that reason possibly be a good one?

She slipped into a robe and padded down the hall, barefoot, to his door. She tapped on it, and heard no response. She knocked louder. This time, she thought she heard something that sounded like a strangled cry. Gripping the knob, she gave it a yank and the door opened. She went in, releasing the door—at which point, of its own volition, it slammed shut behind her.

Stepping into his room was like walking into a bottle of molasses.

Somehow, as soon as she was inside, the room seemed to be miles deep. She could see Gordon's bed off in the far distance, across an impossibly vast empty floor. But she could make little progress toward the bed, because the air was so thick and wet that she could barely move through it. Her lungs couldn't get enough oxygen. She tried to call his name, but when she opened her mouth, it seemed to fill with liquid, so she closed it again.

Pushing herself through the gunk, Cordelia managed to close the gap somewhat. Now, she could see Gordon, at least. But he wasn't in the bed, he was above it, suspended from some invisible height, a rope around his neck. His hands hung limply at his sides, his legs dangling almost to the surface of the bed.

Cordelia did scream now, in spite of the viscous atmosphere of the room. She screamed and screamed, but the sound didn't travel through the heavy air, and sounded even to her own ears like a whisper. She was sure Gordon couldn't hear her at all.

Then she felt a hand on her shoulder, shaking her, and she opened her eyes. Her throat was raw, her ears felt battered by the sound of her own voice. Gordon stood before her in a pair of boxers, a frown of concern on his face. "Cordy, are you okay?"

She tried to smile, but knew it didn't come off right. *No surprise there,* she thought. *Since happy is about the last thing I am right now.* "I'm . . . we're in your room."

"Were you sleepwalking?" he asked. "I woke up and you were standing there, shrieking like there was something terrifying you."

"I . . . I came to check on you," she said.

"No worries here," Gordon replied.

Cordelia, remembering, felt the terror threatening to well up inside her again as she told what she had experienced. "Your room was gigantic, and the air was like pea soup, and you were being hanged, over your bed, just like old Mr. Carstairs, and . . . shouldn't you get some pants on or something?"

"That's not usually my first priority when a beautiful woman sneaks into my room in the dead of night and screams bloody murder," he replied, glancing down at his striped boxers. "But if you're okay . . ."

"Okay?" she said. "'Okay' is a relative term. If I was okay with the things going on in this house, I'm not sure if I'd be okay, you know?"

Gordon tugged on a pair of jeans. "Maybe you should get out," he suggested. "There's a car outside, right?"

"There are only three of us left," Cordelia said. "I've got as much chance to win now as anybody. I'm not going anywhere."

"But . . ." he looked at her, worry evident in his expression. "I haven't seen nearly the amount of strange stuff that you have. It's almost like it's centered on you, for some reason."

"Hey, I'm not the one the bottle picked on," she reminded him. She was concerned, though. Should she leave? If she did, wouldn't the house keep picking on those who remained? *Maybe,* she thought, *it's time I brought some of what I've learned working alongside Angel into play, and started fighting back.* "Unless that's a parlor trick you learned in your wayward youth, I think you should be worried about yourself."

"Yeah, well, who says I'm not?" he asked. "Come on, if we're up to stay, let's make some coffee."

Chapter Seventeen

"Two things," Phil Baxter told Gunn. They had met, this time, at a twenty-four-hour diner off the 405 freeway, near the airport. Phil had explained that turning up the kinds of rocks they were looking under might also turn up the kinds of people who lived under those rocks, so regular meeting places and phone calls were out. They connected by phone only long enough to pick a new meeting place, and then headed immediately there. They could still be observed, but it'd be harder to do it undetected, and impossible to plant surveillance equipment ahead of time. "We got an interesting hit on one of those names your friend gave you. Joan Martin."

Baxter had ordered pie with his black coffee, and he attacked it with gusto. Gunn, who wasn't particularly used to being up at seven A.M., much less out and about, stuck with toast. "What about her?"

"Seems one of her old friends reported seeing her, almost a year after her disappearance. Tried to talk to her, but the woman she swears was Joan Martin denied it, said her name was, according to the report, Sally Truesdale. This friend is absolutely certain that it was Joan she was talking to, but also said that Joan didn't seem to know her. She didn't think Joan was lying. She thought maybe she had amnesia or something. She ended up following Sally Truesdale home to Brentwood and then calling in the report. Detectives went out to the house, interviewed Mrs. Truesdale, and concluded that she was who she said she was, in spite of her definite physical resemblance to the missing Joan Martin."

"Interesting," Gunn agreed. "Sounds like something maybe we ought to check out, and I think I know just the guy to do it. But you said two things?"

"That's right," Phil said. "Saving the bad news for last. I had my friend widen the computer search a little, to see if there were other types of crimes that had a chronological connection to the killings and the disappearances."

"And she found something?"

"She found just about the last thing I would have wanted her to find. Shortly after each disappearance, five days or so after the bodies turned up, there was a mass murder."

Gunn put his toast down, looking at the ex-cop with wide eyes. "Say what?"

"The numbers vary, but anywhere from three to nine bodies, in a single event. Never more than a week after the disfigured corpse turned up."

"So that'd be . . . say, now," Gunn observed.

"If the pattern holds," Phil said. "I'd say today, maybe tomorrow at the outside."

Gunn swallowed, hard. "Why don't things ever get easier? We got to go to the cops." He inclined his head at Phil. "No offense, but I mean the real cops."

Phil shook his head. He looked at Gunn steadily through the narrow slits of his eyes, and Gunn read something there, or thought he did. If he was reading it right, it was a sense of determination, of purpose. "The cops who pulled me off the case in nineteen eighty-three?"

"Can't be the same guys around now, can it?"

"The powers that run the department never change," Phil said. "The names change, the faces change. But the ones pulling the strings—they're the same."

"So what are you suggesting, man?"

"What I'm suggesting, Charles Gunn, is that at least two dozen people have died since nineteen eighty-three because I didn't do my job. Including my partner, Earl."

"Earl capped himself, Phil. You couldn't have done nothing about that."

"He ate his gun because he knew what you were

coming to talk to him about. Because he understood what we're responsible for. Well, I have my own way of handling responsibility."

Gunn nodded. "You lookin' for some redemption? I can respect that. I got a friend works the same way. I think you guys will get along just fine." He shoved his toast away, less than half-eaten. "What's our first step?"

"You said you know someone who can check out this Sally Truesdale."

"That's right."

"Call him."

Anne Steele had slept in her office again, on the cot she kept there for those nights when things were too hectic and she couldn't get away until it was too late to make getting away worthwhile. *And, anyway,* she knew, *what've I got to get away to? An empty apartment, a frozen dinner, and a couple hours of TV before bed? My life is this center, now.*

But she had slept in way too late, exhausted from refereeing some late-night crises. She was just bracing herself to put her feet on the floor, go in the bathroom and wash up and brush her teeth, when there was an insistent rapping on her office door. "What is it?"

"Anne, it's a cop. Says he's got something for you." The voice sounded like Ernesto, a good kid who'd been mixed up with a bad crowd until lately. He'd been around the center a lot for the past couple of weeks, taking on responsibilities, doing various chores. The bathrooms, for instance, had never been cleaner. And he'd washed out the coffeepot, resulting in a thousand percent improvement in the flavor.

"Okay, tell him to wait just a minute," she said. At first she couldn't imagine what a cop might have for her, but then she remembered Angel's anxious phone call. No time for the bathroom, then. She tugged open her top desk drawer, shook an Altoid from the tin, and popped it. Finger-brushing her hair, she opened her door.

Johnny Oakes stood in the rec room, in full uniform. There were always kids in the rec room, and now was no different. But they had young people's innate distrust of police officers, so they were congregated across the room from him, avoiding eye contact.

"Hi, Johnny," Anne said when she entered.

He smiled at her. "Hey, Anne."

"Bring me something?"

He handed her a plain manila envelope, closed with the little metal brad. "Think this is what you were looking for."

She tore it open and looked inside. The envelope contained a slightly out-of-focus black-and-white photo of a limousine passing through an intersection.

"One of our red-light cameras caught this, five blocks from home base," Johnny said. Home base was the address Angel had given her as a starting point, an apartment building in Santa Monica. "Driver must have been in a hurry to get out of the area." He pointed at the photo. "See, there's no one waiting in the other directions, and he just went through a solid red."

"Do you know who this car belongs to?" Anne asked him.

"Ran the plates. It's registered to a law firm. Wolfram and Hart. It's part of their fleet."

"Wolfram and Hart?" she echoed.

"Heard of them?"

"Oh, I've heard of them," she said.

"They've already been mailed a citation."

"Think they'll pay it?"

Johnny smiled. "They'll pay it."

Holding the photo in her left hand, Anne moved closer, throwing her right arm around him in a one-handed hug. "Thanks, Johnny," she said. "You're the best."

"You're welcome, Anne. You need anything else, let me know."

He left the center, and the kids gathered around Anne, wide-eyed.

"You hugged a cop?" Ananda asked her.

"He's not so bad," Anne replied. "He spent a couple of years living on the streets, and some time in a center a lot like this one. You should talk to him sometime. You might find out he's a decent guy."

She went back into her office as the teens discussed the astonishing news that a police officer might have had a rough childhood. Anne knew that adult status wasn't in any way an indication of how one had grown up, but a demonstration of what one had done with the materials one had been given. Johnny had made some hard decisions about his life, set himself a course, and it looked like he was doing okay.

She opened the envelope he'd given her. It looked, to her, like what Angel had wanted to see. She'd have to get it to him. And, judging from the urgency with which he'd asked for it, the sooner the better.

Wesley had called one of his new acquaintances at West Side Limousine, and had a limo and a driver within the hour. Now, having picked up his somewhat reluctant passenger, they were on their way to Brentwood.

"You didn't even give me time to dress properly," the Host complained. "You don't go to Brentwood in just any old thing."

"You won't be getting out of the car," Wesley reminded him. "And if you did, I expect your green skin would generate more remarks than your lack of a proper ensemble."

"Easy for you to say, sweetheart. Look how you dress."

"There's nothing wrong with the way I dress," Wesley insisted.

"Not if you're ninety and living in Miami Beach," the Host said. "But, come on. Look at Angel. He may be the living definition of monochromatic but at least he's got a sense of style."

"You're comparing me with a man who can't even see himself in a mirror," Wesley muttered. "I resent that."

"Yeah, what's up with that, anyway? I mean, I can dig not being able to see himself, but shouldn't his clothes be visible? How does that work?"

"Just one of the many unanswered questions about vampirism," Wesley replied. "Umm . . . the driver can't hear us, can he?"

"I don't think so," the Host said. "But if you're concerned, I have a Patti LaBelle CD in one of these pockets we can blast."

"I'm sure that won't be necessary," Wesley said. He settled back into the comfortable seat to enjoy the rest of the ride in what he hoped was glorious silence.

Twenty minutes later, they were parked in the Truesdales' driveway, and he was climbing from the car. "You're sure you can see?"

"You get her to the doorway, I'll be able to see fine," the Host assured him.

"Because I'd hate to have made this trip for nothing."

"You and me both, brother. I've got to be at work in seven hours. And I still have to shampoo my hair."

"Right, then," Wesley said. "Wish me luck."

"Break a leg, Brando."

Wesley put on a self-satisfied grin and a happy step and strolled up the front walkway as if he owned the place. Reaching the mansion's entrance, he started for the buzzer, but the door opened before he could press the button.

A beautiful woman in her late thirties smiled at him. Her red hair was chin-length and loose, and she wore a simple but expensive dress. "You rang at the gate?"

"Yes, quite," he said.

"And you're from the Brilliant Soap Company?"

"That's absolutely correct. And you must be Mrs. Sally Truesdale," Wesley said. He tried to give it his best salesman charm.

"I'm afraid I didn't catch everything you said over the intercom. Something about me winning a contest?"

"Correct again. You are—if you qualify—our grand prize winner."

"What do I win?"

"A year's supply of Brilliant Soap products," Wesley said grandly. Then, noticing the way her face fell, he added, "And a trip for two around the world!"

"By airplane, I hope," she said. "My husband hates boats. He gets very seasick."

"However you prefer, madam," Wesley assured her.

"What do I have to do to qualify?" she wanted to know.

Wesley gestured to the parked limousine, its blackened windows impossible to see through from here. "We'll be filming this for a television commercial," he said. "All you need to do is to sing the Brilliant Soap jingle, and we'll get your prize package right out to you."

"The Brilliant jingle?" she asked, crestfallen. "I'm afraid I don't watch much TV."

"I'm sure you know it," he said.

"Maybe if you could sing a few bars for me."

Wesley felt his face reddening. *Everyone knows the Brilliant bloody jingle,* he thought. *It's inescapable in this country.* "Umm . . . Cleaner than clean, whiter than white, Brilliant puts clothes in a whole new light?"

"Oh, I think I've heard that," she said. "I know that one, I just forgot. I'm still the winner, right?"

"If you sing it for us," he promised her.

"Where's the camera?"

"It's in the car, pointed at you right now," he told her. "Please face it and sing your heart out."

She took a few steps outside the door and looked

straight at the limousine. With a broad smile on her pretty face, she belted it like a Broadway star. "Cleaner than clean, whiter than white, Brilliant puts clothes in a whole new light!" When she was finished, she took a deep bow.

Wesley couldn't help applauding. "Well done, Mrs. Truesdale," he said. "Congratulations. Very well done."

"Thank you, thank you so much," she gushed. "Do I have to sign anything?"

"Our, umm . . . prize disbursement coordinator will be in touch with you very soon," Wesley lied. "Almost immediately, in fact. Until he is, I wouldn't say anything about this to anyone. So that it'll be a surprise until we air the commercial with your absolutely radiant performance, you know."

"Oh," she said, putting a finger to her lips. In a conspiratorial tone, she whispered, "Mum's the word."

"Perfect, excellent." He was already backing toward the limo. "Thank you so much, madam," he said. "We'll be in touch!"

Reaching the car, he yanked open the door and slid into a seat. "Drive!" he commanded. To Sally Truesdale's diminishing form, he added, "Don't call us, we'll call you."

"Bravo," the Host commended him. "You've just set that woman up for a disappointment of epic proportions."

"I'm sure she'll get over it," Wesley said. "And perhaps when she threatens to sue, the Brilliant Soap Company will give her a year's supply, anyway. The point is, did you get what you needed?"

"Loud and clear," the Host replied. He was an anagogic demon, which meant that he could read people's souls when he saw them sing. That ability had often come in handy.

"And?"

"Brother, that lady is so far off her path, she can't even see the forest."

"Meaning what? In English, if you can."

"Is American good enough? She isn't who she thinks she is. But she doesn't know it. Whoever she really was is so far buried inside, I could barely even get a glimpse of her. Talk about your makeovers—she's been made over from the inside out."

"Well, that fits with what Gunn told us, then."

"I'd say so. And by the way, what was up with that neck decoration?"

"What are you talking about?" Wesley asked.

"The brand, on the back of her neck. You didn't see it? When she took that bow and her hair flopped down, it looked like she had the dictionary tattooed on there. But not a human dictionary, if you get my drift."

"I'm not sure I do," Wesley admitted.

"Demonic writing," the Host explained. "I'm surprised you missed it."

"Yes, well, I was busy lying through my teeth," Wesley said. He'd hated that part most of all. But it had to be done, he guessed, to confirm the suspicions of Gunn's new policeman friend.

And it looked like those suspicions were now confirmed. Which, Wesley was sure, meant that somewhere not far away there were people who didn't know that they were next in line to be the victims of mass murder.

"He's sure it was a Wolfram and Hart limo?" Angel said, looking at the photo Anne showed him,

"That's what he said. The license plate is very clear, but I guess that's the whole point of those automatic red-light cameras. I figured you'd be anxious to know it, given how much you seem to hate those guys."

"It's not that I hate them," Angel protested. "It's just that . . . well, okay. Maybe a little."

"After what I've seen of them, I don't really blame you," Anne said.

Angel walked Anne toward the hotel's doorway, thanking her for the picture and information. When she was gone, he peered out at the sky. Still broad daylight out, and it would be for several more hours. But he needed to get to Wolfram and Hart, now that he had enough confirmation of their involvement in Kirsten's disappearance to confront Lilah Morgan again.

He was considering his options when Wesley hurried in, out of breath and agitated. "Angel," he said. "I've got some rather shocking news."

"Tell me in the car," Angel said. "You're driving. And put the top up."

Forty minutes later they were parked in a slot underneath the Wolfram and Hart building. Angel pointed to a car parked across the garage from them. "That's her car," he said. "So she's here."

"Not necessarily," Wesley reminded him. "She could have walked someplace, she could be out in somebody else's car. For all we know, she could be out in a limousine. There certainly seem to be enough of those involved in this case."

"I guess so."

"At any rate, it won't do for you to risk going inside the building during working hours if you don't have to. I, however, can get in and out unrecognized. I'll go in and see if she's about, and I'll let you know."

"I'll be waiting," Angel said.

It seemed like Wesley was gone for an hour, but in fact it was less than ten minutes, Angel knew. He just felt a sense of urgency, like all the threads of this case were coming together just in time for it to be too late to save anybody. When Wesley returned to the car, he shook his head. "She's not in," he said.

"You know that for certain."

"As certain as I can be without personally ransacking her office," Wesley confirmed. "The receptionist told me that she was out, and then I slipped past her and went straight to Ms. Morgan's door. The door was locked. The receptionist, by the way, has a very shrill voice when she's angry."

"It's probably something they pick up in Wolfram and Hart training sessions," Angel postulated. "We need to find her. Wherever Lilah is, that's where things are happening."

"I'm sure you're right," Wesley said. "But I'm not quite sure how we do that. And I have another question."

"What is it?"

"Do you think I dress badly?"

Angel shook his head and showed a brief glimmer of a smile. "Wes," he said, "you're asking the wrong guy."

Parker McKay was nervous.

"It'll be fine," Larry Mullins assured him. "Trust me, Mr. McKay. Parker. Nothing to worry about."

"I'm just not sure I like the idea of it," Parker said. "Of being there, I mean. I don't even know what tie to wear." He stood in front of his dressing room's full-length mirror, in a white dress shirt, underwear, and socks. His collar was turned up, and he must have held a hundred ties up to his neck so far. "It's not every day one meets one's wife again for the first time. I just want it to be right."

"She'll like whatever you choose, Parker," Larry reminded him. "That's the beauty of the whole thing." But what he was thinking was, *it's a white shirt. You're not wearing pants, but I'm guessing they won't be plaid or paisley, so pretty much any tie you pick is likely to work.*

He knew better than to talk to the client that way, though. At Wolfram and Hart, the client wasn't exactly king, but he or she was still catered to with every possible consideration.

Larry and Lilah had told Parker several times about all the happy clients who had undergone this same process, exchanging aging—and in some cases temperamental, even argumentative—spouses for younger, more attractive, and more malleable ones. Even some of the Wolfram and Hart senior partners had made the same decision, they'd told him. What they hadn't bothered to mention was that part of the same programming that instilled the proper wifely virtues and appropriate memories in the replacement wives was geared toward making sure the women knew whom they really reported to. At opportune moments, these women would find themselves making furtive phone calls to certain Wolfram and Hart phone numbers. Wolfram and Hart would then be forewarned of impending business mergers, hostile takeovers, significant stock transactions, and other important corporate decisions that could affect the law firm's investment portfolio. This inside information had made hundreds of millions of dollars for the firm over the last few decades, above and beyond the rather astronomical fees they charged for the procedure. And in one case Larry knew of, a new wife had warned the firm of her husband's plan to alert the police to what he had done, and of Wolfram and Hart's major role in it. That client—*ex-client,* Larry corrected himself—had met a sudden and unfortunate end, upon which the grateful wife had found herself possessed of his multimillion-dollar fortune. And she, thanks to an intuitive bit of programming, had been only too happy to share that fortune with her good friends at Wolfram and Hart.

The best deals, Larry thought, *are the ones that keep giving and giving.*

"Lilah's waiting in the limo," he reminded Parker. "We really can't be late. She's got to see you first, when the ritual ends. So she can imprint on you."

"You make it sound like she's hatching. Like a baby duckling or something," Parker said.

"That's not far from the truth. At least, the way I've heard it. I haven't actually seen it myself yet, but I'm looking forward to it. And when I dropped in on her yesterday, Audrey was looking exceptionally lovely."

"Was she in good spirits?" Parker asked.

Larry remembered her, limp and feverish, in his hands. "Very much so," he said, lying as easily to this millionaire as he did to his own family and friends. He still fervently believed that it had been the lies he'd told the Wolfram and Hart recruiter at his first interview—both the quality of them, and their sheer number, that had cinched his being offered the position. That, and instead of being put off by an undergraduate incident in which he'd broken a water glass and then inserted it into the ear of a fellow student during a semester-long feud, the firm seemed somehow enchanted by the story, asking him to tell it over and over again during the course of his employment there. These were the things that made him feel like he'd found much more than just a job with Wolfram and Hart. He'd found a new kind of family.

Kat didn't quite understand his devotion to the firm. She wanted him to work regular hours, which few enough attorneys could do, and which was especially difficult at Wolfram and Hart because of the special nature of many of their cases and clients. But he knew that to get ahead at the firm, he had to be at their beck and call, and really, that was the way he preferred it.

Larry knew he had always been considered a little off—manipulative, even violent, through school. He hadn't made many friends, in high school or undergrad. Law school was cutthroat enough to suit him fine, and the reputation he'd earned there had been what had attracted Wolfram and Hart's recruiters to him. He had finally come into a place where he was appreciated and liked for what he was, and that was worth a lot to him.

He rubbed his hands together, more in glee over coming home to Wolfram and Hart than because of Parker McKay's situation. But he grinned at Parker like it was all him. "You're going to be so happy with this, Parker. So happy."

Wesley had started the car and was heading toward the parking garage's exit when Angel had a sudden thought and said, "Stop!" in the middle of the driveway.

"What is it?" Wesley asked, startled by the sudden noise and jamming on the brakes.

"Limousines," Angel said. "Lilah's not in the building, so like we said, she could be out in a limo. Wolfram and Hart owns a fleet of them. So there must be someone, a dispatcher, who sends them out and keeps track of where they are." He nodded his head toward a parking office with a window overlooking a section of the garage filled with limos. Inside, they could see a uniformed man scribbling something in a big notebook. "My guess is, it's that guy."

"I suppose we could find out," Wesley said.

Angel was already on his way out of the car and heading toward the office. Behind him, he heard Wesley scurrying to catch up.

Angel shoved open the door to the small office, and the man behind the desk looked up at him, blinking behind thick glasses. He wiped a hand across his forehead, brushing long, greasy hair away. "What?" he asked.

"You're in charge of the limousine fleet," Angel said.

"That's why I get the big bucks." The man stood then. He wore a blue uniform, almost like a security guard's. But there was no gun at his belt, just a grease-stained rag poking out of one pocket. He was thick, with once-powerful arms that had gone flabby, and a belly that strained his shirt.

"I'm looking for Lilah Morgan," Angel told him. "Where's the car that she's in?"

"I don't know a Lilah Morgan," the guy answered defiantly.

"You didn't look at your records," Wesley put in. "Perhaps you'd know where she is if you checked your dispatch log."

"He knows where she is," Angel said. "I can smell it." He went vampire. "Smells good, too. Reminds me of how long it's been since breakfast." He advanced toward the man.

"Hey, easy," the dispatcher said. "The company, they'd kill me if I gave you anything."

"I might suggest," Wesley said, "that you could get at least an hour's head start on the company, if you cooperate with us. And there's a freeway entrance not five minutes from here. But if you don't cooperate, well . . ."—he cocked a thumb at Angel's fangs—". . . no head start, I'm afraid."

The man had begun to sweat profusely, soaking his uniform shirt at the armpits and the middle of his chest almost at once. "Yeah, the thing is, I'm not lying. I don't know Lilah Morgan. She didn't check out a car."

"How many cars are out right now?" Angel demanded.

"I got three out right now," the guy replied quickly, holding up the log.

"Who's in them?"

"I got one at a charity luncheon in Thousand Oaks, checked out to Roy Neely. I got one at the home of a guy named Parker McKay, checked out to a Larry Mullins. And I got one going long distance, to Palm Springs, with Harold Lance. There was a woman with Mullins, I remember."

"Give us McKay's address," Angel insisted. The guy scrawled something on a scrap of paper and handed it to Wesley.

"Thank you," Wesley said. "I'd take advantage of that head start, sir, if I were you."

Twenty-five minutes later they were parked in front of McKay's gleaming white Beverly Hills neoclassical sprawl. The driveway was empty. When Wesley rang the bell and pounded on the door, there was no response. He returned to the car after standing on the front step for several minutes. He didn't like the look on Angel's face—it mirrored the frustration he felt himself. "The house appears to be deserted," he said.

"Of course," Angel shot back. "Because from the very beginning of this case we've been just a little too late. Why change now?"

"Perhaps we should go back to headquarters," Wesley suggested. "There must be something we're missing, something we just haven't seen in the right way yet."

Angel didn't respond, just scowled at the mansion. Wesley backed the GTX out of the drive, headed for home.

Chapter Eighteen

The night had passed without further incident, unless spectral moanings, the sound of slamming doors in a house that theoretically had no other occupants, and at one point a high-pitched, horrified scream that came from everywhere and nowhere all at once, could be considered incidents.

Cordelia and Gordon passed the night together in the library, since neither of them felt that comfortable in their bedrooms anymore. She had tried to persuade Sharon to stick close to them, but the independent-minded woman had insisted that she wanted to get some sleep in her own room. After the bloodcurdling scream, they ran back upstairs to find Sharon coming out of her room, a little groggy. "Was that you guys?" she wanted to know.

"No, we thought maybe it was you," Cordelia said. "Not that it sounded like you, you know, but maybe how you would sound if you were scared enough to sound like that."

"Wasn't me," Sharon responded. "But it was sure hard to sleep through." She rubbed her bleary eyes. "You two don't look like you've been sleeping."

"We gave up on that long ago," Gordon confessed. "We've been sitting in the library."

"I was starting to doze off," Cordelia said. "When we heard that scream."

Gordon looked at her in surprise. "You were? I was talking."

Oops, Cordelia thought. *Faux pas.* "I know. Sorry. I'm just so tired." Exhaustion from the past nights of badly interrupted sleep, plus vision stress, was really taking a toll on her.

"Face it, honey," Sharon told him. "You are a little on the bland side."

Gordon looked wounded, but didn't reply.

After a moment, Cordelia said, "So, do you think you're getting back to sleep tonight, Sharon?"

Sharon shrugged. "I scare people," she said. "Especially guys like Gordon who are afraid of strong women. But I don't get scared easily."

"That doesn't entirely answer the question," Cordelia pointed out. *Come on,* she thought. *Horror movie cliché number one—don't split up or someone's going down.*

"I guess I could sit with you guys for a little while," Sharon agreed.

They had gone back down to the library, talking and dozing until the sun came up. Or would have come up, according to their watches, since they couldn't see it through the boarded-up windows. The house quieted down then, and the morning passed as the other mornings had. At Cordelia's instigation, the three of them explored further, trying again to find any secret passages or panels the house might be hiding. She was more than convinced now that the supernatural was at work, but it seemed important to the others to rule out fakery of any kind. They didn't find anything definitive, but at least there were no further incidents.

As the afternoon wore on, though, the house seemed to awaken again.

Cordelia had zoned out in front of the cold, empty fireplace. Gordon and Sharon had gone somewhere else—Cordy had a vague memory of them leaving, but didn't know to where, or for what. She felt herself slipping toward sleep again, and went with it, closing her eyes and letting herself relax into sleep's warm embrace.

After a period of time that could have been seconds or an hour, her slumber was disturbed by sounds. She cracked her eyes, unwilling to give up on sleep, and saw the fireplace before her blazing with a roaring fire that crackled and spat. Behind her, she heard distinctive—but unfamiliar—voices locked in an argument. She couldn't make out the words, but the tone was unmistakable.

That's wrong, she thought. *The fire's wrong. And there should not be strangers arguing behind me.*

The fire was wrong because she could feel no heat coming off it. Even holding her hands toward the fireplace, it felt just as cold as when she'd sat down. So the fire was a visual and auditory hallucination, nothing more.

Then she sat up and turned around to view the argument behind her. As she looked, the participants vanished. There seemed to be six or seven of them, hippies, she thought, long-haired and bearded, wearing tie-dyes and fringe and torn jeans and ragged T-shirts, one of them with a huge clenched-fist design emblazoned on the chest. Cordelia remembered contestant Beth, and thought briefly that she would have fit into that scene. But as soon as she catalogued details, they were gone, as if they'd never been there.

When she turned back, the fire was gone, too.

She was about to look for the hippies again when a brass candlestick lifted off the mantel above the fireplace and hurled itself at her.

She saw it coming, and dodged, throwing herself to the floor. The candlestick tore through the back of the couch she'd been sitting in, impaling it.

That would have been me, she thought, *if I hadn't seen it coming.*

She looked toward the ceiling, allowing her face to settle into a mask of concern. "Look, whoever you are," she said. "I know you're angry, you're unsettled, you need something you can't get. Instead of attacking us, let us help you! Instead of trying to drive us away, communicate with us. Tell me what you need and I'll do whatever it takes to put you at rest. What you need now is a friend, not a victim."

There, she thought. *That should buy me some votes with the Internet crowd.* She figured some kind of response had been necessary, in case the WebCams were on—but she really wanted to talk to the other contestants. This was definitely dangerous now, and that was unacceptable.

Wide awake now, she stalked out of the library. "Gordon!" she called. "Sharon!"

After a few moments, Sharon appeared upstairs. "What's going on?"

"A candlestick just tried to kill me," Cordy said. "It totally ruined the couch I was sitting on. But if I hadn't moved, I'd be looking at some serious reconstructive surgery."

"You're kidding," Sharon said. She put her hand on the banister and started down the stairs.

With a groan, the banister gave way under her grip.

"Sharon!" Cordelia screamed.

Sharon began to pitch forward, over the side of the stairway. But she was able to right herself and fall back, instead, onto the stairs, as the banister tumbled over the side and came crashing down to the marble floor of the entryway.

Cordelia dashed up the stairs. "Are you okay?"

Sharon rose, holding onto the wall for balance and rubbing her hip with one hand. "Yeah, I think so," she said. "Takes a lot to hurt this tough old body."

"You're not so old," Cordelia said. Sharon couldn't have been over twenty-five, she was sure. "I mean, you're not old at all."

"Just a figure of speech," Sharon said. Cordy blushed a little, wondering if Sharon did that on purpose. She seemed to enjoy keeping people off-balance—*metaphorically speaking,* Cordelia thought, *not literally, like a breakaway banister. It's almost like a defense mechanism, like she keeps people at a distance by not letting them know where they stand.*

She was about to say something else when the door behind her opened up and four people walked in, three men and a woman. The woman was Raquel, the camera operator, and two of the men wore jeans and T-shirts and carried toolboxes. The third one wore a suit and walked with a harried purpose, running fingers anxiously through his expensively cut silver hair. Cordelia remembered having seen him in the studios when they were going through the audition process. His name was Joel Rayburn, and he was one of the show's producers. His face looked grim.

"Mr. Rayburn," she said, surprised. "What's up?"

"They're pulling the plug," he said.

"What?" Cordelia asked, startled. "What plug? Who?"

"What's going on, Mr. Rayburn?" Sharon queried.

"The network," Joel replied. He walked past them, into the living room, and sank into a chair. They all followed, Cordelia and Sharon sitting as well. The men started to dismantle the light stands, working with practiced efficiency. Raquel came over and knelt next to Cordelia's chair. "I'm so sorry, Cordelia," she said sincerely. "Most of the crew's already gone home, but I wanted to tell you how bad I felt."

"Thanks, Raquel," Cordelia said. She squeezed the camera operator's strong hand.

"What happened with the network?" Sharon asked.

"The ratings started out bad and got worse," Joel said. "The critics hate us. And the audience thinks it's all fake."

"I have some news for the audience," Cordelia said, anger building to a flashpoint in her. After everything they'd been through, she at least knew that it wasn't fake.

"It's not," he assured them. "We haven't rigged any of this stuff. But the network decided, since it looked like things were getting a little too sticky in here, and the numbers were terrible and getting worse, that they didn't want to be responsible if one of you got hurt making a show that was a ratings disaster. Sponsors have been canceling their ad buys right and left, calling us a fraud. The Internet's full of people 'explaining' how we did one trick or another. Basically, if a show nobody is watching can be a national laughingstock, we're it."

"It's not you guys," Raquel assured them. "You were great, really. I think it's just—people are so used to special effects, they think that's all they're seeing. Magic has a hard time on TV for the same reason."

"So that's it?" Cordelia asked, barely able to wrap her mind around the idea that her career was over almost as soon as it had begun. "We're over?"

"The WebCams are already off," Joel said. "Announcements have gone out to the press. The show's canceled. We took a huge bath."

"But what about the prize money?"

"Sorry," Joel said. "If you check your contracts, you'll see that in just such an event, the whole deal is off. You'll be paid union scale for the time you've been on the set—we don't *have* to do that, but we will. But nobody gets the prize money. Believe me, with as much as we've lost on this show, we can't afford to throw that after it."

Cordelia looked at Sharon, who sat with her arms crossed and her face set in a scowl. "My lawyer will be taking a look at that," she said.

"That's fine," Joel said.

"Where's Gordon?" Cordelia asked, suddenly aware of his absence. "He should hear this, too."

"I thought he was hanging with you," Sharon said.

Cordy leaped to her feet. "We need to find him."

"Get him and get your stuff packed," Joel instructed. "The rest of the crew will be here soon to tear down, and we'll get you guys in a car as soon as you're ready to go."

Cordelia and Sharon both headed for the door. "I can't believe this," Sharon muttered as soon as they were out of the living room. "I am going to *so* sue somebody."

"We need to find Gordon," Cordy said, "and worry about that later." She vividly remembered the vision she'd had the night before, of him hanging from the chandelier. "Let's check his room."

Before they could make it to the staircase, though, they heard footfalls coming down from above. Gordon stood near the top of the stairs, looking down at the banister debris. "Someone have an accident? Are you both okay?"

"We're fine," Cordelia said. "We were just wondering that about you."

"No worries here," Gordon said simply. Cordelia realized it was some kind of catch phrase for him.

"Then you're the only one of us the house hasn't tried to kill in the last five minutes," Sharon observed. "And to top it off, the show's been canceled. None of us gets the money."

"Canceled?" Gordon echoed.

"That's right," Cordelia said. "Joel Rayburn, the producer, is here. They're already taking down the lights and things. He told us to pack up so they can take us home."

He came down the stairs then, calmly walking past the two women. His expression hadn't changed. It was like this didn't come as a surprise to him, somehow. "I don't think anybody's going home," he said. He crossed the marble entryway to the big front door and tried to turn the knob. It wouldn't budge. "See?"

"What is this, Gordon?" Cordy asked. "Some kind of joke?"

"No more jokes, Cordelia."

"It's just locked," Sharon said.

"But they said it was always open," Cordy reminded her. "They said anyone could leave at any time. And Joel and Raquel and those guys just came in."

Sharon shoved past Gordon and tried the door herself. "It's really stuck," she said.

Cordy hurried over and took a turn trying the door—shaking it, tugging on it, pounding on it with her fists. Nothing. The door wouldn't budge. Perspiration beaded Sharon's upper lip, and Cordelia didn't think she'd ever seen the woman looking so frightened.

"I'll check with the crew," Cordy said. She went

into the living room, where they were starting to tear down equipment. "Did you guys do anything with the door?" she asked. "Because it won't open."

Joel just looked up from his chair, a beaten figure. The other three stopped working. "We came through it, and it was fine," Raquel said. "We wouldn't have messed with it."

"I didn't think so. But something's going on. Sharon's pretty freaked right now."

They followed Cordelia back to the door and took turns at it, with no luck.

"There a back door?" Sharon asked. "Because now I really want to get out of here."

"I'll try it," the other crewman said. He went down the hall toward the kitchen and back door.

"Heck with that," the man who stayed behind said. He was an enormous man, with legs that looked like telephone poles and rippling muscles on his arms. Cordelia thought his name was Frank, and the other guy, she was almost sure, was Eddie. "I've seen too much weird crap going on in here. Let's open a window."

Frank went back into the living room, and the rest followed him. In there, he picked up a solid-looking chair and drove it into the boarded-over window. The boards held. He raised it over his head and slammed it into the boards again. They groaned, but didn't give way. He picked the chair up once more, lifting it over his head for one last Herculean attempt. But this time, when he had it raised up, some unseen force snatched it from his hands and tossed it easily across the room, as if it weighed nothing. It crashed into the wall, cracking it and kicking up plaster dust, then fell in pieces to the floor.

Frank looked at it and shrugged, but when he spoke again, his voice had a tremulous quality to it that hadn't been there before. "The rest of the crew will be here soon," he said. "They'll get us out."

Sharon sat down on the couch, visibly shivering. "I'm sitting right here till they come. I'm not moving an inch."

Joel folded a cell phone and stuck it into his jacket pocket. "Cell service is still jammed, I guess," he said. "The crew's walkie-talkies aren't working, either."

"Well, I'm not going to sit here and wait," Cordelia said, determined. "I'm going to see if there's some other way out."

"I'll go with you," Gordon said. Cordy hurried from the room, and Gordon dashed to keep up.

"I'm not so sure I want you around me," Cordelia said. "How did you know the door was going to be stuck?" She stopped and faced him. "Do you know something?"

"I know everything," he told her, breaking into a smile. "I'm not really here as a contestant. I'm here to keep an eye on things, make sure it all runs like it's supposed to."

Cordelia felt a sense of outrage wash over her. "So you work for the show?"

"I didn't say that. They don't have the slightest idea what's really happening here. There's more going on than you know about, Cordy."

"My friends can call me that," she retorted. "I don't think you qualify. Tell me what's going on."

"I can't." For a moment, he looked genuinely sorrowful. "I liked you, Cordelia. I really did. And I recognized you from the start. As soon as I saw you, I started trying to get you out of here. I wanted you gone before it was too late."

"Too late for what?" Then his words registered. "You voted against me? You recognized me?"

"Sharon and I had a secret alliance," he admitted. "You thought we were voting with you, but we were trying to get you safely out."

'What do you mean, 'safely'? Too late for what?"

"You should have gone when you had a chance," he said simply. "You had every opportunity to save yourself."

Now she grabbed the collar of his shirt, anger boiling over in her. "Save myself from what?" she demanded. "Gordon, what is going on here? Ohh, I can't wait until Angel gets his hands on you."

"You should have gone when you had the chance," he said again, apparently unfazed by her fury. He tugged his shirt free, and straightened it. "Now you're just a sacrifice, like the others."

"A sacrifice?" Cordelia exploded. "If you don't—"

But before she could finish, he broke and ran down the hall and around a blind corner. Cordy raced after him, but by the time she made the corner, he was gone. She hadn't heard any doors close—there weren't any doors visible; it seemed to be an empty bit of hallway. *Which means there has to be some kind of secret panel,* she thought. *Because he went somewhere. He's no ghost. I don't know what he is, but he's no ghost.*

She began to tap and listen at the walls, searching for the panel. She had only covered a couple of feet, though, when a crash and a horrified scream came from the direction of the living room. She gave up and ran back in there, hearing unrestrained sobbing from inside.

As soon as she cleared the doorway, she saw Frank. Somehow he'd fallen from a ladder with a cord tangled around his throat, it seemed. Raquel and Joel knelt around his body, and Sharon sat where she had been, on the couch. But Frank was clearly dead already, tongue extruding from his mouth, head cocked at an impossible angle.

"He . . . he wanted to keep working until help came," Raquel explained tearfully. "That's the kind of guy he is. But as soon as he got up the ladder, the cord seemed to tangle around him, and then the ladder just pitched him off. We couldn't do anything."

Cordelia didn't like this at all. She sat beside

Sharon, putting her arm around the shaking, sobbing woman's shoulders, to wait for whatever came next.

The pale demons chanted. The woman who had been named Kirsten but now thought of herself as Audrey watched them. They seemed to have been doing this for hours, perhaps even days, without tiring. She couldn't make out any words—they weren't singing in English, or in any other language that she could recognize. Before, she remembered, they had stood still as they'd chanted, but now they walked, remaining exactly equidistant from one another, in a circle around her. Each carried an object—one a small brazier that burned incense, smoke wafting from its holes; one a wooden construction of some kind that he carried as a priest would a crucifix, except it was a seemingly random pattern of joined sticks; and one a pure white, glowing ball. Then she noticed that he wasn't actually carrying that at all—his hand was held flat, and the ball or orb or whatever it was floated an inch or so above his palm. She almost thought the orb was leading them in their slow, steady circle around the room, but it was impossible to tell who led and who followed.

The back of her neck itched like mad, but otherwise she felt pretty good, she thought. She was confused and disoriented. She felt like she had been away somewhere, and was just on the verge of coming back. But she didn't know where she was coming back from, and she didn't know what she was coming back to. It was as if she'd taken a long trip but had no memory of her destination, and now knew only that she was on the way home.

Where home was, she didn't know. But the concept of going home held a certain appeal. She felt like she would be more comfortable soon, when she got there.

She knew, somehow, that she wouldn't be allowed out of this small room until whatever ritual these chanting beings were performing was finished. She knew that it was very important that they finish. She even knew, though she couldn't have said how, that the end was coming soon. She had a feeling that things were racing toward some kind of conclusion, and when that conclusion was reached, all the questions she didn't quite dare to ask would be answered for her, anyway.

Chapter Nineteen

There was no part of Los Angeles that could be confused with the steppes of Siberia, one of the coldest and most forbidding landscapes on Earth. Bextrian demons could function in warmer environments, but preferred cold ones, which Angel believed was a large part of the reason they rarely visited. But Salvatore insisted that there was one in town, and had called Angel with an address he'd learned. When Angel arrived at the downtown address, he found a building that had once been a supermarket. It had been closed for a couple of years, its signs taken down, its windows painted over. The front doors were chained shut and padlocked from the outside.

But around back, Angel found a loading dock with a sliding door that was not locked. The door was cold to the touch. Angel pressed an ear against it for a moment, but heard nothing inside except the steady hum of some kind of motor. He slid the door open just enough to slide through, and then closed it behind him.

The vacant store was freezing. In here, the sound was much louder—motors running air conditioners and cooling units at full blast. Angel was in a darkened back room receiving area, with high ceilings and tall metal shelving units. Twenty feet away, double swinging doors, propped open, led into the main store area. Because the windows were painted over, it was just as dark in there.

The coldest place, Angel thought, *will be the meat locker.* Since it wasn't on this side of the back room, it had to be on the far side, through the maze of shelving units and abandoned equipment that cluttered the storage area. Moving silently, Angel wove between shelves and dusty shopping carts and cash registers with sprung drawers, until finally the heavy, stainless steel door of the meat locker came into view.

That door, unlike the others inside the store, was closed. Angel guessed the Bextrian spent most of its time inside its frigid interior but kept the rest of the place as cold as possible for when it had to venture out.

His experience with supermarket meat lockers was limited, but he didn't expect that there would be a lot of room inside it, or a lot of places to hide. *Which means,* he thought, *that when I go through that door, I need to expect trouble.*

His biggest concern was the Bextrian's claws. He'd seen the photo of Curtis's severed head, and Salvatore had described the claws in considerable detail, his professional fascination with edged weapons giving him a unique insight. They were basically fingernails, except thicker and harder, and they grew naturally with an edge that, while not sharp enough to meet Salvatore's high standards, were certainly keener than most common meat cleavers or kitchen knives. Bextrians prized their claws, and had become well known in demonic circles as excellent assassins—and sometimes, bodyguards—because of their built-in weaponry and the enjoyment they took in using it.

He braced himself for anything, and tugged down on the handle. The door's heavy seal broke, and he went in.

Inside, the meat locker was dark and freezing, and even over the cold the stink of spoiled meat assailed his nostrils. The place must not have been cleaned after it was abandoned, he thought. Old blood and bits of fallen meat had rotted here and then been iced over by the Bextrian when he'd restarted the coolers.

But there was no Bextrian to be seen.

Angel ventured farther into the dark locker, peering into the corners. There were shelves here too, crusted with frost, and he examined each one. On two different shelves he found bundles of heavy clothing, also frosted, that might have belonged to a very large man or a demon, but not the demon or demons who owned them. He was about to turn away from the shelves when the door slammed shut behind him. He whirled around. Standing at the door was the Bextrian.

The demon was a foot taller than Angel, and broader through the shoulders. It was hard to make out colors in the dark meat locker, but his skin seemed to be a mustard yellow, very wrinkled. Long dark hair hung in frozen locks around his face. He held up both hands, the blade-like claws twitching as he regarded Angel.

"What do you want?" the demon asked. Its English was heavily accented.

"You chopped the head off a kid who worked for a TV company," Angel said. "I want to know why."

Instead of answering, the demon charged him. Angel sidestepped, his foot almost slipping out from under him on the icy floor. But he got out of the Bextrian's way and grabbed the big demon as he rushed past, using the creature's own momentum to slam him into one of the shelving units against the wall. The demon shook off the impact and spun around, his claws slicing the air. Angel ducked away from them as they whistled uncomfortably close to his head. He was still smarting a little from the Branichor attack and hoped to avoid another demon-inflicted wound.

The small space didn't give him much room to maneuver, though. The Bextrian jabbed at him, and Angel leaped back to dodge. He ended up against the wall, though. No place left to go. The Bextrian closed in again, and drove both hands forward at once. Angel caught the creature's wrists and stopped their forward momentum, the claws an inch from his gut. The Bextrian bore down with all his weight. Angel's arms shook, but held the claws away from him. Slowly, he turned the claws away from him, putting everything he had into it. The Bextrian kept leaning forward, not realizing until it was too late that he was just helping Angel do what he intended, anyway. When it did strike him, his eyes widened, but it was too late.

Angel bent the demon's wrists forward, using the creature's own weight to help, until the bones snapped. The Bextrian screamed and collapsed onto the floor. Angel leaned against the wall, gathering his strength in case the demon had another attack planned. But the thing seemed to be in genuine agony.

"You . . . you broke me . . ." the demon moaned.

"That's right," Angel said. "Now I want to hear about the guy you decapitated. Who sent you to do that?"

"Not . . . not me," the Bextrian claimed, voice breaking. "I did not—"

Angel took a step forward. "Don't make me hurt you more," he said angrily.

"Was . . . my brother," the demon insisted. "I stay here to protect home. Brother do the job."

"Sounds like he's better at his job than you are," Angel said. "Where is this brother?"

The demon groaned and shook his head. Angel put his foot on the demon, willing to press against the broken wrists if necessary. This creature was definitely connected to the kidnapping of Kirsten St. Clair, and Angel needed to find her to bring Cordelia some peace. He'd do whatever it took.

"No!" the Bextrian cried. "Brother is . . . doing last part of job. At the television house."

"Television house?" Angel repeated, a sudden, sick feeling in his gut. "The haunted house?"

"Yes, correct," the demon quickly confirmed. "Haunted television house."

Angel turned away and opened the meat locker door. If that was true, there was no time to waste.

Returning to the Hyperion Hotel had not helped track down Lilah Morgan or Kirsten St. Clair, Wesley was sorry to realize.

All the way here, they had talked over theories—*well,* he thought, *mostly I talked and he listened and then pointed out what was wrong with them.* Upon arriving at the hotel, Angel had found a telephone message from an informant and had headed back out while Wesley had parked himself at the computer, trying to find out what he could about Parker

McKay, to see if that raised any possibilities.

An Internet search on Parker McKay turned up hundreds of listings. He was wealthy enough to make the society pages, and there were various pictures of him and his wife, Janine, an attractive blond woman some years younger than him, possibly in her mid-forties to his mid-sixties, at functions around the city. There were business-page profiles of him and articles about his companies. There were reports of various philanthropic activities. Again, his wife seemed to figure in a lot of these; Wesley got the idea that she was the one interested in causes, and he was the one whose money went to support them.

Wesley even found, in a brief notice in one of the legal reporter newspapers, a story about McKay hiring Wolfram and Hart to do all of his personal legal work. His various businesses had their own legal departments, of course, but for matters of his personal estate, his taxes, and any other individual issues, Wolfram and Hart was now the law firm of record. Wesley considered calling Angel, but when he thought it through, he realized that it didn't tell them anything they couldn't have guessed. They knew there was a connection between McKay and Wolfram and Hart, since Larry Mullins, and presumably Lilah Morgan, had gone to his house in a firm limo and had taken him someplace. What they needed was something that might indicate where that "someplace" had been.

Wesley gave up. This wasn't panning out at all. He decided to check in on Cordelia, via WebCam, to watch the events leading up to the night's shooting. He knew she'd managed to stay in the house until the bitter end, and he didn't want to miss out on the opportunity to vote for her. He clicked over to the WebCam's URL.

But instead of a selection of viewing possibilities, he got a gray screen and a notice saying that the site was down. *How could that be?* he wondered. He reconnected a couple of times, to see if it was just busy, but he wasn't getting an error message—just a box telling him that the site was gone. He went to a phone and dialed the offices of Laughing Pig Productions. After a few rings, a voice mail message answered. He hung up.

"*There's something very wrong,*" he thought. As he stood there, wondering what to do next, the telephone he had just put down rang, startling him. "Angel Investigations."

"Wes, you need to find out where that house is, that Cordelia's in. What was it called, the Carson place or something?" It was Angel, and from the sound, using his cell phone.

"Carstairs, I believe."

"Whatever, just find out where it is and meet me there."

"Angel, the Website that is supposed to show WebCam feeds from the haunted house is down," he said. "And the production company isn't answering their phones."

"Just locate the house," Angel said. "It's somewhere off Mulholland, I think, in the hills. I'm headed that way but I need you to find out exactly where I'm going." He hung up.

As Wesley returned to the computer, Gunn burst through the front door with a stranger in tow. The tall, fit-looking man had "cop" written all over him, so Wesley assumed this could only be the police officer that Gunn had been working with.

"Gunn," Wesley said. "I'm afraid that Cordelia's in trouble."

At the same instant, Gunn was saying, "What are you sittin' around for? Cordelia's in trouble!"

"You know?" Wesley asked.

"Phil has a police-band radio in his car," Gunn said. "We were headed this way when we heard the report."

"What report?"

"There's a TV production company locked outside of a house," Phil Baxter explained. "A few crew members got in, but when the others showed up, they couldn't open the doors. They're stuck outside, and their contestants are inside. Gunn said one of the contestants worked for Angel."

"For me, actually," Wesley said, realizing even as he did so that it didn't matter. "Did the police report say where the house is?"

"Off Mulholland, in the Topanga Canyon area," Phil said.

"Let's go," Wesley said. "Just let me grab some books on haunted houses. Oh, and weapons would be a good idea."

Raquel shook Cordelia's arm. It had gone to sleep, wrapped around Sharon's shoulders. Now that she looked, she realized that Sharon was in a state of shock, almost catatonic. Around them, the house whistled and moaned and screamed. Objects flew seemingly at random, furniture, sculptures, plates. Cordelia had resolved to stay with Sharon until they were rescued, but that hadn't happened, and it had to be later than six by now.

"I'm worried, Cordelia," Raquel said. Her pretty brown eyes were bright and moist with terror. "Joel went to look for Eddie. But I haven't seen either of them for a long time."

"How long have I been sitting here with Sharon?" Cordelia asked, realizing that she'd had no real sensation of the passing of time. "I guess I was in kind of a daze or something."

"I don't know, maybe twenty minutes or so," Raquel said. "My watch stopped a long time ago. All the clocks are stopped, too."

Cordelia extricated her arm and shook it to restore the blood flow. "So what do you want to do? Go looking for them?"

"I think we should all stay together," Raquel said. "In the beginning, Joel told us to ignore anything we saw, that there'd be special effects teams working to scare you guys. But now he says there weren't, so maybe they were just trying to make sure we left you guys alone. This . . . this is pretty freakin' scary, you know?"

"It is that," Cordelia said. "God, that's just about the closest to sleep I've had in ages, it seems like. I must look awful on WebCam."

Raquel ignored her. *Which is just as well,* Cordelia thought. *I wouldn't want her to think I'm so vain that I'm more concerned with my looks than with her dead friend. Frank,* she remembered. *His name was Frank.*

She realized that she was the only one here who had experience dealing with the supernatural. She encountered things on an almost daily basis that would frighten other people to death, she knew. So she had to hold it together, try to get Raquel and Sharon and Joel and Eddie through this. There would be an end point. Someone would show up to help them. She was sure of that. "Okay," she said. "Let's find them."

Sharon came along willingly. She was still not visibly alert, but she followed when Cordy tugged on her hand. "Do you know where they were going to look?" Cordelia asked.

"No," Raquel replied. "They just said they'd be

back in a few minutes. But that was a long time ago."

Cordelia led them toward the entryway, figuring the best way to go would be through the dining room and kitchen. *If there is a back door, it would probably lead off the kitchen,* she thought. She had a vague memory of having seen one, though she'd tried to leave kitchen duty to those who could actually cook.

But they had just made it into the entryway when Raquel let out a scream. She pointed toward the ceiling. Cordelia looked up, dreading what she would see. And it was exactly what she had expected.

Gordon hung from the giant crystal chandelier, a noose around his neck. There was no ladder about, no visible way for him to have gotten up there, and they had heard no noise, no sounds of struggle. His legs swayed gently as if in a passing breeze. He was definitely dead.

"Don't look," Cordelia said. She grabbed Raquel and shook her. "Just don't look at him."

But that meant letting go of Sharon, who kept walking blindly. Cordy tugged Raquel after Sharon, caught up to the dazed woman and grabbed her arm. Sharon stopped.

"This way," Cordelia said. "It's going to be okay, I promise." She didn't know how she could keep that promise, but she was determined to try.

She led the catatonic Sharon and the now sobbing, semihysterical Raquel through the formal dining room. It was a mess, as the rest of the house was. Chairs were upended. One of them was on top of the dining table, skittering around under its own power in a twisted tap dance. Paintings had flown from the walls, and dozens of dishes had been hurled toward the fireplace.

She led the other two women through there as quickly as she could, hoping against hope that the kitchen was in better shape. She knew that if Raquel flipped out, too, then all their chances would be minimized. The more control they all had, the more likely they'd survive. *Until we're rescued,* she thought. *But rescued by whom? Who even knows we're in trouble?*

Whoever Gordon was working for, for one, she realized. *But they're probably the least likely to want to help us out.* And she knew that if the production company was involved, then they'd be able to keep the whole situation secret for as long as they wanted. Especially now that the show had been cancelled.

The kitchen, as it turned out, was relatively calm after the chaos of the dining room. Everything was in its proper place, no furniture was moving, nothing flew through the air.

The only thing wrong was that there was blood everywhere. Spattered on the walls, dripping from the ceiling, pooled on the floor.

Joel and Eddie were here, too—or their parts

were. Both men had been cut—or torn—in half, by some incredible force. Legs on one side of the room, torsos and heads on the other, blood between and around.

Raquel screamed again, and this time, through her catatonia, Sharon awoke enough to join her.

Cordelia wasn't too far from following suit.

Chapter Twenty

Phil Baxter drove his Taurus like it was a squad car and had a siren, weaving in and out of traffic, shooting through intersections, roaring onto the freeway and barreling down the fast lane, then suddenly cutting across three lanes of traffic to catch an exit that came upon him by surprise. Wesley was amazed that they didn't get stopped, but figured that Baxter could probably pull some strings if they did and dodge a ticket. He had called Angel with the information Phil had given him, and they were supposed to meet at the house as soon as possible.

As Phil drove, Gunn tried to explain what they'd found out.

"That body in the lot," he said, "with all the identifying marks removed. That's happened before—a whole lot of befores, you go back far enough."

"How far back?" Wesley interrupted.

"We have similar—I might as well say identical—cases going back more than forty years," Phil replied.

"Good lord," Wesley said. "How many women?"

"Over that time period, sixty-two corpses," Phil said. He aimed the Ford's nose between two semis. Wesley tried to make himself smaller, as if it would help, but the car squeezed between them and shot out the other side.

"And that's not all the corpses," Gunn added. "Within a week after each of these bodies turning up, there has been some kind of mass killing. Three, four, eight people, it varies each time. But over the same sixty-two incidents, we're looking at a total of two hundred and seventy-one bodies. And that doesn't include the missing."

"There are missing?" Wesley asked.

"That's why we think the body is related to the Kirsten St. Clair case," Gunn said. "In each of these cases, a young woman has gone missing the same time the body turns up. Or within a couple of days, either way."

"So there are sixty-two missing girls as well."

"All in the same boat as Kirsten St. Clair."

"And Joan Martin," Wesley said. "The Host and I paid a visit to Sally Truesdale."

Gunn cracked a smile. "You got her to sing?"

"Like a bird," Wesley said, grabbing onto the seat as Baxter swerved and the car swayed like a hammock in a high wind. "But the thing is, Sally Truesdale is not Sally Truesdale."

"So she's Joan Martin?"

"That seems like the best guess," Wesley agreed. "The Host couldn't tell much about her, because she's so much not who she thinks she is, her aura was quite confused. Gave him a bit of a headache, I believe."

"That shut him up?" Gunn asked.

"Heavens, no," Wesley replied. "It would take more than a headache to do that. But he complained about it quite vociferously."

"I bet," Gunn said. "So here's what we think's goin' on. Someone is kidnapping young women, killing older ones, and somehow replacing the older ones with the younger ones. Like trading in used cars."

"Yes, well, that's a crude but not inaccurate way to put it," Wesley admitted.

"And this has what to do with Cordelia in a haunted house?"

"There's only one element missing so far," Phil reminded him. "There hasn't been a mass murder in town this week."

"Drive faster," Wesley said grimly.

In less time than he'd have thought possible, they were stopped outside the gates of a deserted estate off Mulholland Drive. From the road, they couldn't see the house, but they could tell there was activity down the driveway. Police cars and paramedics turned through the gates on a regular basis, and a handful of civilian cars had stopped to see what was going on. The sun had begun to set, and here in the hills, deep shadows already covered most of the land. As they sat at the gate, Angel pulled up in his GTX. He'd been farther away, all the way at the southern end of downtown, so Wesley could only imagine he'd driven even more dangerously than Phil Baxter had.

When Angel approached the car, Wesley was frantically thumbing through some books on the way. Angel glanced at him. "You find anything in those?" he asked.

"I think so," he said. "I believe I can unseal the house momentarily. Long enough to get in. The only way to permanently unseal a house that's been sealed by a haunting spirit is from the inside, though."

"Then I guess I'm going in," Angel said.

"Not alone," Wesley argued.

"Why not?"

"For one thing, you haven't been reading the books. You wouldn't know what to do once you got in there."

"I find the ghost and I hit him a lot," Angel said. "Until he unlocks the door."

Gunn looked at Phil. "Angel's always got a plan."

"We'll all go in," Wesley said. "We'll need to find

Cordelia. I'll work on unsealing the house. Someone might need to protect me while I'm doing so."

"You're the boss," Angel said.

"That's right. And I say we all go in." He remembered then that Phil Baxter didn't work for Angel Investigations. "By all, I mean me, Angel, and Gunn," he clarified. "You're welcome to join us if you'd like."

"I've come this far," Phil said. "You'd have to put me in the ground to keep me out of there now."

"Well, welcome aboard, then."

"How do we get past the cops?" Angel asked.

"I'll take care of them," Phil Baxter said. "Being an ex-captain doesn't have as many privileges as being captain, but it's still got its advantages. Hop in."

Angel climbed into the backseat with Wesley and an array of weapons. Phil started the car again and pulled across the street. A uniformed officer stood at the gate now, letting emergency vehicles in and shooing away the curious. Phil pulled up next to him and rolled down his window. "Hey, Loomis," he said. "What's shaking?"

"Got a situation here, Captain Baxter," Loomis said.

"I know," Phil said. "My associates and I were asked to come in and lend a hand, on kind of a consulting basis. They're experts at this kind of thing."

"What kind of thing?" Loomis asked, puzzled.

"Haunted houses, what else?"

Loomis laughed nervously. "Yeah, gotcha, Cap. You go for it." He pulled the gate open for them, and Phil drove through.

"You know every cop in L.A.?" Gunn asked him.

"Not all of them," Phil said. "I don't know the new ones. But if they've been around for a while, I've probably met them once or twice. If not, most of them recognize me, and they wear their names on their chests, so it's easy to pretend I know them."

At the bottom of the drive, the house stood, wooden panels covering all its windows. Crews tried to get the wood down, but without success. Police cars and fire trucks and other emergency vehicles were parked haphazardly, many with roof lights still flashing. Cops and paramedics and firefighters milled about aimlessly.

"Wait here," Phil said. He got out of the car and hiked down to the police officer in charge of the scene. A few minutes of animated conversation ensued, after which Phil started back up the hill to the car with a smile on his face.

"I just realized something," Angel said.

"What is it?" Wesley asked.

"No limo. There should be a Wolfram and Hart limousine here, but I don't see one."

"Not necessarily," Wesley said. "We don't know that Lilah is involved in this."

"Sure we do," Angel said. "We know that Wolfram

and Hart is. They hired the demons who attacked me when I broke into the production offices and that obnoxious kid saw me. This whole thing stinks of them."

"And more than half of the missing women over the past dozen years or so had auditioned for Laughing Pig," Gunn said. "They were selling their rejects out the back door. We figure they're tied to Wolfram and Hart because they hired the suicide demons that attacked Angel. So there should be a car here. Maybe there's some other way in we can't see."

Phil reached the car then and got back into the driver's seat. "They're going to let us take our shot," he said. "They're pulling back to give us some privacy, too."

"How did you do that?" Wesley asked.

"Same thing I told Loomis," Phil replied. "Told them you guys were haunted house experts."

"After this is over," Wesley said, "I'd like to talk to you about joining our team. We could use a man with your powers of persuasion."

"I'm retired," Phil said. He started the car and drove slowly between the police cars and emergency trucks. As they neared the house, the police officers and firefighters who had been standing near it were walking away. "I'm here for this because I didn't do anything to stop it when I should have, and I think I need to make some payback. But after this is over, I'm going back to fishing and soap operas."

"He leads a very full life," Gunn explained.

Near the front door, Phil stopped the car again, setting the emergency brake. "Last stop. Everyone out."

The house was silent, as if whatever had sealed it up kept all sound within its walls as well. There should have been people shouting, banging on doors or windows, Wesley thought. But there was nothing. He only hoped that didn't mean what he feared it might: that there was no one left alive inside. *I can't even consider that,* he thought. *It's not an option.*

Wesley took up a position in front of the door, one of his books open in his left hand. As he read out loud, he moved his right hand in a carefully choreographed sequence. At first, Angel thought he was reading Latin, but then he realized that it wasn't all Latin. There were a few Greek words mixed in, some he recognized as Mesopotamian, and a handful that didn't sound human at all.

"He know a lot of languages?" Phil asked quietly.

"He knows a lot, period," Angel replied.

"You know, I catch those soaps once a week, I can pretty much keep up with what's going on. They move pretty slow. I don't really have to watch every day, I guess."

Angel smiled. "Talk to the boss later."

"I will."

As Wesley progressed, his voice grew louder and louder until finally he was shouting at the house, or more likely at the spirit or spirits inhabiting it. His arm motions became more pronounced, too, jerking from position to position almost as if pulled by invisible strings. His face was turning red from the effort.

Finally, he stopped and closed the book. He stared at the front door for a moment.

And then it swung open slowly.

"Let's go!" He dashed through—Angel, Gunn, and Phil close at his heels. He carried a crossbow, Angel a broadsword, Gunn a two-handed ax. Phil had his service revolver in his fist. As soon as they were all inside, the door slammed shut behind them.

They found themselves in a marble-floored entryway with a grand staircase sweeping up and away. Wesley felt someone grab his arm, and turned to see Gunn, gripping him and pointing up.

Hanging from a chandelier at the top of the staircase was a young man. Wesley had seen him on the show, and believed his name was Gordon. "Oh, my God," he breathed. *What if that had been Cordelia? Where is she?*

"Cordelia!" Angel shouted, desperation in his voice. "Cordy!"

There was no answer.

"We should split up," Wesley suggested. "To cover more ground. Angel and I can go together, through there," he said, pointing out a doorway. He ticked his head in the opposite direction. "Gunn and Captain Baxter, you go that way. Find Cordelia."

This is not good. This is not good at all, Cordelia thought. She had to get Raquel and Sharon out of there fast, before they both went mad, or something similarly horrible happened to them. She thought she could hear faint sounds from elsewhere in the house, but it was as if the air were too thick to let sound travel.

"Come on!" she said, tugging on their arms and trying to back them out of the kitchen. Sharon had snapped out of her catatonia—the spark of life was back in her eyes, but was partially obscured by tears and terror. She took a huge breath and let it out in yet another bloodcurdling shriek. Raquel had stopped screaming but sobbed uncontrollably.

"Let's go," she said, increasing the pressure on their arms. With each hand she held a different woman's arm, which she hoped to use to lead them to some other part of the house. Getting outside would be good, but leaving the scene of carnage in the kitchen behind was more important right now.

They were almost back out the doorway, when they heard Joel. "Wait," he said, his voice a liquid gurgle. "Don't go yet." Cordelia turned as Joel—his upper half, at least—pushed itself semi-upright, palms of his hands hitting the tile floor with a wet slap.

Cordelia felt her eyes widen in horror. Joel held himself up on his hands, mouth moving, blood dripping from between his lips as he spoke.

"Don't look at him," Cordy warned the others. "It's not real. None of this is real."

But Raquel started to pull away from Cordelia's grasp, trying to get back to Joel. "No, he needs help. Joel is alive, he just needs help."

"He's not," Cordelia insisted, struggling to maintain a grip on the camera operator. "Come on, Raquel. We have to go."

Sharon, in Cordelia's other hand, had gone silent again. Cordy could feel her quaking like a leaf.

Raquel jerked her arm from Cordelia's grip. "Joel, you'll be okay," she shouted, running to his side.

Cordelia let go of Sharon and followed Raquel across the blood-slick tile floor, nearly slipping on the way. Before she could reach Raquel, though, Raquel reached Joel, and Joel threw his arms around Raquel's legs. As if realizing then what was happening, she screamed again.

Cordelia caught up a half-second later, grabbing Raquel's shoulders. "Raquel, no! Come on!" She shook the woman, trying to free her from the dead man's grip. Then she felt a wet hand on her own ankle, and looked down to see that Eddie had also reanimated and scooted himself across the floor toward her.

"Get off me, you bifurcated freak!" she shouted, kicking at him until she broke free of his clutches. *He's half the man he used to be,* she thought crazily, almost breaking into a giggle in spite of the bizarrely horrific scene. *Or maybe because of it,* she knew. *Defense mechanism.*

Eddie made another grab at her, tumbling forward when he missed. His head and face slammed against the tile floor, hands scrabbling for purchase but failing to find any. Cordelia wrenched at Raquel's shoulders and kicked past the woman's legs, her heel landing squarely against Joel's chest. He slipped back, losing his precarious balance and falling over. "Come on!" Cordelia insisted again, and this time Raquel came willingly. They ran from the room, picking up Sharon at the doorway, and not looking back.

Larry Mullins stood quietly in a corner of the room. At the door, a tall, muscular Bextrian demon with wicked knife-like claws stood guard. To Larry's right was Parker McKay, breathing heavily through his mouth and sweating profusely from nerves. Next to McKay, Lilah Morgan was as cool as ever in a sleeveless white silk blouse and a battleship-gray skirt. She watched the scene almost impassively, as if it was nothing she hadn't seen a dozen times before. *Maybe it's not,* Larry thought. *But it's a first for me.*

Before them, Audrey—the new Audrey, he noted—sat in a chair that was centered inside a circle. She appeared to observe with a detached sort of interest the goings-on around her. Standing right beside her—two just behind her shoulders, one directly in front of her, all three mere inches away—were three ghastly looking white demons. The one in front of Audrey held a stone bowl filled with some clear liquid that he used to dab on Audrey's forehead and neck. It was colorless like water, but seemed thicker, more viscous, the consistency of jelly. The demon by Audrey's right shoulder had his hands in the air, quivering, fingers trembling independently, and he kept up a steady chant in a language that Larry had never heard. The one at Audrey's left shoulder stood statue-still, eyes closed, but every now and then he spoke a few words in English. "One has fallen," he said at one point. Later on, he added, "Another has fallen," and so on. By Larry's calculations, four had fallen at this point.

Larry knew, of course, what that meant. The ritual required sacrifice to be completed. Upstairs, the sacrifice was taking place. Each of the "fallen" was another victim down, another person whose life-force was being taken from them and transmitted by the demon with his hands in the air—as if reaching through the ceiling and the floor above—to the demon with the bowl. The gelatinous liquid was a transferal agent by which the life-force was—metaphorically, at least—given to Audrey, awakening the person who dwelled inside the body that had formerly belonged to Ms. St. Clair. There was, he'd been told, no specific number of sacrificial victims necessary to the completion of the spell, but the more the merrier. The demons performing the ritual would know how many they had to work with, and would tailor the ceremony accordingly so that it reached its climax when the last victim fell. That was when Parker McKay would have to stand before Audrey, so that she would imprint on him. Then Parker would have a beautiful new wife with many of his favorite attributes of the old one, and many, though of course not all, of her memories.

Parker would have some explaining to do, of course. He would claim that Janine had gone on a long trip, after filing for divorce. His new wife, Audrey, would be accepted into his circle after a while—money and prestige would have a lot to do with that, and it wasn't at all uncommon for wealthy and powerful men to attract young women. If any of Janine's closest friends pressed for more, they could always meet with "accidents," he knew. Those weren't hard to arrange.

"Four have entered," the statue-demon said.

The one with the stone bowl glanced at him,

seemingly in surprise. Larry got the impression that this was not in the game plan—he'd thought the house was sealed, anyway, so it shouldn't have been possible for anyone to enter. Suddenly, he felt a flash of panic. *Did something go wrong? Is this all going to fall apart?* Lilah glanced at the ceiling without concern, though, so he forced himself to relax.

But the demons recovered and continued their tasks, the one with the bowl dabbing his gunk on Audrey's nose and cheeks with the ends of his chalk-white fingers. Larry relaxed again. They didn't seem too distressed by this new development. After all, if four more people really had entered the house somehow, that would just give them four more victims for sacrifice, and would cement the spell that much more firmly.

No worries here, he thought.

Chapter Twenty-one

After finding the body hanging from the light fixture, Gunn and Phil Baxter had peeled off from Angel and Wesley, going through a doorway at the back of the entryway that led into a kind of warren of what would have been, in the house's prime, servants' passageways. They called for Cordelia and tried door after door, most of which led into empty rooms, rooms that had been servants' quarters or pantries or storage areas. But in one of the rooms there was another doorway, half-hidden by a jumble of unused furniture.

"Look at that," Phil pointed out, showing Gunn fresh scrape marks on the floor. "Looks like someone was trying to move this stuff away from the doorway, and got interrupted."

Gunn touched his own neck, right where a noose would encircle it. "Let's hope it wasn't that guy we just met," he replied.

"Come on," Phil said, holstering his gun. "Help me get this stuff out of the way." He and Gunn went to work on the pile of chairs and tables and in a few moments had it far enough to the side to get to the door. "I always figure the hardest door to get to is probably the one you want to look through first."

Phil drew his .38 service revolver again. "You don't have a gun?" he asked Gunn.

"Hate 'em," Gunn said. He raised the ax. "Anyway, I'm pretty handy with this."

"Stay behind me, then," Phil instructed. He pulled open the door and swung into the doorway, his revolver pointed into the black hollow beyond. The door opened onto a narrow, unlit stairway that led down. Moving at a half-squat, gun held close to his feet, Phil descended first. Gunn came behind him, one hand against the wall for balance. Below them, light leaked around the edges of the door.

At the bottom, Phil pressed his ear against the door. Gunn couldn't see the man's expression in the dark, but after a moment he stepped back and turned the knob. This door opened out, and Phil poked his gun through into the light as he pushed the door.

This doorway led them into an ancient-looking stone hallway, illuminated by two glass bulbs powered by exposed wires hanging along the ceiling. There was a door on each end of the hall, and nothing else but old, dry stone. Phil turned his head quickly in both directions.

"That way seems like it's away from the house," Gunn whispered, pointing down the hall. "So that one must be under the house."

"That's the one we want, then," Phil said quietly.

"Why?" Gunn questioned. "It's so hard to get down here, how could Cordelia be down here?"

"I don't know if she is," Phil said. "But something is. Lights are on, and somebody else was trying to get down here before."

"Let's check it quick, then," Gunn insisted. "We got to get Cordy."

Phil showed Gunn the revolver again. *As if I forgot about it already,* Gunn thought. "Me first," Phil said. He walked down the hall, ramrod straight, pistol at the ready, and put his hand on the door at the end.

Angel and Wesley made a left out of the entryway into what looked like a once-grand dining room that had suffered a destructive rampage that even a score of teenagers couldn't have equaled.

Before they were all the way through the room, Cordelia came from the other direction, leading two young women with her. One of them Angel recognized as one of her fellow contestants, while the other woman, in a blood-spattered T-shirt and faded jeans, was a stranger.

"Cordelia!" he shouted.

"Oh, thank God!" Wesley said.

Cordelia eyed them both suspiciously. "Are you

really you?" she asked. "Because I'm beyond the point where I'm willing to trust anyone or anything."

"Of course we're us," Wesley replied firmly. "Who else would we be?"

"Cordelia, are you okay?" Angel asked.

"I'm fine. Nothing that can't be fixed by a couple of months in a rubber room, I'm sure." She hesitated, as if thinking of something. "Or maybe a trip to the Caribbean, all expenses paid—"

"You've just had a week's paid vacation," Wesley responded automatically.

"Oh, you are you!" Cordelia said happily. "Because no fake Wesley would be so small-minded as to remind me of that at a time like this!" She ran to them, throwing her arms around Angel, and then Wesley.

"Guys, we need to get Cordy out of here," Angel said. "We need to find Gunn and Baxter and figure out what's going on here."

"Right," Wesley agreed. He flipped open the book he carried to a page marked by his finger.

"How did you even get in here? And who's Baxter?" Cordelia asked.

"Long story," Angel offered.

The door was heavy—reinforced and soundproofed—but Gunn helped Phil open it, and Phil went through first, his .38 stuck out in front of him. Just inside the doorway, he stopped. Gunn crowded him, looking over his shoulder to see what was going on. A wave of smoky, incense-flavored air washed out over them.

The small room was crowded. Three nasty-looking pale demons surrounded a woman sitting on a chair—a woman who looked just like the photos of Kirsten St. Clair. A bigger, dangerous-looking demon was already in motion toward them, claws clicking against one another as he charged. Two people who could only be lawyers stood off to one side, flanking a short, older guy wearing expensive casual clothes. *That's probably what's-his-name, McKay,* Gunn thought. *Which makes these two chumps Lilah Morgan and Larry Mullins. And that means Angel's right, there is a limo parked somewhere around.* He figured that the long hallway probably led to a secret entrance at some remove from the house, so people could come and go to this secret room without the contestants upstairs knowing about it.

"Whatever you're up to, it's over!" he barked. "We're shutting this down!"

Without a moment's hesitation, the big demon slammed into Phil. Phil pumped four shots into it, but it didn't even slow him down. It pressed Phil against the door jamb with a forearm across the cop's throat. The other three came toward the blocked doorway, chittering in what Gunn figured must be their own language—it sounded like crickets chirruping on a summer's night, and he found the sound of it extremely disturbing.

The big ex-cop twisted and writhed and kicked, but he couldn't break the demon's grip. Gunn tried to help, punching at the big creature. The doorway was too narrow for him to get through with their struggle blocking it, and the three inside couldn't get out. Realizing that he was having no effect, he tried to pull Phil backward.

"Come on, man," he said. "Let's get Angel."

But the demon holding Phil's neck just increased his pressure, silently bearing down. Then, with a quick movement, it sank the claws of its other hand deep into Phil's belly. The cop gave an anguished croak and went limp. The demon tossed his body to one side.

Gunn started to back down the hallway, fast, not wanting to turn away from the demons. He hoped for a moment that they were bound to the small room and couldn't come out.

They weren't.

"Gunshots," Angel said. "Sounds like they're downstairs. How do we get down there?"

"How do we get down?" Cordelia echoed. "If the gunshots are down there, aren't we better off being someplace like up here? Or better yet, out of the building altogether?"

"Baxter and Gunn could be in trouble," Angel explained.

"We're all in trouble as long as we're in here,"

Cordelia said. "But, okay, if Gunn's in trouble, we have to save him. *You* have to save him." She indicated Raquel and Sharon, who stood by watching the exchange with a silent but definite lack of comprehension. "I'll stay here and keep them safe. But, hurry."

"We still don't know how to get down," Angel pointed out.

"I didn't even know there *was* a down," Cordelia said.

Wesley pointed back toward the entryway. "Gunn and Baxter went through a door in there," he said.

"Let's go," Angel said.

As they ran for the entryway and the door through which Gunn and Phil had disappeared, Wesley began to read out loud from the book he carried, intoning the strange words as clearly as he could while trying to keep up with Angel. Angel led them through the door into the maze of little rooms, finally finding the open door that led into the narrow stairway. At the bottom he could see part of a lighted hallway, and the sounds of a struggle wafted upstairs.

"Down here!"

Wesley followed him, still trying to keep his place on the page and continue the spell he read as he jostled and jolted down the dark stairs. Reaching the bottom, Angel charged into the lighted stone hallway. Gunn was there, halfway to another doorway. He was on his knees, doing his best to fend off three skeletal but seemingly powerful demons who looked intent upon ripping him to shreds. His ax was abandoned on the floor. A fourth demon—*a Bextrian,* Angel realized, *no doubt the brother*—had been hiding near the doorway, and came at Angel as soon as he showed himself.

Angel didn't hesitate. He hurtled down the hallway and leaped into the air, sword out. The Bextrian put up its own claws to parry, but Angel had all of his force behind the leap, and the sword slipped past the demon's claws, driving deep into his chest. Angel yanked it out, and blue Bextrian blood spurted toward him. The thing still hadn't gone down, though, but swung his arms wildly, a couple of the claws finding Angel's face, slicing the skin on his cheek. Angel swung the sword again and severed one of the clawed hands. It bounced off the ceiling and then hit the floor, and the demon started to slump, weak now from the wounds and the massive blood loss. Angel took one more swing, his sword slicing into the demon's neck. Finally, the thing fell.

But Gunn still struggled with the others. Angel ran past the fallen Bextrian and leaped, sailing over Gunn's head and crashing into one of the demons. They went down in a tangle, and the sword bounced from Angel's fist. The thing got a grip on one of Angel's arms, and its grasp felt like a steel vise. *No wonder Gunn was having a hard time with three of them,* Angel thought. The strident, subvocal sound the thing made as they fought was almost as bad as its strength. *Sounds like a hundred rats' feet running across a grave,* he thought.

As they both regained their feet, Angel scrabbled for a purchase on the demon, but his fingers kept slipping off the thing's pale skin. The surface felt like soap, and he couldn't get a decent grip. At the same time, though, its fingers clawed at him. Finally he was able to gain enough leverage to slam the demon's back against the stone wall. The thing lost its grip, then, and Angel turned away from it, shooting an elbow hard into its ribs. The demon grunted in pain and Angel clenched his fists together, following up with a double-fisted uppercut to the demon's jaw that snapped its head back. It hit the wall again, and this time it fell.

"We have to get out of here," Lilah said urgently.

"How?" Larry asked her. "They're between us and the door."

"They're a little preoccupied right now, if you haven't noticed," Lilah said. "We need to go, while the demons have their attention. The demons work for us, they'll make sure we get out."

"I don't know," Larry said. "We may pay them,

but I always get the feeling that demons work for themselves, and if their interests coincide with our own, that's just a fringe benefit."

"I'm senior here, Larry," Lilah hissed. "I say we go. Now."

Larry turned to Parker McKay. The man looked as if he was on the verge of a stroke. His skin was bright red, with white splotches on his forehead and cheeks. His mouth was working, opening and closing, but no sound was coming out.

"What about him?" Larry asked.

"He's a client. He comes with us."

"And the girl? Audrey?"

"Forget her," Lilah ordered.

Larry shrugged. This was Lilah's deal, he was just assisting her. So he'd go along with her instructions. He hoped she was right about them getting out past the battle royale in the hallway. "Come on, Parker," he said. "Time to go."

"But . . . my wife—"

"Your wife's dead," Larry snapped. "You had her killed."

Parker looked at Larry, eyes brimming with sorrow and anger. "You . . . you betrayed me!" he shouted. "You guys promised me a wife. Better than before, you said. Young and healthy and beautiful."

"Didn't work out, Parker. Come on, now, while we can still get out!"

Larry noticed that Lilah was already on her way.

He followed. Parker could come with them if he chose.

Angel turned his attention back to Gunn, still wrestling with the other two demons. Gunn bled from his nose and mouth and a dozen cuts from their sharp fingers, and one of the demons had his head in the crook of its arm, trying to twist it off. The two of them still made that awful noise.

Remembering the difficulty of getting a good hold on their skin, Angel threw his arms around the neck of the one who was trying to behead Gunn. He got a similar hold on that demon, with its head in the bend of his elbow, and tried to pry it off Gunn. It turned its head, trying to protect its throat, and suddenly its eyes, pale, almost transparent gray with tiny veins and a haunted aspect, were right in front of his own. They were nightmare eyes, horrible to look into, as if to see into them was to see one's own worst fears. Angel closed his own eyes rather than look at them, and increased the pressure on the demon's neck. He felt its fingers clawing at his face, trying to get to his eyes, and he whipped his head to the side, shaking the demon.

A rustling sound made him open his eyes again, and he saw Lilah Morgan and someone else, a young man he didn't recognize, wearing a dark suit, slipping down the hallway past them while they were occupied with the demons. He knew he should try to stop them, but if he let go of the demon now, it would kill Gunn. He tried to warn Wesley, who stood by the door to the stairway, still reading aloud from the book, his crossbow dangling from his arms, trying to complete the spell that would eliminate the haunting spirits from the house. When he opened his mouth to shout, though, the demon's fingers slipped inside and grabbed his tongue.

Angel bit down, hard, and in his anger he wrenched the demon's head. The thing screeched once, but the screech was cut off by Angel's arm, and it went limp in his hands. He dropped it, spitting out bits of its skin and blood. *Not tasty,* he thought.

Angel turned back to Gunn to see if he needed any help. But he'd overcome his own demonic opponent and, face fixed in a mask of rage, slammed its skull over and over into the stone wall. "You killed Phil!" Gunn hissed at the creature.

Angel drew up behind Gunn and put a calming hand on his shoulder. "It's okay, Gunn," Angel said quietly. "He's finished."

Gunn looked at him, eyes wide, lips drawn back in a snarl, and for a moment Angel thought he would lunge. But, recognizing Angel, Gunn relaxed and released the last demon. It slid to the ground, lifeless now, leaving only a stain on the wall. The last of the demons' chittering noises were stilled.

The only sound was Gunn, breathing hard and unevenly, Wesley reciting words that human voices were never meant to speak, and the slamming of the door at the far end of the corridor. Angel thought for a moment that he should go after the lawyers, but he couldn't bring himself to bother. In another few seconds he heard the sound of a car's motor starting and the crunch of tires on gravel as it raced away.

Limo, no doubt, he thought.

As he was helping Gunn to his feet, there was another loud, sharp report, from the near end of the hall, followed by a horrified scream. *Gunshot,* he knew.

"Baxter's gun," Gunn croaked. "The girl."

Angel ran into the room at the end of the hall, stepping over Phil Baxter's corpse to get in. Kirsten St. Clair stood in front of a chair at the center of a circle painted on the floor. She was crying and pointing at the room's only other occupant, an old man who looked very small and frail in death. Near his outstretched arm was what must have been Baxter's service piece. Blood pooled on the floor beneath his head. The scent of it argued with the overwhelming smell of incense, and after tasting that demon's blood, it smelled tantalizing to Angel. He put it out of his mind.

"What happened?" Angel asked her.

"He . . . he shot himself," Kirsten said. "He put the gun against his head and just . . . just . . ."

"Who is he?"

"He's Parker McKay," she said, holding back a sob. "He's my . . . he's my husband."

Epilogue

"Nothing," Wesley said. He wadded up the newspaper in disgust and threw it into the trash. "Five days, and still not a single word about what went on in that house."

Gunn walked into the room. His voice had mostly recovered, although the marks were still visible on his neck. "Ain't gonna be," he said. "Anne's cop friend said there's nothing being done within the LAPD. No investigation, nothing. Not even of Phil Baxter's death." The murder of the ex-cop had been especially hard on Gunn, who had grown to like and respect the man a great deal in a short time.

"But Parker McKay was practically a billionaire," Wesley argued, frustration evident in his tone. They were in the office in the hotel. Angel watched them both, silent. He had his own problems with the whole case. "They can't just sweep that under the rug."

"They are," Gunn said. "Believe it. Wolfram and

Hart pulled some major strings this time. They got the cops, the fire department, and the press to all work together—maybe a first in the history of L.A. But what they're workin' on is a big whitewash."

"Perhaps we should go to the press ourselves," Wesley said. "Tell them what we know."

Gunn laughed and sat down in one of Angel's chairs. "And prove it how? They'd think we were crazy. Then we'd tell them how we know, and they'd *know* we were crazy. Can't even take them back to the haunted house and show 'em that, since it imploded after Wesley finished his spell."

"Yes, well, at least I accomplished that," Wesley said. "My mouth still feels strange from trying to pronounce some of those words. From now on it's Latin or nothing for me."

"You have to use whatever works," Angel offered.

"Well, true," Wesley agreed. "I'm certain that if I'd had a bit more time I'd have been able to find an anti-haunting spell in Latin, though. Perhaps even in English."

"I just can't get over that whole plan," Gunn said. "If what Kirsten says is true, then she was being set up to replace McKay's wife. That's just sick."

"The police could run a DNA test on the Jane Doe, compare it with some of the real Mrs. McKay's hair or something, and make a positive ID," Angel suggested.

"But they won't," Gunn said.

"As far as I'm concerned," Wesley offered, "the simple

fact that Mrs. McKay hasn't shown up to claim her husband's fortune is evidence enough for me. But what about the other replacement wives, over the decades? Should we try to do anything about them?"

Angel shook his head. "By now, they really are who they think they are, for all intents and purposes. The people they were are long gone. We'd only be opening a lot of people up to heartbreak, even if we could somehow convince those women of their real identities."

"But, Angel," Wesley argued, "the people who lost loved ones are the people who knew the missing girls. Their families and friends. The men who are enjoying their new, young wives are the bad guys here, right? They contracted with Wolfram and Hart to kill their wives and replace them with kidnap victims. Surely you don't intend to let that stand."

Angel folded his fingers together, elbows on his desktop, resting his lips against his hands. "Look into it, Wes. If there's a way to restore their memories, it's worth doing. Otherwise, we should let those people live with whatever accommodations they've made. You think Sally Truesdale wants to know that she's really Joan Martin?"

"I think Sally Truesdale wants to know when she's getting her plane tickets," Gunn speculated.

"And her soap," Angel added with a chuckle. "Don't forget the soap."

* * *

"Nathan Reed is not a happy man right now," Lilah told Larry Mullins. She paced around his desk as she talked. "Not happy at all. Especially with us. And by us, I mean you."

"Me?" Larry echoed. "What did I do?"

"You left a very wealthy client alone in a room with a loaded gun, for starters," she said. "I told you to get him out and you just abandoned him there with the woman he knew he could never have. After, I might add, blaming him for his own wife's death. Use a little Psych 101 and figure out how many things are wrong with that picture."

"But he was to blame," Larry protested. "He paid us to have her killed."

"Key word, 'us,'" Lilah pointed out. "That absolves him of any blame. That's the Wolfram and Hart way."

"So what's going to happen to me?" Larry asked. He was already seeing, in his mind's eye, his Ferrari or Lamborghini driving away into the sunset, leaving him stranded by the side of the road.

Lilah shrugged. "Fortunately for you, he's feeling like the body count in this case is already high enough." She ticked them off on her fingers. "We lost Curtis, our man inside Laughing Pig Productions who scouted potential brides for us. We lost Gordon, who posed as a contestant to make sure none of the real contestants figured out what was going on downstairs. We lost a valued client. And somewhere along the way, our limousine dispatcher decided to make a run for it."

"He did?" Larry asked. "What happened to him?"

"No one knows. Security caught up to him at a gas station outside Las Vegas. They didn't bother asking any questions before they took care of him."

"So what you're saying is, you don't think Reed's going to have me killed."

"Not today," Lilah said. She pried his blinds apart with her fingers, peeking out his windows at the city below. "Which leaves you an opportunity to get back in his good graces. Whatever your next assignment is, don't screw it up."

"Hey, Gordon should have recognized that Cordelia Chase worked for Angel," Larry said. "That wasn't my fault."

"Maybe he did," Lilah agreed. "But what good did it do? She was already in the house. He wasn't in a position to keep her off the show. His job was to keep people away from the stairs."

She cut off his next attempt. "There's no way you can deflect the blame onto them, Larry. This one's on you."

"So without Curtis at Laughing Pig, is the trophy wife project over?"

She shrugged again. "The haunted house made a good cover, even though it could only be used once every few years. Now that it's gone, we need to find a replacement. The production company is out. We can put something new together, but it's going to take time. Wolfram and Hart hates to walk away from a proven earner, though, so I'd guess it'll be back, sooner or later. More likely later."

"I could . . . I could work on that," Larry said, nervous about his prospects. He had thought his future was golden; now he'd be lucky to have a future at all. "Make some connections, pull together a plan."

Lilah leaned on his desk, bending close to his face. "One thing you should learn about this firm, Larry. They don't really like it when you take initiative. They like it when you follow orders. And they especially like it when you don't screw up." She straightened, turned, and headed for the door. "That's my best advice to you, Larry. Don't screw up."

"I really appreciate everything you've done for me, Cordy," Kirsten St. Clair said. "And your friends, too. I mean, I guess I put you guys through a lot of trouble, from what you say."

Cordelia waved her fingers at her friend dismissively, just glad that Gunn and Phil had interrupted the ceremony before it was totally complete. "That's what we do, Kirsten," she said. "Angel Investigations, I mean. We help the helpless. For a while I wanted to say 'we help the hopeless,' but I kept saying 'homeless' instead, and that didn't really sound right. Although we've done that, too."

"Your friends are so cool," Kirsten said. "And cute, too."

"They're okay," she admitted. "If you like those

types. Which, I guess, between Angel, Wesley, and Gunn, there's a lot of types to choose from."

Kirsten pulled the car up in front of the Hyperion Hotel. "This is the place, right?"

"That's right," Cordelia said. "Thanks for the ride. And the dessert. Scrumptious."

"It's the least I could do," Kirsten said. "I can't believe you're not getting any money from the show, after you stayed all that time. You should have been the winner."

"Sharon lived as long as I did," Cordelia said. "Although splitting it two ways would have been okay with me. But the letter I got from their attorneys says that Laughing Pig Productions has declared bankruptcy. Wesley thinks they're trying to shield their assets from any lawsuits that might come out of the whole *Haunted House* mess, though the way they've managed to hush everything up, I don't see that ever happening." With the show an unmitigated disaster, no one in the industry press had even bothered to follow up on it. Rich Carson had already gone to New York and taken a job at a local station. Less than a week after the event, Cordelia's name was already out of the papers and the industry consciousness, and her phone hadn't rung with a single job offer.

All in all, a rough way to earn exactly nothing, she thought. *Good thing the time off work was paid.*

She'd framed the letter from Laughing Pig's law

firm, though. It was always good for a laugh. *Who ever thought I'd get official legal correspondence from Wolfram and Hart?*

Through the lobby doors, Angel watched Kirsten St. Clair drive away and Cordelia come toward him, smiling from some private thought. He was pleased that Kirsten's memory was returning. *If the ritual had been finished* . . . He didn't complete the thought.

Mostly, though, he was pleased at the way Cordelia had come through. Hurting from vision-brain, she had still pulled it together well enough to not only function but thrive in the haunted house. She had made a friend—sure, he turned out to work for the enemy, and when Angel heard that, he wasn't so sorry the guy had ended up hanging from the chandelier. But more than that, when things got really dangerous, she had managed to protect the lives of two other people and get them safely through when everyone around them was being killed by malevolent spirits. Wesley was only guessing, but his speculation was that the ghosts who haunted the house were agitated, or perhaps specifically prompted, into acts of violence by the ritual being performed in the basement. If it hadn't been for Cordelia, the house would have claimed at least two more victims.

He backed away from the door before she reached it, so she wouldn't think he'd been watching her. By the time she entered, his back was turned. "Hi, Angel," she said brightly.

"Oh," he said, trying to sound startled. "Hi, Cordy."

"What are you doing?" she asked.

"Me? Just . . . um . . . thinking."

"Because standing there in the middle of the floor, facing a blank wall, is where you do your best thinking, right?"

"It's a good thinking spot. Nothing to distract me, you know. Good for serious contemplation."

"No brooding?"

"No brooding."

"What are you really doing?" she demanded.

"Okay," he said. "I was watching you."

"I knew it!" she said triumphantly. "You had that same 'I wasn't watching you' pose my dad used to have when I came in from a date, in high school. I didn't believe it when he tried it, either."

She has me pretty well trapped, Angel knew. "Okay," he said again. "I missed you, all right? Happy now?"

Cordelia crossed the floor and put her arms around Angel in a strong, friendly hug. He returned it, glad she was back safely once again.

"Yeah," Cordelia said. "Definitely. Happy now."

About the Author

Jeff Mariotte is the author of two previous Angel novels, *Close to the Ground* and *Hollywood Noir*, as well as, with Nancy Holder, the Buffy–Angel crossover trilogy *Unseen*. He's published several other books, and more comic books than he has time to count, including the popular horror-Western series *Desperadoes*. With his wife, Maryelizabeth Hart, and partner, Terry Gilman, he co-owns Mysterious Galaxy, a bookstore specializing in science fiction, fantasy, mystery, and horror. He lives in San Diego, California, with his family and pets, in a home filled with books, music, toys, and other examples of American pop culture. More about him can be gleaned from www.jeffmariotte.com.